WYCHWOOD

WYCHWOOD

GEORGE MANN

TITAN BOOKS

Wychwood
Mass-market edition ISBN: 9781785651403
Ebook edition ISBN: 9781783294107

Published by Titan Books
A division of Titan Publishing Group Ltd
144 Southwark Street, London SE1 0UP

First mass-market edition: July 2018
10 9 8 7 6 5 4 3 2 1

What did you think of this book? We love to hear from our readers.
Please email us at: readerfeedback@titanemail.com,
or write to us at the above address.

To receive advance information, news, competitions, and exclusive offers
online, please sign up for the Titan newsletter on our website:
www.titanbooks.com

WYCHWOOD

CHAPTER ONE

Shesensed movement, and risked a glance over her shoulder.

Around her, the Wychwood seemed silent and still. Even the shrill cawing of the crows seemed distant, now: the laughter of an audience that had already moved on to the next joke.

Had she shaken him off? Had he given up and fled in fear of discovery?

Her heart was hammering, her breath coming in short, sharp gulps. She felt lightheaded, disorientated. How long had she been running? It couldn't have been more than a few minutes, but she'd lost all sense of passing time.

She'd torn her dress on a branch and laddered her expensive stockings. She'd abandoned her high heels in the car park, along with her handbag, containing her phone. She cursed, wishing she'd held onto it long enough to call for help. Sweat was beaded on her brow, pooling in the soft hollow at the base of her throat. Her hands were trembling and her head was pounding. Blood was matting her hair, trickling down the side of her face where he'd struck her in the car park.

Frantically, she fought her way through the undergrowth, feeling the damp earth oozing into her stockings. What did he want? Why *her*?

She let out an involuntary whimper. She was going to die here, out in the middle of nowhere, in the cold and wet. Her body was going to be dumped amongst the mossy tree roots, to be found the next day by a dog walker or a rambler, covered in blood and dew.

She fought a wave of panic. She had to keep her wits about her. Her attacker was still out here, somewhere, lurking amongst the trees. She might not be able to fight him off again. Last time she'd surprised him, giving him a sharp punch to his gut as he'd dragged her into the woods. This time, though, he'd be ready.

She could still smell his cheap aftershave; see the snarl as he'd reached out to grab her. She'd known then that he meant to kill her.

She couldn't allow that leering face to be the last thing she saw. She had to find somewhere to get help.

Up ahead, she could see the dim lights of a building through the willowy fingers of the trees. If she could make it to the house, she'd be safe. No one would turn her away. She'd call the police, and everything would be all right.

Something rustled in the dry leaves behind her. She felt suddenly nauseated. She knew it was him. She could hear his thin, reedy breath, whistling between his teeth as he ran. He was gaining on her.

Tears pricked her eyes. She glanced behind her to see him rear up out of the trees like some nightmarish spectre.

He was cloaked in shadows, as if he'd somehow wrapped the darkness around him to form a downy mantle.

"No!" she moaned, forcing herself to run faster, digging for any final reserves of energy. Branches whipped her face, drawing beads of blood, but she barely noticed them as she fought her way towards the light. So close now…

She felt a hand on her shoulder, fingers digging into her flesh, and she twisted, trying desperately to shake him off. And then suddenly she was falling, spinning towards the ground as he shoved her hard in the back. She threw her hands out to break her fall.

The heels of her hands slipped on the slick mud, and she rolled, jarring her elbow. She cried out, scrabbling quickly to her feet, expecting him to grab her at any moment, to burst out of the shadows and strike her again.

She glanced around, desperately looking for something – anything – she could use as a weapon, but there was nothing but the trees, silent and still. She balled her hands into fists. She wasn't about to give in now.

He loomed out of the trees before her. His arms were outstretched, beckoning for embrace.

"No…" she murmured, her voice wavering. "Stay back."

"Shhh," he said, and his voice was eerily calm and reasonable. "It'll all be over soon. It'll be so much easier if you just let it happen."

He came for her, and she thrashed out, striking him hard in the chest. He staggered back, surprised by the ferocity of the blow. She pressed her advantage, pummelling him again and again, raging breathlessly until he was forced to raise his arms to protect his face.

She felt a sudden surge of hope. Maybe she could do this. Maybe there was still time to get away.

And then he was lurching forward again, grabbing her by the upper arms, pinning her in place. She tried to kick, but he twisted out of the way. She fought to free herself from his grip, but he was too strong. He forced her back against a tree.

She parted her lips to scream, but he clamped his palm over her mouth, squeezing painfully. She tried to bite down as he twisted her head to one side, tasting something bitter on his fingers, but his other arm shifted, and she felt a sharp prick in the exposed side of her neck.

"There," he said, his voice calm and level. He almost sounded reasonable. "That wasn't so hard, was it?"

She thrashed, but he pinned her there as the warm liquid spread into her shoulder, flushing through her bloodstream, and as the sedative took hold and the woozy feeling overcame her, the last thing she heard was the rustle of feathers as he gently laid her down amongst the fallen leaves.

CHAPTER TWO

She was only a few hundred yards from her mother's house, and they hadn't moved for nearly half an hour.

Elspeth sighed and peered in the rear-view mirror. The line of traffic snaked away into the distance, stretching as far as she could see. Directly behind her, the driver of the white Fiat – a tired-looking woman with two young kids in the back – was growing increasingly frustrated, gripping her steering wheel so tightly that her knuckles had turned white. Elspeth could see the kids squabbling in the rear seats, arms flapping as they tried to resolve their spat. She could imagine the tension in the vehicle, growing more taut with every passing second.

Up ahead, a hulking lorry blocked her view of the road. The driver had left the engine running, and oily smoke chugged from its corroded exhaust. She'd already turned off the intake fan in her car, but the stink of burning fumes lingered. She wrinkled her nose and leaned back against the headrest.

Anna Calvi was singing about desire on the car stereo. All that Elspeth desired was a cup of tea, and maybe a Kit Kat, if her mum still kept a stash of them hidden behind the breadbin. She was craving something sweet – she'd run out of mints back on the motorway. She rummaged in the glovebox on the off-chance, but aside from a heap of CDs, a pair of sunglasses and an errant lipstick, it was empty.

She'd been driving for hours. It had taken her twice as long as it should have to clear the London Orbital, and then she'd been snarled up in *this* for the last thirty minutes. Wilsby-under-Wychwood was supposed to be rural, too. They didn't *get* traffic problems. She considered ditching the car by the side of the road and walking the rest of the way, but decided against it – it wouldn't go down well with the police if she prompted a mass walkout. She had sudden visions of Michael Stipe singing 'Everybody Hurts', and grinned.

The lorry nudged forward a few feet, belching more sooty fumes, and she caught a glimpse of flashing police lights in the distance.

It was clear there'd been an accident, or at least an incident; an ambulance and two police cars had come screaming by a short while earlier, and now they appeared to be letting the cars through one at a time. She guessed it was probably a car that had taken the bend too quickly and careened into the trees – the small wood behind her mum's house had seen its fair share of accidents over the years – although there did seem to be rather a lot of police.

She edged forward behind the lorry, and the white Fiat inched in behind her, as if pulled along by an invisible tether. Now one of the kids had unbuckled himself and was attempting to scramble through to the front passenger seat to escape his sister.

Elspeth played with the stereo, searching for something to lift her mood, and grabbed her phone. She quickly dismissed the string of messages from her London friends asking where she was and flicked through the music player. Moments later, Stevie Wonder was crooning away over the Bluetooth, and Elspeth was already beginning to feel better. She sang along for a minute, drumming against the steering wheel with her fingers.

Finally, the lorry ahead of her pulled away, waved through by the police, and she had a clearer view of what was going on. The police had formed a cordon along the left-hand side of the road, to block the entrance to her mum's cul-de-sac, and, as she'd anticipated, had partially coned off an area of the road ahead in order to allow the ambulances through. They were waving people through one at a time, and evidently redirecting people who were coming in the opposite direction. It was complete chaos.

She noticed that a constable in a high-visibility jacket was beckoning her forward, and she eased the car slowly towards him, lowering her window and cutting the sound from the stereo.

"Hello, officer, can you tell me what's going on?"

"It's a crime scene, miss. You need to move along as quickly as possible."

"A crime scene?" She'd expected him to confirm her suspicion there'd been an accident. Come to think of it, there was no sign of any overturned vehicle in the ditch. "What sort of crime scene?"

The police constable raised an eyebrow, as if to say 'you really expect me to answer that?'

Elspeth sighed. "Look, I live in that house over

there." She pointed at the back of her mum's house, just visible beyond the trees, backing directly onto the woods where two women in uniform were marking out a boundary with white and blue striped police tape. "I'm trying to get home."

"Alright, miss," the man nodded. "The boys will let you through." He straightened up, calling over to the driver of the police car that was blocking the entrance to Stanford Road. The sirens had been turned off, but the lights were still flickering relentlessly, causing her to look away. "Resident," he said, patting the roof of her car.

The driver nodded and put his vehicle into reverse, backing onto one of the neighbours' driveways. Mr Harrison wasn't going to like that very much, Elspeth knew – he'd always been a stickler for chasing them off his property when they were kids.

She thanked the constable and swung her Mini around into the road, pulling to a stop outside her mum's house. In her rear-view mirror, she saw the police car slide slowly back into position, blocking the end of the road. She fought the sudden sensation of being trapped here again; a feeling she'd battled with for over half her life, before she'd finally escaped to London nearly a decade ago. Now, after all this time, she was back. Perhaps there really was no escaping the place.

She decided to leave her cases in the back of the car for now, and snatched up her handbag from the passenger seat and trudged up the driveway towards the house. It was a glorious old place, really; a detached eighteenth-century cottage, constructed from the same butter-coloured stone as the rest of the village, with a slate-tiled roof and strands of ivy clambering haphazardly over the walls. There was a small garden at the back, which looked out onto the wooded area that was presently garnering so much attention from the police.

She stood before the door for a moment, took a deep breath, and then tried the handle. It yawned open. She went in, closing the door behind her.

The old family home hadn't changed much. In fact, Elspeth couldn't remember the last time her mum had decorated the place. It still retained its old-fashioned charm, with its wonky walls and terrible phone signal. The hallway was filled to bursting with bric-a-brac and strange objects her mum had bought from car boot sales and antique fairs – a brass bedpan hung on the wall like a pendulum; chipped plates, decorated with gaudy landscapes of Oxfordshire, stood on wire stands atop the dresser, alongside little porcelain models of houses; a Victorian nursing chair was piled high with soft toys, and a gilt-framed mirror hung above the telephone table, which still housed a red Bakelite handset from the era before time began. There was the familiar ticking, too, of the long case clock her grandfather had made after the war. It had taken him years, apparently, to fashion the new case, chipping away at the wood with his gnarled fingers.

"Mum? Are you home?"

She heard the creak of floorboards from the landing.

"Ellie?" A surprised face appeared over the top of the banisters. "Is that you?"

"Hi, Mum. Made it at last."

Elspeth dropped her handbag on the telephone table

as her mum, Dorothy, bustled down the stairs. She was still young, really – in her mid-sixties – and had kept her youthful complexion and wavy blonde hair. She looked well, and her face lit up at the sight of Elspeth, her lips parting in a huge grin.

Elspeth went to her and bundled her up into a big hug. "Good to see you, Mum."

"And you, love." Dorothy held her by the shoulders and looked her up and down appraisingly. "Not *too* thin. So they're still feeding you in London."

Elspeth shook her head. "Don't ever change, Mum." She glanced over her shoulder. "What's going on out back? I had to queue for over half an hour and then persuade the police to let me through."

"Apparently there was an incident in the night. One of the constables has been round already asking if we'd seen or heard anything. He wouldn't say what had happened, exactly, but they seem to be taking it seriously."

"Yeah, they're not giving much away, are they?"

"No. Come on through to the kitchen. I'll pop the kettle on and you can tell me all your news."

Elspeth followed her mum through to the kitchen, cutting through what they'd always jokingly referred to as 'the study' – a small room piled high with more bric-a-brac, a couple of bookcases, and a desk that she'd never seen anyone sitting at.

The kitchen was a large, square room, with a big farmhouse table and all the mod cons – her mum's one concession to modernity had been to have it updated about five years earlier – with a door leading through to the living room, and a set of French doors leading out to the patio and garden. Light was streaming in through them now, pooling on the tiled floor, where the ginger cat, Murphy, was stretching languorously.

While Dorothy was filling the kettle, Elspeth peered out into the garden, trying to see into the woods beyond. These were part of the ancient Wychwood, a dense forest that had once covered much of the area and had subsequently given its name to a number of local villages. The old forest had long ago been eroded, felled to make way for farms, settlements and roads – but what remained of it now was largely protected, a series of small wooded areas nuzzling the edges of villages or towns, or scattered around the local countryside.

"So, are you going to tell me what's brought you home all of a sudden?" said Dorothy.

"Hang on a minute, Mum," said Elspeth. She opened the French doors and stepped out onto the patio.

The garden was pretty, and in full bloom. Gardening was a passion of Dorothy's, and always had been; she still worked at the local garden centre three days per week, where she'd been for over a decade.

Elspeth breathed it all in. Even now, the heady scent of the flowers took her straight back to her childhood, and lazy days spent running in circles on the lawn, chased by her dad, or kicking a ball about with her friends, trying to avoid the flowerbeds and subsequent scolding.

At the end of the lawn, a low drystone wall formed a border between the garden and the wilderness beyond. As a child, Elspeth had practised over and over until she'd been able to vault it in a single leap, escaping into the strange fairyland beyond, amongst the bracken and the moss, the babbling streams and skeletal, angular trees. To her the woods had been like the fantasia beyond the back of the wardrobe, a land of wild disorder and exploration, a place of adventure, where the ancient past intersected with the present. Here, she'd dreamed of the ancient Wychwood, filled with warring Saxon warlords and wizards, of highwaymen and runaway princes, of nymphs and elves and centaurs. The thought of it being invaded now by the police seemed entirely wrong. And yet, she wanted desperately to know what was going on.

Elspeth walked towards the end of the garden, listening for any activity from the woods. She could hear voices in the trees, just make out the flashes of more high-visibility jackets through the branches, bright and unnatural.

"Sod it," she said, approaching the wall. She wasn't about to let another story get away from her, especially one on her own – albeit temporary – doorstep. This could be the lead she'd been looking for, her chance to be the first journalist on the scene of a murder.

She hitched her skirt and threw her leg up over the wall, hoisting herself over. Either the wall was higher than she remembered, or she was a little less supple than she'd once been. She'd have to find a new gym in Heighton or Oxford, so at least she could assuage her guilt by paying the monthly membership fees.

She dropped down into the mulch on the other side, and had to grip hold of the wall as her feet nearly slipped from under her. She righted herself, smoothing down the front of her skirt.

"Ellie, what are you *doing*?" She looked round to see her mum was standing at the bottom of the garden, her hands on her hips. She was wearing a disapproving look. "It's a crime scene. The police are everywhere. That young constable said we had to remain in our houses until they were finished."

Elspeth put her finger to her lips. "Shhh. I'll be back in a minute," she whispered. "Just a quick look."

Dorothy gave an exasperated sigh. "You don't change, Elspeth Reeves."

Elspeth gave her best attempt at a beatific smile, and then turned and crept slowly through the undergrowth towards what she presumed was the scene of the crime.

She wasn't about to go charging in like a bull in a china shop, blurting questions and getting herself into trouble. She'd hang back, take a look at what was going on; see if she could find an angle for a story. It would be a great start, a way in with one of the local newspapers. Assuming, of course, that whatever was going on here was even newsworthy. She couldn't imagine there'd be so many people if it wasn't.

The police seemed to have gathered in a natural glade in the woods up ahead. She crouched behind the bough of an oak tree and peered in, trying to ascertain what was happening.

Four uniformed policemen milled around the perimeter, their radios crackling, while a woman in a grey trouser suit, with a bob of dark hair – presumably the inspector in charge of the scene – spoke in hushed tones to a man in a blue coverall. This latter was, Elspeth assumed, a forensic pathologist. The rest of his team – two women and a rather young-looking man – were across the other side of the glade, unpacking the contents of several silver cases. They were also wearing blue coveralls.

Then, in the centre of the glade, was the body.

Elspeth had seen only two dead people in her life. The first had been her father, in the cancer ward at Churchill Hospital, six years earlier. He'd looked rested and peaceful, lying in her mum's arms as if he were simply dozing. Dorothy had been cradling him as he died, and he'd looked so pale and thin, as if the cancer had leeched the life right out of him. She remembered a shaft of sunlight streaming through the window, dust motes swirling, silence.

The second had been during a brief, ill-considered holiday to Benidorm with her friend Julia, when she'd seen a young woman lying face down in the road, having drunkenly stumbled into the path of an oncoming car. She'd only caught a fleeting glimpse as her shuttle bus had sped past on its way to the airport, but the image of the barely dressed young woman had been emblazoned in her memory, still clinging on to her zebra-print handbag, her clutch of friends all standing around her, mascara running in black tributaries down their tanned cheeks.

The sight that greeted her here, in the woods, however, was something else entirely. She supposed she'd expected to see something gory and horrific – the result of a struggle, spilled blood, even a gunshot or knife wound – but the view before her was nothing of the sort.

It wasn't so much a murder scene as a tableau, a piece of theatre, or an installation of contemporary art. The entire glade had been *dressed*.

The victim – a blonde-haired woman in her mid-forties, Elspeth estimated – had been laid out upon a bed of leaves. Her head lolled to one side, limp and lifeless. She was naked, save for a cloak of bright white feathers, which had been carefully draped across her shoulders, a small cord looped around her throat to hold it in place. A crown of holly and thistles, wound with red roses, had been placed upon her head. The only obvious sign of a wound was a thin line of dried blood on the side of her face, stark and obscene against the pale flesh. Seven dead crows had been placed on the ground close to her head.

Elspeth stared for a moment, unable to tear her eyes away. The woman's skin was milky white and smooth. She looked strangely beautiful, draped in her coat of feathers and wearing her floral crown; like something from a Pre-Raphaelite painting. It was an appalling sight, nevertheless, and she gaped at it with a mixture of sadness and fascination. She was grateful she couldn't see the expression on the woman's face. She hoped she hadn't suffered, although she knew that was a ridiculous thing to think in the circumstances. The woman had been *murdered*. No matter how it had been done, she'd been brought out here, and she had lost her life.

Elspeth fought a wave of nausea, and turned away from the corpse. The fact that someone had done this to another human being, so close to her childhood home, in the place that she used to play as a child… it just seemed so unreal. And what did it all mean? There was something disturbingly familiar about the symbolism, but she couldn't place it. It had to bear some occult relevance, or else some relation to the Arthurian myths she'd been so obsessed with in her youth. Her mum probably still had all her books in her old room. She'd have to dig them out.

Elspeth stood, careful to keep out of view of the police officers and pathologists. She'd seen enough. There was definitely a story in this – she just had to find out a bit more about what had happened.

She turned back towards the house, and directly into the path of a man in a suit. She almost yelped in surprise, but just about managed to retain her cool.

"What do you think you're doing? This is a mur—" The man stopped short, a confused expression crossing his face. "*Elspeth? Elspeth Reeves?*"

Elspeth swallowed. Her mouth was dry. This was the last thing she needed – being recognised by one of the policemen. She painted on a smile. "Yes, that's me…" She peered at him a little more closely.

He was tall and slim, his grey suit crumpled, his blue tie slightly askew. The top button of his shirt appeared to be open at the collar. He had a mop of unruly auburn hair, and a broad, lopsided smile. He was wearing a thin layer of stubble, and he smelled vaguely of cigarettes. It was the green eyes that seemed most familiar, however – sharp and insightful, alert. She would have recognised them anywhere.

"*Peter?*"

He laughed, and kicked at the ground with the tip of his boot. "It's been a long time," he said. "*Years.*"

"And you're a *policeman*? What happened to your plans to be the world's greatest rally car driver?"

Peter shrugged. "We all grow up, don't we?" He cleared his throat, seeming to remember himself. "But more to the point, what are *you* doing here? You can't just go sneaking around crime scenes, you know."

Elspeth held up her hands in a parody of surrender. "I know, I know. I'm sorry. I've just arrived back at Mum's. I saw there was something going on, and hopped over the back wall to take a look." She sighed. "I kind of wish I hadn't, now." She nodded in the direction of the corpse.

"You never get used to it," said Peter. "Trust me."

"I don't suppose you'd ever want to."

"Not really. But were you really only being nosey? Only, it seems a bit unlikely, and I *am* a detective sergeant..." He shrugged.

"I suppose it does seem unlikely, doesn't it. Alright. I wanted to be the first on the scene, to see if there was a story. That's the truth. I parked up at Mum's and hopped over the wall. I've only been here for a minute. I... well, I used to work for a newspaper and—"

"DS Shaw?" She was saved by the sound of the dark-haired inspector calling Peter's name.

He put a hand on her shoulder. "Listen, you need to *go*, before we both get it in the neck. She's... a bit prone to overreacting. She'd have you straight down to the station for questioning, and probably charged for interfering with a police investigation, or worse, murder."

"Okay," said Elspeth. "I'm going." She took a couple of steps, then turned back to see he was still watching her. "It was good to see you, Peter."

"You too," he said. The inspector was calling his name again. "See you around."

Grinning, Elspeth made a dash for the garden wall, scrambled over in a most unladylike fashion, and was back in her Mum's kitchen a few moments later, trying to take stock of what she'd just seen.

CHAPTER THREE

"So, love, are you going to tell me what all this is about?"

They were sitting at the kitchen table, and Elspeth was playfully teasing the cat with the edge of her boot. He scrabbled for her laces, and then skittered away across the tiles in search of more meaningful entertainment.

Dorothy had made her a strong black coffee with a shot of brandy in it. She sipped it gratefully. "A woman's been murdered, Mum. Right behind our house, in the trees where we used to play as kids."

"Yes, yes, I realise that." Dorothy perched on the edge of her chair. "But I'm talking about *you*, Ellie, coming to visit like this, with only a day's notice." She looked worried. "Not that I *mind*, of course. It's just... well, it's a bit unusual. A bit *unexpected*. Is something wrong?"

"So I can't even visit my mum without something being wrong?"

Dorothy gave her the *look*. This was a particular glare of incredulity the woman had perfected over many years – one that had always been proven to make Elspeth squirm.

"Alright, alright," she said, placing her empty mug

on the coaster. "I need a place to stay for a while. I was hoping I could have my old room?" She hadn't wanted to get into this now, especially with everything else going on out in the woods, but her mother was shrewder than she appeared.

"Of course you can, love. Like I said on the phone, a couple of days' rest will do you the world of good. You've been doing too much. I've been saying that for a while. It'll be nice to have you around, cheering the place up. Especially after all *this*." She nodded in the direction of the French doors, and the garden and woodland beyond.

Elspeth chewed her bottom lip for a moment. She felt as though she were sixteen again. "It might be more than a couple of days, Mum. I'm sorry. I should have said on the phone. This isn't a holiday."

Dorothy looked dubious. "Ellie, are you going to tell me what's *really* going on?"

"It's all gone a bit wrong, Mum," said Elspeth. She fought back the pricking tears. She'd told herself she wasn't going to cry, but now she was here, about to lay it all out... She steeled herself.

"*What's* gone wrong?"

"Things haven't been right between Andrew and me for a while. We've both known it. We've not been happy. He's been spending more and more time with his friends, and I've been throwing myself into work... and the other day it all just came to a head."

"You'll sort it out. Maybe a little time apart is what you need."

"No," Elspeth shook her head. "It's too late for that.

I've left him. Turns out… well, you don't need to know all the sordid details. But it's over. He's staying on at the flat, and I…well, I'll have to go back and fetch my stuff, once I've found somewhere a bit more permanent."

Dorothy put a hand on her shoulder. "Oh, Ellie. You should have said."

"I know. It's just… if I say it out loud, it means it's true." She felt her bottom lip trembling. "I don't want to have to start again, Mum. I'm not sure I can face it."

"Of course you can. You can bloody well face anything. You're Elspeth Reeves."

Elspeth laughed, wiping away tears on her sleeve. "I really loved him. I thought…" she trailed off. "Well, I don't suppose it matters *what* I thought, now. But you might have to wait for those grandkids you wanted."

"And you're sure that's it? That there's no way the two of you can sort this out? Maybe give it a few days, then give him a call…?"

"Mum, it turns out he'd been cheating on me for years."

Dorothy bristled. "I see. Right." She squeezed Elspeth's arm. "The little sod."

"I just need to get my head straight. Work out what I want to do." She grabbed a tissue from the box on the table.

"What about work? Are they okay with you taking some time off?"

Elspeth swallowed. "Oh, yeah, as much time as I want. *All* the time, in fact. Like I said, everything's just come at once. Turns out they were looking to 'downsize', and since I was the last person to join the team…"

"Oh, Ellie dear. Come here." Dorothy swept her up

in a warm embrace. Elspeth felt numb. Here she was, back at her childhood home, and everything falling apart around her.

"Well, look, you were right to come home. It's the best thing for you. You can take a bit of time now; decide what you want to do. Your room's just where you left it, and it's yours for as long as you need it, alright?"

"Thanks, Mum."

"You've had a long drive, and you're tired. Why don't I run you a bath, and you can throw some of your things in the wardrobe and flop. No need to worry about anything else today."

"Sounds blissful."

"Alright. I'll give you a shout when it's ready."

She watched as Dorothy placed her empty mug in the sink and hurried off to start the bath running. Then, after pouring another shot of brandy into her own mug, she opened up the French doors again and stepped out onto the patio, staring up at the trees and feeling distinctly uncomfortable, as if, somehow, they were staring right back.

An hour later, she sat by the dresser in her old bedroom, running a brush through her damp hair and staring at herself in the mirror.

What was it about coming home that made her feel like a failure? She'd once heard it said that re-entry was the thing astronauts feared most about going into space. Not sailing out into that great, infinite unknown, not rocketing through the airless void inside a tiny metal can, but the return to the familiar, the terror of burning up as they came home. Sitting there in her childhood bedroom, staring at her own reflection, she thought she might understand how they felt.

She heard the flutter of birds on the tiled roof above her head, and crossed to the window, looking out at the gloomy expanse of the Wychwood. The police had gone, leaving behind reams of blue and white tape, intended to deter any errant dog walkers or trespassers. The light was fading, the last of the sunlight poking inquisitive fingers through the upper branches of the trees. Above, birds wheeled in a silent, stately dance. A lone car drifted down the road, headlamps bobbing with the uneven surface. It all seemed so quiet compared to the bustle of London. She wondered how long it would take her to grow used to it again. Perhaps she wouldn't stay that long. She was already wondering if she'd done the right thing. It was just… her entire life down there revolved around Andrew. Most of their friends were the same, she'd lost her home, and now, without a job to go back to, she had to wonder what *was* waiting for her in London. She didn't want to be in Andrew's orbit any longer, didn't even want to talk to him… except, she was missing him already. She just felt as if everything had been turned on its head. She had to figure out what she wanted.

Maybe she'd stay for a few days, and then see how she felt. The distance would help. And she'd start looking around online for freelance work in the morning. She wasn't going to sit idle, and she might be able to sell a piece about the murder.

Her mind drifted back to the sight of the dead woman, strangely serene in her downy cloak and crown

29

of thorns. She'd looked to Elspeth as if she'd been sleeping, like an enchanted princess from a fairy tale. There was something about the image that felt oddly familiar, and she hadn't been able to shake the notion that she'd seen it somewhere before.

She recalled her plan to search out her old books on the Arthurian legends, and so, tightening the belt on her borrowed dressing gown she decided to have a ferret around.

She started with the wardrobe first, which had long ago been given over to storage, rather than clothes. It was heaped with boxes of old junk – soft toys, records, baby clothes, school exercise books. She didn't know where to start. She rummaged around for a few minutes, shifting a couple of the boxes and moving things around to see what was inside them all, but none seemed to contain any books.

She lost ten minutes to a dusty photo album she'd filled one summer when she'd been given a Polaroid camera for her birthday. She'd loved the way all the photographs had come out first as indecipherable blurs, and had slowly resolved in their white frames, becoming sharper with every passing second. It had seemed like magic, and she'd wasted cartridge after cartridge snapping pictures of her friends and family, which she'd glued into this book, scrawling little messages into the margins.

Peter was in there, too – chubby in those days, with his mop of bright red hair, wandering about with his poetry books. He'd seemed so sophisticated at the age of fourteen, reading Wilfred Owen and Siegfried Sassoon, carrying around a little reporter's notebook in which he jotted down all of his observations. Thinking now, it made perfect sense that he'd go on to become a detective. She wondered if he still recorded his thoughts in iambic pentameter.

She dropped the photo album back into the box, and stuffed it back into the wardrobe, careful not to place anything on top of the records. She'd look forward to sorting through those in the comings days, maybe hooking up the old turntable and giving some of them a spin. She'd never quite given up on vinyl in the same way she'd abandoned cassettes; she adored the warm crackle of dust, the fact you were forced to consume the album as a piece of art in its entirety, as the artist intended, unable to skip or fast forward or play everything through on a random shuffle. She and Andrew had assembled quite a collection back in London. That was going to take some sorting out, too. She sighed.

The wardrobe door wouldn't close properly, now that she'd disturbed Dorothy's carefully arranged stacks. She left it hanging open and glanced around the room, wondering where else her mum might have secreted her old stuff. Under the bed was the most obvious option, particularly for a box of heavy books. She dropped to her knees and grabbed her phone off the bed, using the torch function to take a look. Sure enough, there were three boxes under there, nestled in a sea of dust. She reached under and grabbed one, sliding it towards her. It seemed to contain nothing but ancient school uniforms, wrapped in plastic bags. She shoved it back under and grabbed the next one.

This time she knew she was in luck. The weight of

the box made it difficult to drag out, and when she peered inside, she caught a glimpse of an armoured knight standing at the gates of a castle; the lurid watercolour on the front of one of her most fondly remembered books, *Le Morte D'Arthur* by Sir Thomas Malory.

She pulled back the cardboard flaps and pulled it out, spluttering at a plume of disturbed dust. She was certain that somewhere inside this old tome there'd be another watercolour describing a similar scene to the one she'd seen that afternoon in the woods.

Half an hour later she'd finished leafing through *Le Morte D'Arthur*, *The Mabinogion*, and a handful of illustrated histories of the Dark Ages. She'd found nothing that even resembled the picture she remembered, and was beginning to wonder if she'd simply imagined the whole thing. Ellie placed the books in a heap on the floor and leaned back against the bed.

Her phone had buzzed a couple of times, and she glanced at the lock screen, seeing two messages from her friend, Abigail. She sounded worried. Elspeth thumbed the button and dashed off a quick response:

Visiting Mum in Oxfordshire. All good. Speak soon. X.

She hit send, and then tossed the phone back onto the bed.

There were still a handful of books in the box. She put aside a gazetteer of Roman Britain and a book about the Celts. At the bottom of the box, buried beneath a never-opened textbook on the interpretation of Ancient

Egyptian hieroglyphics, was an old book with a familiar cover. The title *Myths and Legends of Oxfordshire* was emblazoned on the front in bold yellow typeface. She remembered poring over it for endless hours as a girl of twelve, daydreaming about all the bizarre creatures and characters contained within, imagining they were real, and still living in the woods at the bottom of the garden amongst the ancient boughs of the Wychwood.

She turned the pages slowly, smiling at the primitive illustrations of local pixies and dragons, ghostly spirits and doppelgangers. The book held almost as many memories as the album of Polaroids. But it wasn't until she turned to the chapter entitled 'The Carrion King of the Wychwood' that she realised what she'd missed.

There, on page fifty-six, was the picture she'd been looking for. It was a primitive woodcut of a woman laid upon a bed of leaves, a crown of thorns and roses upon her head. She was wearing a cloak of feathers, and above her head, seven crows circled in flight, their beaks parted as they called out, silent and still. Beneath the picture was the caption: THE KING'S CONSORT.

Elspeth shuddered. She felt suddenly cold. There was something chilling about seeing the old picture like this, only hours after bearing witness to its very real, very visceral reconstruction. What was more, there were further, similar pictures in the same chapter, of other bizarre characters, including a man with antlers and an arrow in his chest, and another woman on her knees, as if in prayer, her lips sewn shut with twine.

She knew at once that she had to show the book to Peter in the morning. It was growing late now, though, and she no longer had any idea where he lived, or how to contact him. The only thing she could do was read the chapter through in full, and then take it over to Heighton first thing in the morning and see if she could get hold of Peter at the station.

Elspeth loaded all of the other books into the box, and then pushed it back beneath the bed. Then, after selecting an Angel Olsen song on her phone and dumping it on the nightstand, she propped up the pillows, tied up her still-damp hair and sank into bed with the book.

CHAPTER FOUR

As a child he had practised on birds.

He'd grown quite adept at it: finding just the right kind of smooth-sided pebble, fitting it to the pouch of a catapult he'd stashed in his secret place in the woods, choosing exactly the right target.

He'd started with pigeons, but soon gravitated to magpies, and then ravens and crows. The bigger birds rarely died when they were struck by the stone, but were injured or stunned, making them easier to catch. He'd scoop them up with an old fishing net he'd stolen from another child's back garden and find somewhere safe amongst the trees to hide. He'd turn them out from the bright green net and hold them in his cupped palms, thrilled at the terrified fluttering of their hearts, at the way their warm bodies shuddered as he wrung their necks; that final, juddering spasm of life.

He'd never felt guilt. More a crushing sense of disappointment that it was over so quickly; that the creature had died so easily, that its grasp on life had seemed so tenuous. He'd known death – he'd seen it visited upon others – and he was constantly amazed by how quickly, how willingly, the living embraced it.

It wasn't so much a fascination with death that had inspired him to such acts, however, but more a need to understand how to control it, how to exert power over it. If the taking of a life was such a simple act, couldn't the reverse be true, too?

He'd experimented with rituals to stir the creatures back to life, to breathe vitality into their silent corpses, but of course, he had failed. Real power, he had learned much later, was far more difficult to attain, and his juvenile efforts had been naive, ignorant, misguided. There was a toll to pay for mastery over such things. Sacrifices to be made.

Now, though, decades after his search had begun, he had found what he sought: the tools of his vengeance and the path to real power. He had pieced the rituals together from fragments, painstakingly interpreted every word, every symbol. Soon, he would put them to proper use. This was to be his finest hour, the summation of his life's work. All he had to do was tread the path that had been laid out. The process had already begun.

The first two had been nothing, not really. The woman had nearly escaped, but once he'd caught her, it had been just like snuffing out another bird, holding her in his arms as she shuddered and died. He would be more careful next time, though. He couldn't afford for them to get away.

It wasn't that he'd *wanted* to kill them, more that he had no choice. These were the sacrifices, steps along the path towards transcendence. Steps towards being reunited with the one he had lost.

Out here, amongst the gnarled boughs of the Wychwood, he felt close to him, as if he could almost hear him whispering amongst the shushing of the leaves, urging him on. He would visit properly, soon. Tonight, however, he had a different task. Tonight he was here to watch.

He peered into the mirror he had propped upon the stump of the tree, and felt nauseous at the sight of the woman preening, peering out through the silvered glass as though she were looking right back at him. She brushed her hair, smeared ointments and creams upon her aged flesh, and he noted it all, monitoring every moment of her nightly routine, aware of every deviation from the norm.

This one was different from the others, so much more than a simple sacrifice. History had already chosen a far more terrible death for her. If he wished to follow in the master's footsteps, then he had to free himself of those who had wronged him, destroy them through their own vanity. She would be the first.

CHAPTER FIVE

Heighton was one of those idyllic Oxfordshire towns that still retained its turn-of-the-century charm. It boasted tree-lined avenues of Victorian villas, a market square with its weather-worn medieval cross, and a bustling high street filled with antique shops, bookshops, upscale furniture showrooms and bistros.

Heighton had always been *the* destination when she'd been a child – a short bus ride from Wilsby-under-Wychwood, and a small taste of the wider world. Where Oxford had its obvious charms, it had always seemed a little removed from her life in Wilsby-under-Wychwood, and while she'd visited regularly with her parents, she'd only really got to know it as a teenager during cinema and bowling trips, and then later, on drunken nights with her friends from college. Because of this she'd never felt the same attachment to the city as she did to Heighton.

She'd forged so many memories here, and while a lot of the fascia boards had changed in the last ten years, the streets and alleyways remained the same. The smell of the place, too: the fresh fruit and vegetables from the market, the stale beer as she walked past The Fletcher's Arms, the rich aroma of steaming coffee and frying bacon from Lenny's Café. She was pleased to see the big chain stores hadn't moved in and overrun the place like they had in so many of the market towns around London.

It was a dry, overcast day with a sharp chill in the air, so she'd borrowed one of her mum's sweaters and grabbed a pair of jeans from her case. She'd had to scrape the mud from her boots, too, after the previous day's endeavours. She'd tied her hair up and spent a little time making herself presentable – after being caught lurking in the woods, she wanted to at least make something of a reasonable impression on her old school friend, assuming, of course, that he was able and willing to see her.

While the place might not have changed all that much, Peter clearly had. As a child he'd been plump and bookish, rarely engaging with the other boys, who'd passed their summers playing football or racing their bikes down the old, abandoned railway tracks. Peter had always preferred to climb a tree and sit amongst the branches with a tatty old paperback or comic, if and when he could be dragged away from his games console.

Elspeth had been bookish too, but her mum had insisted on kicking her out of the house during the holidays, telling her the fresh air would do her good, that if she wasn't careful the TV and games machines would give her square eyes. Together with Helen and Benedict – two other neighbourhood kids – she and Peter had spent these summer days wandering the woods, climbing trees and getting up to mischief.

And now she'd met Peter again in that very same place, after all these years. She wondered what he'd make of her discovery. She wondered what he'd make of *her*.

She considered all of this as she ambled up the incline towards the station. At least the walk would give her chance to stretch her muscles; her old single bed wasn't quite as comfortable as she'd remembered.

The police station was a squat, single-storey building at the top of the hill on the way out of town, with an old-fashioned blue lamp outside, and a clutch of ivy strangling the brickwork. It was opposite a small park, and close to a primary school. She could hear the children playing in the schoolyard, cheering and laughing and galumphing about.

She was a little out of breath when she reached the top of the hill, so she stood for a moment in the car park, watching the traffic whizzing by. There were more cars than she remembered, too.

Inside, a cadaverous-looking man sat behind the reception desk. He must only have been in his late fifties, but his face was lined and gaunt, his hair was thinning, and he had dark yellow stains on his fingers from years of nicotine addiction.

There were two other people sitting in the waiting room – a middle-aged woman with a carrier bag full of shopping, and a young man in a hoodie and tracksuit bottoms, listening to music on his phone. His foot tapped in time with the rhythm of whatever atrocious dance beat she could hear through his tinny in-ear headphones.

"Can I help you, miss?"

"Yes, I'm here to see DS Shaw. Peter Shaw."

"Do you have an appointment?" The man peered at her along his aquiline nose, narrowing his eyes.

"No, I don't have an appointment or anything. Just some information that I thought might be useful to him."

"Right then, miss. You can leave that with me if you like, and I'll be sure that he gets it." He opened a drawer and took out a notepad, then looked at her expectantly.

Elspeth considered this for a moment, and then shook her head. She wasn't supposed to know any of the details of the murder investigation. She didn't want to get Peter into trouble for letting her leave the scene yesterday. "I'm sorry, but it's rather... sensitive information. I should really speak directly to DS Shaw. If he's not available at the moment I can come back later."

She heard voices as two men in suits came bustling into the station behind her, and turned to see Peter laughing with one of his colleagues – a man with a bushy black beard and smiling eyes. They were carrying takeout coffee cups from Lenny's.

When Peter caught sight of her, he clapped the other man on the shoulder and made his way over. The desk sergeant *tutted* somewhat indiscreetly, and put his notebook back in the drawer, turning his attention to the computer monitor on his desk.

"Elspeth? Is everything okay?" Peter looked concerned, his brow furrowed. The surprise of bumping into her the previous day had clearly diminished, and he looked worried.

Now that he was here, she felt a little foolish. They probably knew all of this stuff anyway – all she'd done was look something up in an old book, join a few dots. She felt her cheeks flush. "Yes. Everything's fine." She lowered her voice. "It's about the murder. Or more specifically, about the body." She caught the slight look of panic in his eyes, the fact he was glimpsing from side to side to make sure no one was listening. "Is there somewhere we can talk?"

"Um, yeah. Sure," he said. He ran a hand over his stubbly chin. He clearly hadn't shaved that morning. "Let's step outside for a few minutes, shall we?" She nodded and followed him back out into the daylight. "Over there, in the park." He indicated a bench with a tip of his coffee cup. They crossed the road.

"It was good to see you yesterday, Ellie," he said, dropping onto the bench. "I mean the circumstances were a bit unusual…"

"I know, I know. I shouldn't have done it. Sometimes I just can't help myself, and I end up getting into trouble."

"Is that what's going on with you? Is that why you're back? You said you *used* to work for a newspaper…" He took a long swig from his coffee.

"God, you *are* a policeman, aren't you?" She laughed. "Yeah, something like that."

"Is it just a visit, to see your mum?"

"No. I mean… maybe. I'm not really sure yet. It's complicated. Let's leave it at that."

He smiled. "But you've enough time on your hands to be helping me with my investigation?"

"Looks like it." She reached into her bag and took out the book. "Do you remember when we were kids, and I used to go on and on about all the Arthurian legends?"

Peter laughed. "Yeah. I used to have to pretend to be Lancelot. *All the time.*"

Elspeth felt her cheeks flush. "Yes, well. I went

through a phase of being obsessed with different myths from the Dark Ages. My mum bought me this book. I must have been about twelve." She handed it to him.

"*Myths and Legends of Oxfordshire?*" he said.

"Turn to page fifty-six." She watched while he leafed through the pages. His eyes settled on the illustration, and widened. "Oh, God. That's *her*. That's Lucy Adams."

"The King's Consort," said Elspeth. "That's why it seemed so familiar. Someone knows the story of the Carrion King of the Wychwood."

Peter looked up from the book for a moment. He was frowning again. "You'll have to jog my memory, Ellie. This was all a long time ago."

"I read up on it last night. There's tons of stuff online, too. He was a pagan magician, who was said to have lived in the Wychwood towards the end of the ninth century."

"Like a magical Robin Hood?"

"Well, he lived in a forest, but was far less magnanimous. He declared himself a king and took in followers, forming a sort of primitive cult. There were five members of his court: The Confessor, The Master of the Hunt, The Master of the Pentacle, The Fool and—"

"The King's Consort," finished Peter.

"Precisely," said Elspeth. "The Carrion King had been cast out of his village as a boy, by the ealdorman, after the child had begun to manifest strange powers that terrified the other villagers. He fled into the Wychwood, where he encountered an old hermit, who cared for him, and urged him to embrace his burgeoning powers.

"When the Carrion King finally came of age, he sought revenge against the ealdorman who had banished him, first by establishing a kingdom deep within the Wychwood that would rival any domain of the Saxon lords, and then by using his ritual magic to murder the ealdorman. He knew the ealdorman was vain and kept a mirror in his house; the Carrion King used it to seize control of the ealdorman's reflection and cause him to plunge a dagger into his own chest."

"And what about the members of his court?" said Peter. "What happened to them?"

"That's the tragedy. They all betrayed him. All except the Consort."

"Go on," said Peter.

"She was a 'fallen' woman, a whore from one of the local villages who had fled into the Wychwood to escape the abuse of the Saxon warriors. The Carrion King took her in, and promised to make her pure again, to cast off all traces of her previous life. He dressed her in a coat of white swan feathers to represent her rebirth, and gave her a crown of thorns and roses to make her his queen."

"Then how did she end up like this?" said Peter, tapping the picture in the book.

"Because the Carrion King himself was tainted by the abuse he'd suffered in his past, and that impurity spread, slowly poisoning her. She died in his arms, and he laid her upon a bed of leaves deep within the Wychwood, and called upon seven crows to watch over her body so that it might never be desecrated again." Elspeth shrugged. "It's all nonsense, of course, but there's no doubt the dead woman had been dressed to resemble the woman in that woodcut. Whoever your killer is, he's referencing that story."

"The Carrion King," said Peter, looking thoughtful. "Someone else has mentioned that recently. Or I've seen something, somewhere. I think the Winthorpe Players are putting on a play about him."

"Winthorpe? I haven't thought about that place in years. I used to go all the time with Mum when I was growing up."

Winthorpe was an open-air theatre on the grounds of Winthorpe Manor, out on the edge of the old Wychwood boundary. The Players were the local amateur company, with a revolving lineup of cast and crew, who put on a succession of shows each season.

Peter had already got to his feet. "Can I borrow this?" he said, holding up the book.

"Of course," said Elspeth.

"Thanks." He tossed his half-full coffee cup into the green litterbin beside the bench. "Look, I'd better take this straight to DCI Griffiths. I'll see you later, alright?"

Elspeth nodded, waving him on. "Go! It's fine."

"You always were the clever one," he said, before spotting a gap in the traffic and darting off across the road.

Elspeth watched as he jogged over to the police station and ducked inside.

She decided it was time for a coffee, before popping into the offices of the *Heighton Observer* for a quick chat with the editor.

CHAPTER SIX

Meredith Stokes was a fierce woman with a reputation for burning through employees – or so Elspeth's mum had explained to her over a cup of tea that morning. She'd made a name for herself on Fleet Street during the Thatcher years, before returning to Oxfordshire in the late nineties to set up her own small office, from where she ran a successful website, weekly newspaper and monthly *Oxfordshire Life* magazine.

Elspeth liked her immediately.

"We don't have a great deal of call for freelance work," said the woman, removing her glasses and eyeing Elspeth suspiciously. She must have been in her mid-fifties, with long dark hair shot through with distinguished streaks of silver-grey. Her make-up was subtle and applied with perfection, and her eyes were bright and perceptive. Elspeth felt as though the woman was peering into her soul. "Although I admit, it's a reasonably impressive CV."

"I've just returned from London and I'm looking to place a few articles," said Elspeth. She met the woman's gaze. "I've got a story."

"Oh, you do?" said Meredith, with an amused half-smile.

"The murder yesterday in Wilsby-under-Wychwood. The body they found in the woods. It's right behind my mum's house. I've got an angle. I could cover the story for you."

Meredith smiled wistfully. "An angle? So I suppose you think people would be interested in hearing how you used to play there as a child, how it used to be such a safe place, how things like this never happen in Wilsby-under-Wychwood..." She waved a dismissive hand. "We've heard it all before, dear. That's not a story."

"No," said Elspeth. "But I was *there*. I saw the body."

"You did?"

"Yes. And there's more to it than the police are letting on." Elspeth knew she'd have to choose her words carefully. She didn't want to go behind Peter's back or go blurting out something that might compromise the investigation – or blow her advantage. If Meredith took the bait, she'd have to tread with caution, talk it over with Peter and pick her timing.

"Alright," said Meredith. She tapped her finger against her lips. "I'm interested. But the police have been down here about these murders already. They've asked us to stick to the official line for now. They're worried if the details get out, it could lead to complications. I don't want to be responsible for impeding their investigation."

Murders. Plural. Elspeth hadn't been expecting that. Peter hadn't said anything when she'd shown him the book... but it would explain why he'd been so keen to get back to the station. Were there other murders that corresponded to the legend of the Carrion King, too? She decided to play it cool for now. "Not a lot of editors would go along with a request like that."

Meredith shrugged. "This is Heighton, not Soho. I want them to catch the bastard."

"Yes, I can see that. Look, I have a contact in the police. I could talk to him, gather all the information, post regular updates to the website as the investigation develops. And let's face it – other news agencies aren't going to be so scrupulous. The details are going to get out, one way or another."

Meredith was nodding. "Alright. I'll take a look. Send me your story, and *if* I think it's worth printing, then we'll talk fees."

"I can do that," said Elspeth. "And if you need anything else, I'm looking for work."

Meredith laughed. "And persistent, too. There is one thing, if you're really that keen. I suppose you could save me a trip out on a Sunday. There's an old dear called Patricia Graves who's just won a local wildlife photography competition. I need an interview. She's expecting one of our reporters tomorrow afternoon. If you can have the piece on my desk by the end of the day, I'll pay you our standard freelance rate – which I warn you, is piss poor. How about it?"

"Done," said Elspeth, trying to hide her grin. The interview was a bind, especially on a weekend, but if it got her a foot in the door, it would be worth it. She'd have to keep looking for work elsewhere, too, but it was something, and it would help to keep her busy and her mind off Andrew.

"Right then," said Meredith. "See Carl on reception on your way out. Leave your contact details, and I'll have him send you the address for tomorrow."

"Thank you," said Elspeth.

"Good to meet you, Miss Reeves." She stuck out her hand, and Elspeth shook it. She had a good feeling about the *Heighton Observer*. It was a minor victory, but it was a start – the first step on the road to taking back control of her life.

Now all she had to do was write the actual story.

CHAPTER SEVEN

Three black coffees later and Elspeth had a draft of a piece on the murder of Lucy Adams.

Lenny's had been heaving with weekend shoppers, but she'd managed to find a table in the corner near a power outlet, and had bashed the story out over the course of a couple of hours. She'd backed it up to her online account, and she'd take another pass through it later that evening before sending it over to Meredith. She just hoped that she wasn't wasting her time. If Meredith didn't bite, she supposed she could try it elsewhere, maybe head over to Oxford and see if any of the papers there might be interested.

Now, it was early afternoon, and she was back in her car, feeling a little wired. She'd grabbed a takeout sandwich and was heading over to Winthorpe for a bit of a nose around.

It had been years since she'd last been to the theatre there, but she had fond memories of the place. Back in her early teens her mum had dragged her along to a performance of *A Midsummer Night's Dream*, hoping to instil in her a little culture, away from the Nintendo and the TV and her mobile phone. Elspeth had gone along expecting to find the whole thing as dull as ditchwater, but was surprised to find herself utterly entranced.

Out there, nestled amongst the trees, watching these strange figures cavorting in the woods, it had seemed as if she'd been transported to a different world. She'd been eager to attend ever since, and Dorothy had made a point of buying tickets two or three times a year during the spring and summer months. It had become something of a ritual: staying up late sipping tea from a flask, eating boiled sweets from a paper bag, wrapping up warm in a blanket against the evening chill as they watched the story unfold.

The theatre programme seemed much the same this year as it always had – she'd looked it up briefly on her phone – only they were clearly attempting to appeal to a broader audience, with additions such as *An Inspector Calls* and *The Importance of Being Earnest* to the lineup. One of these additions was a new play entitled *Corvus*, which was due to premiere the following week. It claimed to chart the rise and fall of the mysterious Carrion King of the Wychwood, and was clearly what Peter had referred to that morning.

She'd decided to see if she could write a local interest piece on the play – maybe even blag some free tickets – but also to surreptitiously investigate any links she could find between the theatre and Lucy Adams. It seemed a little too coincidental that the woman's murder should have been staged in the way it was, just when a new play about the Carrion King myths was preparing for its opening night. She'd seen the look in

Peter's eyes, too – he'd had exactly the same thought.

Elspeth turned the car down a quiet lane, swerving to avoid a cavernous pothole and eliciting a furious beep from the driver of an oncoming Range Rover. She fought the urge to gesture out of her window, and carried on into the heart of the small village.

Winthorpe was on the very edge of the old Wychwood territory, and looked as if it had barely changed since the end of the eighteenth century. Just like Wilsby-under-Wychwood, the houses here had all been built in local stone and capped with slate-tiled roofs, but despite that fact the roadsides were lined with gleaming modern cars, their private registrations suggestive of the wealth in the village. In fact, it looked no different than it had ten years ago, the last time she'd been up here with her mum: just a small collection of cottages and a single pub in the rural outskirts of Oxfordshire.

It had always seemed an odd place for a theatre, although she supposed that was what gave the place its charm. The theatre itself was set in the grounds of Winthorpe Manor, in a natural copse on the edges of the woodland that still covered much of the estate. The owners of the manor house had begun to put on shows there over thirty years ago – or so her mum had told her – looking for ways to generate revenue to help pay for repairs and maintenance of the house. It wasn't until the eldest son took over, though, that it had become the draw it was now, pulling in people from all around the region. It offered something different to the theatres in Oxford – something more primitive, perhaps, both in terms of the performance and the overall experience.

The eldest son – Elspeth had forgotten his name – had invested in the theatre, building tiered seating around the edge of the copse and erecting a permanent scaffold and canvas roof over it, allowing paying visitors to watch in relative comfort, even if the cast themselves were forced to soldier on through whatever the elements decided to throw at them, stuck out in the open air amongst the trees.

The trees provided an unusual, atmospheric backdrop, particularly as the sun went down and the electric lights and smoke effects were deployed to their full effect. Practically, too, it meant that the stage area could be easily accessed from almost any direction, with the actors leaping out from between the trees whenever they were required for a scene. She recalled there was a small brick building off to one side of the stage that served as the backstage and storage area, although she'd never been inside.

Elspeth was close now, and she slowed down, trying to spot the correct turning. She saw the sign for the theatre a moment later and turned off to the left, driving through a set of wrought-iron gates and along a narrow track towards the car park. She churned the gravel as she pulled up beside a rather battered-looking silver Ford Focus and turned off her engine. There were seven or eight other cars here, suggesting that rehearsals were still taking place. She'd hoped that would be the case, given it was the Saturday before opening week.

She grabbed her notebook and phone off the passenger seat and climbed out.

In the distance, beyond a large expanse of meticulous

lawn, the manor house loomed, morose and silent. She had no idea how old it was, but it had been 'improved' during the Victorian era, when a large orangery had been added, along with crenellations on the roof and a rather ostentatious neo-Gothic portico.

Ahead of her the path fell away down a gentle incline towards the auditorium. Its stretched canvas roof looked stark against the sea of trees beyond, which stirred in the breeze, scattering birds. This was one of the largest remaining areas of woodland that had once formed the ancient Wychwood, although it was largely out of bounds to ordinary folk like Elspeth. There were around two hundred acres of it on the estate, if she remembered correctly.

She picked her way down beneath the canvas, expecting to see people from the theatre company milling about, or rehearsing scenes, but the place seemed completely empty. Peering in both directions, she decided to head around to the backstage area to see if anyone was about.

Much to her relief, she found a tall, thin man leaning against the wall smoking a cigarette. He looked up when he saw her approaching, the cigarette dangling from the corner of his mouth. He couldn't have been older than twenty-five, and had long dark hair that curled behind his ears, and a vaguely androgynous look that Elspeth found rather appealing. He was wearing black eyeliner and tight black jeans, and was hugging himself against the chill.

"Can I help you?" he said. He blew smoke from the corner of his mouth.

"I hope so," said Elspeth. "I'm a journalist. I…"

she hesitated, trying to figure out how best to present herself. "I'm planning to write a piece about the play, *Corvus*, and was looking for someone who might be able to answer a few questions."

He narrowed his eyes, as if suddenly suspicious. Then, having evidently weighed up his options, he tossed his cigarette butt on the floor, ground it under his heel, and nodded towards the door in the wall behind him. "You'll be wanting Vanessa. She's in there. Although… if you're here about, you know, you're not going to get any salacious gossip. Not today."

Elspeth frowned, and her look of confusion must have convinced him of her sincerity, as he stepped forward and opened the door for her. "Be it on your own head, then."

Unsure what the hell he was talking about, Elspeth stepped through the door.

It opened directly onto a large room, with polished wooden floors, a bunch of chairs and foldout tables, and two large rails of costumes on hangers. Doors led off to changing rooms, lavatories and what appeared to be a small kitchenette. Someone had opened a bottle of red wine and it was standing nearly empty on the nearest table, surrounded by a number of crumpled plastic cups.

Elspeth counted ten people sitting around in a loose circle, some of them on chairs, some of them perched on the edge of tables or cross-legged on the floor. Most were sipping wine from plastic cups, and as one, they looked around when they heard her enter. For a single, dreadful moment she thought one of them was Andrew – but then he frowned, and she saw that it wasn't him at all, but just another man in his late thirties who bore a faint resemblance. She swallowed, her mouth suddenly dry, and tried to put the thought out of her mind.

A pretty black woman in jeans and a red sweater glanced accusingly at the man who'd shown her in. "Oscar?"

"She's a journalist," he said from behind her. "Says she's here about the play. Wants to do a piece on us, apparently."

The woman glowered disbelievingly at Elspeth. "Look, have you people got no decency whatsoever? We're all in shock."

"I'm sorry," said Elspeth, taken aback by the unexpected vehemence. Her heart was thrumming. Had she been right? Clearly *something* was going on here. "I don't mean to be insensitive, but I have no idea what you're talking about. I'm looking for someone called Vanessa, to talk about the play. Look, if it's a bad time…"

The woman frowned. "I'm Vanessa," she said. "And you really don't know, do you?"

Elspeth shrugged.

"The owner of the theatre was found dead yesterday," said one of the other women. She was rosy-cheeked, as if she'd already indulged in a little too much wine. She had long dark hair shot through with streaks of blue, framing a round face. She had a friendly demeanour. She glanced at Vanessa, as if seeking approval. "Murdered. None of us can believe it."

"You mean Lucy Adams?" said Elspeth.

The owner of the theatre. She hadn't been expecting that.

"So you *do* know," said a scruffy-looking man, at least a decade older than most of the others, who was sitting on the floor with a ring binder open on his lap, containing what appeared to be a script.

"She was found behind my mum's house. I didn't know who she was. I'm so sorry. No wonder you're all in shock."

Vanessa got to her feet. "Let's talk outside." She gestured to the door, and Elspeth nodded and followed her out, still feeling a little shaken after the initial shock of seeing the man she'd taken to be Andrew.

"I'm sorry," said Vanessa, when the door had shut behind them. "It's just… we're all a bit jumpy, you know."

"Understandable," said Elspeth. "Did you know her well?"

"Unfortunately," said Vanessa. "I had to work with her." She looked suddenly regretful. "That sounded worse than I'd intended. It's just… Lucy was a difficult woman. Always trying to get too involved. She was the owner of this place – or, at least, her husband was. But *I'm* the producer. It's my responsibility to organise everything. As the owner she's supposed to sit back and take her cut of the proceeds. But Lucy isn't…" She paused to correct herself. "*Wasn't* like that. She wanted to know what we were up to all the time. Even sat in on rehearsals sometimes and gave the actors notes. Last week, Oscar was furious…" She stopped herself suddenly, as if realising she'd said too much. "Look, this is off the record, okay. You've caught us at a bad time."

"Don't worry," said Elspeth. "Look, my notebook is still shut. I genuinely do want to know more about the play. I've only recently moved back to the area and I'm writing a few pieces for the *Heighton Observer*. I thought a short article might help to generate local interest. I'm interested to find out more about the mythology, too, the stories the play is based on."

"Okay," said Vanessa. "Well, we can do with all the publicity we can get." She gave Elspeth a half-hearted smile. "I didn't even ask your name."

"Elspeth Reeves." She stuck out her hand. "Ellie."

The other woman took it. "Vanessa Eglington. Nice to meet you. You've already met Oscar, who's playing the Carrion King, and Rose, our stage manager. And the chap with the folder is David Keel, the writer-cum-director of this fine endeavour. He's a little spiky, but he'll be able to help you with all the mythology stuff. I'd introduce you to the others, but I don't think now is a good time…"

Elspeth held up her hand. "Say no more. I'll come back later. Although… I'm sorry to ask, but is the play still going ahead? You're supposed to be opening on Friday, aren't you?"

Vanessa nodded. "John – that's Lucy's husband – has given his blessing for us to continue. Says it's what Lucy would have wanted. So yes, we're still going ahead. The show must go on and all that. We've all put so much work in. Lucy included."

Elspeth smiled. "I don't suppose you have a spare copy of the programme I could take away? Just so I can read up in advance, prepare some questions."

Vanessa nodded. "Of course. They're back inside. Come on, I'll fetch you one. I'll give you my number, too, so we can sort something out. We're going to be rehearsing most nights this week."

They turned back towards the dressing rooms, just

in time to see Peter and another man coming along the path. Peter locked eyes with Elspeth, and she couldn't quite tell whether it was a look of wry amusement or disapproval. She offered him her most charming smile.

"Are they with you?" asked Vanessa.

"No, we're not," said Peter. "Detective Sergeant Peter Shaw, and Detective Constable Ravi Patel," he said, holding up his identification. "I'm looking for Vanessa Eglington."

Vanessa gave an audible sigh. "That'll be me," she said.

"And the rest of the cast and crew? Mr Adams said you would be rehearsing down here. We've just come from the house."

"No one felt very much like rehearsing this afternoon, DS Shaw. Now, what can I do for you?"

"Let's step inside for a moment, shall we?" said Peter. Elspeth grinned. It was strange to see Peter acting so confident and forthright. She followed them inside and waited by the door, trying to keep out of the way. Vanessa shot her an apologetic look, but quickly indicated a pile of glossy programmes on the table, the covers emblazoned with a stylised crow motif. Elspeth grabbed one and tucked it under her arm.

"Everybody, this is DS Shaw," said Vanessa.

"You're here about Lucy," said David Keel.

Peter nodded. "We just have a few questions. We need to establish everyone's whereabouts on Thursday evening, just so we can eliminate people from our enquiries. DC Patel is going to come around and speak to you all individually."

"That's easy," said Oscar, from across the other side of the room. He was perched on the edge of a table, rolling himself another cigarette. "We were all in the pub. Together. Thursday's rehearsal night, and we all went up to The Horse and Cart for a few drinks afterwards. It's tradition."

"All of you?" said Peter.

There was a murmur of agreement from amongst the cast and crew. "Well, all except Vanessa," said one of the women whom Elspeth had yet to be introduced to.

Peter glanced at Vanessa, a question in his eyes.

"No, that's right," said Vanessa. "I stayed here. There was a lot to finish up. We're opening next week."

Peter nodded. "DC Patel will speak to everyone in turn. It won't take long." He crossed to where Vanessa was standing beside the costume rails. "Is this where you keep all of the costumes for the show?" he asked.

"Yes, that's right. For the current production. Everything else is in storage."

"It's the current production I'm interested in," said Peter. "Can you just confirm for me that everything is where it should be, please?"

Vanessa gave him a quizzical look. "I really can't see what you're driving at, Detective."

"If you could just check if anything is missing, Ms Eglington."

Reluctantly, Vanessa began scanning the rails, at first arbitrarily, but then with an expression of increasing confusion. She repeated the action, going through each garment again – an assortment of mediaeval robes, furs, and cloaks – before turning to the others, who were still sitting in a loose circle, while DC Patel spoke to Rose over in the corner. "Alice, you haven't taken your costume today, have you?"

A young blonde woman in leggings and a T-shirt, who was sitting beside David Keel on the floor, looked over and shook her head. "No. I haven't touched it today. Why?"

Vanessa glanced at Peter. "I can't seem to find it on the rail," she said. "Elizabeth, you haven't taken it for repair?"

An older woman, whom Elspeth guessed to be in her mid to late forties, got up from her chair and went over to join Peter and Vanessa by the rails. "No. I've not seen it since rehearsals on Thursday."

Vanessa took a deep breath, and looked at Peter. "Then it's missing," she said. "Look, has this got something to do with Lucy? How did you know one of the costumes was missing?"

Peter looked at Elizabeth. "Can you describe it for me? The missing garment."

"Yes, it's a coat made of white swan feathers. But I don't understand. It should be here, on the rail."

"Thank you," said Peter. He turned back to Vanessa. "I'm going to need details of everyone who has access to this backstage area," he said. "And details of exactly what happened on Thursday evening. I think it might be better if we continue this at the station. DC Patel can finish up here."

"Well... alright," said Vanessa. She looked terrified. "I'll just fetch my coat." She crossed the room and disappeared for a moment into the kitchen. Peter took the opportunity to walk over to join Elspeth.

"Look, you'd better go," he said. "I'm going back to the station, but I'll give you a shout later, okay?"

Elspeth nodded. She could see the way things were going here. She lowered her voice to a whisper. "Okay. But you don't really think Vanessa is involved, do you?"

"At the moment, I'm keeping all of my options open," he said. "Now, I'll see you later." He leaned around her and pointedly opened the door. She smiled brightly, before ducking out, the programme for *Corvus* still clutched tightly beneath her arm.

CHAPTER EIGHT

"It's nice to have someone to cook for, for a change," said Dorothy, as she dolloped out a portion of shepherd's pie and slid it over to Elspeth, who was sitting at the kitchen table, scrolling through an impenetrable website on her tablet.

"What was that, Mum?"

"I said it's nice to have you here, love. That's all. Despite the… well, you know."

"I know," said Elspeth. She took a swig of wine. She'd been attempting to absorb a particularly onerous academic article on the mythology of the Carrion King, but was faltering at the unnecessary obfuscation and reams of footnotes and references.

Her mum slid into the seat opposite. "I had a little bit of a tidy around while you were out today. I thought that if you're going to be staying for a while you might need a bit more room, so I sorted out all that stuff in your old wardrobe into boxes."

"What, *all* of it?"

Dorothy nodded. "I thought you might drop it down to the charity shop. There's a box of old records there for starters. Some kids' books, a few T-shirts, a bag of teddy bears. That sort of thing."

"I'll take a look later. I want to try to get through this first."

"What are you up to?"

"It's for the story I'm working on. Just a bit of research."

"You're not still poking into that horrible business from yesterday, are you?" She could hear the distaste in Dorothy's voice. "Everyone at work was talking about it today. That poor woman."

"She was called Lucy Adams. She and her husband owned Winthorpe Manor, and the theatre. Did you ever meet her?"

"Oh, that's awful," said Dorothy. "No, I don't think I ever did. And to think, all those times we went up there."

Elspeth nodded. "I drove over there today. They're all in shock."

"I'm not surprised. But what were you doing up there?"

"I've written a piece on Lucy Adams's murder for the *Heighton Observer*." She'd emailed it to Meredith soon after getting back from the theatre. "Meredith Stokes said she'd take a look at it. Plus I'm helping the police. Well, sort of."

"Helping the police? You mean Peter?" Dorothy smiled. "I remember him from when you were kids. You always did get on well. I see him about the village quite a bit."

"Well, yeah." Elspeth shrugged. "I think I might have given him an idea this morning and—"

"So *that's* why you were up and out so quickly. I

wondered if perhaps Andrew had called…?"

Elspeth shook her head. "No. I found something in one of my old books last night. I thought it might be useful, that's all. I don't think Andrew's going to be calling, Mum. And to be honest, I'm not sure that I want him to." She took a forkful of shepherd's pie. "This is lovely."

There was a rap at the door. Dorothy pushed her plate aside and got up to answer it.

"Ah, good evening, Mrs Reeves. I was wondering if, um, if Elspeth was in."

Elspeth glanced over at her mum, who was standing in the open doorway, grinning. "Peter wants to know if you're going out to play, Ellie?"

Elspeth laughed. "Let him in, Mum."

Dorothy stood aside to let Peter pass. He had to duck beneath the ancient lintel so as not to bang his head. He offered Elspeth a rueful grin. He was dressed in his civvies – a pair of skinny jeans, and a black and white paisley shirt beneath a green jacket. "Sorry to bother you. I didn't realise you were eating. I can come back."

"No. No, it's fine," said Elspeth. "Pull up a chair for a minute. Do you want some? Mum always makes too much."

"I won't, thank you. I ate earlier." He pulled out a chair, which scraped upon the terracotta floor tiles, causing them all to wince. Sheepishly, he sat down. "I was just wondering if you fancied coming out for a drink?"

Elspeth placed her tablet down on the table, weighing him up.

"You know, to discuss the case," he added hurriedly. He produced a manila folder from inside his jacket and placed it on the table. "I wanted to say thanks for earlier."

"Okay," said Elspeth. "Let me grab my keys." She took a final forkful of her shepherd's pie, and then stood and placed the dish by the sink. She left Peter and her mum chatting about the old days as she ran up to her room to get ready.

She was forced to manoeuvre through the slalom of boxes on the landing – spotting a copy of Duran Duran's *Rio* poking out of the top of one of them as she passed by, and making a mental note to rescue it later – before quickly changing her top, freshening up, and grabbing her handbag. Five minutes later she was back downstairs. "Ready?" she said, laughing at the sight of Peter, who'd been forced to succumb to Dorothy's shepherd's pie after all. He looked like a deer caught in headlights.

"Yes, well, I…"

Elspeth shook her head, laughing. She grabbed her coat off the hook by the door. "See you later, Mum."

"Don't worry, Ellie dear. I won't wait up."

After a decade frequenting the bars and pubs of Central London – which were sometimes so busy that the patrons would be forced to huddle in the street outside, irrespective of the weather – The White Hart seemed like a strange throwback, a relic from the previous century, somehow preserved for the modern day. If it weren't for the trilling of the fruit machine in the corner or the ancient jukebox belting out a song by The Clash, it would have been easy to imagine they'd just walked into a time warp.

The place was stuffed to the rafters with memorabilia: an old wheelbarrow; an unwound grandfather clock;

a portrait of a gentrified landowner with his hounds; a rusting claymore mounted on the wall in iron brackets; and scores of dusty barrels and demijohns. A small black dog was curled up before an open fire, and a row of grey-haired men sat at the wooden bar in companionable silence, sipping their pints. Unlike most modern pubs, the décor hadn't been updated, and the walls had not been knocked through – there were still several interconnected rooms, wood panelled and gloomy, each of them smelling of stale beer and damp.

"What would you like?"

"Better make it a G&T," said Ellie, as Peter leaned over the bar and caught the landlord's attention. "I'll go find us a seat."

She chose a nook towards the back of the pub, away from prying ears. Not that she thought any of the old gents would be the least bit interested in what she or Peter had to say; they'd barely acknowledged them – or each other – since they'd arrived.

Ellie checked her phone. There was no signal. She slid it into her bag.

Peter found her a couple of minutes later. He was carrying a bag of pork scratchings between his teeth. He placed her drink on the mat before her.

"What?" he said, as he pulled out a stool. "They'll put hairs on your chest."

Elspeth laughed. "Give us one, then." He grinned and tossed her the packet.

"So, you didn't tell me there'd been more than one murder."

"Straight to business, then," said Peter. He took a

swig of his beer. "You know I'm not supposed to talk about this stuff, don't you? I really shouldn't have let you leave the scene yesterday, either."

"My lips are sealed."

"You're a *journalist*!"

She laughed. "Well, alright. But if we're going to solve this, you can't go holding that against me."

Peter grinned. "We?"

"Well, it doesn't hurt to pool resources, does it? Especially as you're going to be stuck with me for a bit."

"I am?"

Elspeth smiled. "Full disclosure. I'm going to cover the story for the *Heighton Observer*. Assuming they like what I do, that is. But they're being dutiful and won't publish anything until your lot gives them the okay, so you don't have to worry. I'm going to keep your secrets."

"The *Heighton Observer*," said Peter. "So you *are* sticking around for a while."

Elspeth sipped at her drink. The bitter tonic was sharp and refreshing. "No more prevaricating. Murders. *Plural*. Are you going to tell me what's going on?"

Peter took the folder from inside his jacket. "I hope I can trust you, Elspeth." He handed it to her.

"Bit late for that now," she said, with a wicked grin. "I've told you, I'm not going to say a word. And besides, I want to *help*. If I'm going to go poking around for a story, I might as well make myself useful."

She went to open the folder, but Peter leaned over and caught her wrist. His grip was firm. "Before you open that, are you sure you want to see what's inside? It's worse than what you saw yesterday."

She nodded. "I'm made of sterner stuff than you think." He released his hold on her arm, and she opened the folder.

The first page was a form, covered in indecipherable typescript. She skipped over it. Behind this was a sheaf of photographs. She cocked her head to one side as she tried to make sense of what she was seeing. It looked like an animal slumped at the base of a tree. She leafed through, peering more closely, until she happened upon a picture of a man's startled face, and she finally realised what she was looking at.

The subject of the photographs was a man in late middle age. He'd been shot in the chest with an arrow – the stem of the projectile still protruded from his left breast, presumably buried in his heart, and blood had trickled down his pale chest, stark and unsightly. Like the woman, he'd been stripped naked, but rather than feathers he'd been dressed in animal skins, with a thick fur collar wrapped around his neck. Antlers – evidently removed from the carcass of a stag – had been affixed to his head with a wire skullcap, giving him a bizarre, otherworldly appearance. His lined face was fixed in a grimace of shock and pain, his eyes still open but clouded over.

Elspeth flicked through the rest of the photographs, grimacing.

"His name was Geoffrey Altman," said Peter. "A gamekeeper over at Ascott-under-Wychwood. He was found like that almost two weeks ago, in the woods on the grounds of Ascott Manor. So far we've drawn a total blank. He was a widower who'd disassociated himself with his family over twenty years ago, and no one with any motive or anything obvious to gain from his death. He was close to retirement. Until today, we couldn't even make sense of the symbolism. We just assumed it was some bizarre ritual, cooked up by a crackpot obsessed with the occult."

"You might still be right on that count," said Elspeth, closing the file. "But it seems very clear that this poor man has been dressed to resemble another member of the Carrion King's court."

"The Master of the Hunt," said Peter.

"Precisely," agreed Elspeth.

Peter closed the file. "There are going to be more, aren't there? More deaths. Who were the other members of the Carrion King's court again? The Master of the Pentacle, The Confessor…"

"The Fool," said Elspeth.

"The Fool," echoed Peter. He looked thoughtful as he took another swig of his beer. "So we're looking at another three potential victims for starters. Unless we can find the killer first."

"So what about the Winthorpe lot?" said Elspeth. "It seems too much of a coincidence that Lucy was the owner of a theatre putting on a play about the Carrion King. Especially as it looks like she was dressed in the missing costume, too. Do you suspect someone from the theatre?"

Peter shrugged. "I suspect everyone until I can prove otherwise. That's my job. But it seems likely that one or more of them have something to do with it. Although they claim they were all in the pub until late on Thursday night, and Patel says it all checks out with the landlord. All of them except Vanessa Eglington, who says she stayed behind at the theatre to finish up. Alone. There's no way of corroborating her story."

"And she did say that things were a bit tense between her and Lucy," added Elspeth. "Although… she just doesn't seem the type. To be a killer, I mean."

"There *is* no type. Not in my experience. But there are other considerations. She'd have had a hard time manoeuvring the body on her own. She's only slight. Although she might have had an accomplice."

Elspeth nodded. "What about Geoffrey Altman? Is there any link there, between him and the theatre lot?"

"Not as far as we can tell. They all have alibis for the night he died, and there's no history of any contact between them – or at least not any that we've uncovered so far. Patel was pretty thorough, and he's spent today confirming everyone's movements. But we can't rule out anything yet. They could be unconnected – although that seems unlikely – or there could be more than one killer, working together." He shrugged. "We'll just have to keep digging."

"What about the other costume? It looks as though Altman was dressed in similar stuff, too. Had that come from the theatre?"

Peter shook his head. "No. It's different from the one they're using in the play. But it's much less elaborate than the coat, and therefore easier to copy – just a bit of fur and some antlers. Anyone could have done it, if they'd had the inclination."

"I suppose," said Elspeth. She took another sip of her drink. "The husband?"

"John Adams? It doesn't seem likely. Although he's not

sure where Lucy had been on the night of her death. She'd told him she was going out with a friend from Heighton, but the friend says they had no such arrangement."

"And where was he?"

"He has a watertight alibi. He was at the snooker club all evening. We found her handbag in the car park with her phone in it, and the history shows that he called her three times before going to bed, but couldn't get an answer. When he discovered she still wasn't home in the morning he called the station."

"So what now? I suppose you're trying to find out where she'd been, tracking CCTV, that sort of thing?"

"As far as we can," said Peter, "while we wait for the autopsy results. We've got uniforms searching the woods, too, looking for her discarded clothes, or anything left behind by the killer." He reached for a pork scratching and munched on it loudly. "I keep going over what you said, though. About the Consort being a 'fallen woman'. That could have some bearing. I mean – it seems obvious now why Geoffrey Altman was chosen as The Master of the Hunt, being a gamekeeper and all…"

"So you think Lucy might have some sort of sordid past?"

Peter shrugged. "Again, too early to tell. But we're looking into it." He drained the last of his pint. "But thanks to you we have another line of inquiry, too."

"The Carrion King," said Elspeth.

Peter nodded. "Whoever the killer is, they clearly have a deep fascination with the legend. So that's where we look next. We try to pin down anyone in the area who might be able to point us in the right direction.

The theatre group is a start. But there might be others. People who can help shed a little more light."

"Ah, now that's where I can help," said Elspeth. "I've been looking into the legend in a little more depth. There's quite a bit online, and one of the websites I found pointed me to a bookshop in Heighton. The owner is a man named Philip Cowper, and he runs a small imprint from the back of the shop, publishing local interest books. Apparently he's authored a book on the Carrion King called *The King in Shadow*. I was planning to call in tomorrow to pick up a copy and see if I could get anything useful out of him."

"Then we should go together," said Peter.

"Alright. But I think I've earned another G&T, don't you?" She held up her empty glass.

"You're on," said Peter, getting to his feet. "And then you can tell me what you're *really* doing back."

Elspeth sighed. She supposed she should have seen that coming. She tucked a strand of loose hair behind her ear, and smiled. "Okay, DS Shaw. I'll submit to questioning. But it's going to cost you some crisps, too."

He went off to the bar, laughing.

Elspeth leaned back in her chair, chewing on her bottom lip. All she could think of was Geoffrey Altman's blank, slack-jawed expression.

CHAPTER NINE

Had it always been this way?

Had he always harboured such bitterness?

After so long, he could no longer be sure. Memories, he'd found, became dulled with overuse, like a favoured blade. What once cut deep and clean now left only a ragged, uneven scar. Equally, the mind was prone to flights of fancy, or at the very least, to colouring the events of the past with the learning of the present, twisting those memories until they were no longer pure.

Back then he'd been a different person. He'd known confusion, sorrow, fear, the burning need to belong – but he could never have imagined he would develop such a capacity for loathing. And yet, as he watched the woman preening in the mirror, he felt that hatred swelling inside of him, bursting to get out.

Soon, he would let it. He would harness it.

Around him the Wychwood was silent and still, save for a gentle breeze stirring the treetops and the shrill cawing of a crow, somewhere deep amongst the twisted boughs. It was dark, and only a thin sliver of moonlight breached the canopy above, casting the copse in a weak silvery light. The nearby branches became sinister jagged silhouettes, taking on eerie, human qualities, as if the trees themselves had gathered in a circle around this place to watch while it was done.

Being here, in the place where it had all happened – it made him feel alive. The heady scent of the damp earth seemed somehow primeval, transporting him to a simpler time. Here, he felt connected to the past in a way that he never had elsewhere. That he never *could*. Here, he felt part of something bigger than himself.

He knelt in the soft loam, scoring channels in the dirt with the end of a stick, describing the ancient sigils that would allow him to enact his vengeance. It was a surprisingly simple ritual, its success predicated on the will of the caster. And willpower was something he had in abundance. That was something *they'd* forced him to learn.

He glanced again at the mirror, propped upon the ancient stump of a tree. The woman in the silvered glass was leaning close, studying her own reflection as she made her preparations for bed.

She looked gaunt and tired. Ugly.

Even now, despite days of studying her pathetic routine, the sight of her shocked him – how time had ravaged her once-delicate features, leaving her craggy and lined and downtrodden. Here was a woman who had been beaten by life, who dragged her miserable carcass around her house each day without a single ambition beyond her own survival. And soon, he would take even that from her. It was no less than she deserved.

He watched as she tugged a brush through her wiry

mop of hair. It was thinning now, with age and mistreatment, and peppered with strands of dull grey. It was unkempt and uncared for, much like the woman herself.

She had wasted her life. That was, perhaps, her greatest crime – that she had lived for so long, free from prosecution, and that she had done *nothing* with those stolen days.

He realised he was grinding his teeth. There it was again – that sickening hatred, boiling up inside of him. He wanted only to be free of it. And he wanted her to suffer.

He drew a deep breath. His heart was racing. The time had come.

He locked eyes with the woman in the mirror.

She seemed to recognise immediately that something was wrong. Her face creased in panic, her eyes widening. He felt her trying to turn away, but he held her gaze, forcing her to remain before the mirror. He always had been stronger than she'd given him credit for.

Slowly, he raised his arm and opened his hand.

Confused, horrified, the woman mirrored his action, dropping her hairbrush to the floor. She had no idea what was happening. Tears were forming in the corners of her eyes, trickling down her cheeks.

He grinned, and the woman grinned back at him, gormless and hollow. Her eyes told a different story.

Carefully, almost delicately, he puppeted her hand, reaching out for the pair of scissors she had left upon the top of the dressing table. Her fingers closed around the handles. He raised his arm again, and she followed suit, holding the scissors high above her head, the tip of the blades pointing towards her belly.

She emitted a tremulous sob as realisation finally struck.

He exhaled, savouring the moment. Then he brought his fist down violently against his belly, and watched, fascinated, as the woman plunged the scissors deep into her own flesh.

Blood welled instantly, spilling out over her fist.

He didn't even allow her to cry out, before raising his arm again, and again, and again, causing gouts of thick, oily blood to rupture from her veins. He didn't stop until her body crumpled to the floor, unable to support itself any longer, a patchwork mess of blood and ruptured flesh.

Then he kicked away all traces of his sigils, collected his mirror, and left.

Behind him, the trees whispered excitedly as the breeze stirred their leaves.

CHAPTER TEN

It was late when she finally got home, feeling a little worse for the wear. Her mum had already gone to bed, and the house was still and silent. She crept along the landing, trying to avoid the floorboards that creaked. She was surprised she still remembered where they were – like a muscle memory, returning to remind her of her misspent youth.

She reached her room, clicked the light on, and collapsed onto the bed.

Peter had walked her to the door, claiming that he'd never hear the end of it from her mum if he let her walk back on her own, after what had gone on in the woods the other night. He'd given her a peck on the cheek, and she'd been more than content to leave it at that.

She wasn't stupid, of course – she'd seen the way he looked at her. But he was *Peter*. A childhood friend, and the only one she had left around here these days. He'd told her tonight about Helen, who'd been struck down with a debilitating motor neurone disease at the age of twenty-seven and was living in a nearby hospice, and Benedict, who'd made a name for himself in computer games and was in LA, making the most of the sunshine. She'd felt shock, and a momentary pang of regret on hearing the news. She'd never been good at keeping in touch with people from her past, and she'd never really been able to understand why. She had a habit of compartmentalising things, and always running at the future, never taking enough time to look back. She'd done that to her mum, and she'd done that to her friends. Maybe what she had now was a chance to put some of that right.

There were friends in London, of course, but at the moment, they just felt too associated with Andrew. They all knew what had happened, and somehow that just got in the way. Everything was just about the breakup. There was no getting away from it. Even if they weren't talking about it, she could see it in their eyes. And they were also so damn happy, too – married with young kids, in high-flying jobs in the city. Being around them at the moment just made everything a bit too raw.

She knew they cared, that they all really did have her best interests at heart, but right now, she needed to be as far away from Andrew, and London, as possible.

She dumped her clothes on the chair in the corner and turned the music on her phone on low, lying back while Natasha Khan sang her to sleep with a gentle lament.

Sunday morning brought with it a headache to end all headaches. Elspeth squeezed her eyes shut and rolled over, trying to ignore the light streaming in through a crack in the curtains. She was going to have to do something about that. Her back ached from sleeping in an awkward position, and her tongue felt as if she'd been licking the carpet.

She heard footsteps on the stairs, followed by a rap at the door, and sighed.

"Cup of coffee for you, love." The door opened and Dorothy bustled in, already dressed and smiling brightly. "Thought you could probably use it."

"Hmmm," mumbled Elspeth.

"Didn't you say you had to be up for something this morning?"

Elspeth frowned, waiting for her brain to engage. There was the interview that afternoon in Heighton, with the woman who'd won the photography competition, but her mum was right. There was something else she'd planned to do, too... "Oh, the bookshop," she groaned.

"I'll leave you to it then," said Dorothy, placing her coffee on the nightstand.

She couldn't face breakfast, so after a quick shower, a couple of ibuprofen and another mug of coffee she hopped in the car for the short drive to Heighton. She hoped she wasn't still over the limit. And that Philip Cowper wouldn't be able to smell the alcohol on her breath.

She parked the car in the marketplace and fed coins into the machine, poking at the buttons with bleary eyes until it spat out a ticket. She grabbed for it, still feeling a little queasy.

"You could have parked at the station, you know," said a voice from behind her.

She turned to see Peter holding two takeout coffees. He looked remarkably together, given the amount he'd had to drink.

She grinned. "I'm not going within a hundred yards of a breathalyser until after lunch. You led me astray. You're a bad man."

He laughed and proffered one of the cups. "Well, in that case, here's a peace offering. Although I must say in my defence, you were easily led."

"Thanks." She took the coffee and walked over to the car, placing it on the roof while she affixed the ticket to the windscreen.

"So, does your inspector know about this little outing?"

"DCI Griffiths?" Peter looked a little sheepish. "She knows I'm following up on the Carrion King lead, and that I'm enlisting the help of some experts to do so."

Elspeth laughed. "So I'm an expert now, am I?"

"Well, you were the one who spotted the connection in the first place. But probably best we don't let her know about your clandestine visit to the crime scene."

"It all feels a little underhand," said Elspeth. While it was exciting to be working so closely with Peter on the investigation, she had to admit, the thought of going behind the inspector's back made her feel a little uneasy. "I mean, don't get me wrong. If I'm going to be writing this story I want to help, but shouldn't we be upfront about it?"

Peter laughed. "I would have thought your time in London might have cured you of such idealistic notions, Ellie. We do what we need to do to get the job done. That's how this works. As long as I stay within the law and follow due process, DCI Griffiths won't care. Promise. Like I said before, she's interested in results. A little too much, sometimes. Besides, it's only a visit to a bookshop."

Elspeth nodded. "Well, if you insist. Shall we get on with it, then?"

Peter nodded. "Lead on, lead on."

Elspeth led him along the high street, then cut down a small passage between two charity shops, across a courtyard in which the patrons from a café sat smoking cigarettes over greasy bacon rolls and black coffee, and out onto Westgate, where Westgate Books was nestled between a haberdashery shop and a jeweller's.

It was an old, narrow building over three floors, with an impressive garret window. The exterior had been recently painted in bright green gloss, and a fresh sign, its legend written in swirling gold, hung above the door. A small table of yellowing paperbacks had been placed before the ground-floor window, along with a handwritten sign declaring them '3 FOR £1'. A small black tin served as an honesty box on the table beside them.

Through the window and its heaped display of faded, curling books, she could see a grey-haired man inside, shuffling about between the stacks of books.

"I think you'd better go first," said Elspeth, gesturing toward the door.

"It's your natural habitat too," countered Peter, but did as she asked. A bell trilled somewhere deep in the bowels of the shop, and the man looked up from the heap of books in his arms.

"Good morning," he said. "Come on in, feel free to browse. If there's anything you're looking for, just ask." He turned his attention back to his books. He was an untidy-looking fellow, with unkempt grey hair, wild eyebrows, and a scratchy beard that might have just been a couple of days' worth of growth he hadn't dealt with. He was wearing a red sleeveless pullover, nicked with holes, and a pair of semi-circular reading glasses. He was short, but seemed taller because of his outlandish hair.

"Actually, it's more 'anyone' than 'anything'," said Peter. "Would it be possible to speak with Mr Philip Cowper, please?"

The man's demeanour shifted. His wiry eyebrows knitted into a frown. He placed the pile of books on the countertop behind him, and made a steeple with his hands, as if carefully considering his answer. "I am Philip Cowper," he said. "And *you* are?"

Peter reached for his ID and handed it to the man. "The police. I'm DS Peter Shaw, and this is Ms Elspeth Reeves."

Cowper was still frowning. "Well, happy to oblige, of course, but I haven't reported any crimes. Nor," he added hastily, "have I knowingly committed any." The man's voice had an annoying clipped quality, and he made a point of enunciating every syllable. He was the sort of man, Elspeth decided, who was going to respond to flattery.

"We're hoping to make use of your expertise," she said. "We understand you're something of an authority on local mythology."

Cowper seemed momentarily taken aback. Then a broad grin spread across his face, and he puffed out his chest like a prize cock. "Well, it's a very broad subject, of course, but I certainly have *some* insight I could share. I wrote a book, you know…?"

"On the legend of the Carrion King, yes," said Elspeth. "I'd like to buy a copy if I may."

"Well, yes. Yes, indeed!" said Cowper. "There's a display of them over here. These are all books that I've published." He waved at a table piled high with five or six different titles, and then took a slim volume from the pile and handed it to her. The garish cover showed a photograph of a crow in flight, superimposed over a shot of local woodland. She smiled. "He's a fascinating figure. Our own Merlin, if you like, although with something of a darker temperament."

"Do you believe he was real?"

"Oh, yes," said Cowper. "Without question. I don't believe for one minute that his occult practices had any legitimacy – that he was, for want of a better word, a *magician* – but there's no question in my mind that he existed, and that he gathered a cohort of followers in the woodland nearby. He was a great orator, and people were taken in by his promises." He looked wistful, as if remembering better times. "So, what precisely can I help you with?"

"Well, I'd also like a copy of your book, and it would help a great deal with my enquiries if you could tell us where you were the night of the twenty-third?" Peter said.

Cowper narrowed his eyes. "Is this about those murders? I can assure you, they have nothing to do with me."

"I'm afraid I'm not at liberty to disclose that, sir, but I assure you, this is just a routine enquiry."

"I, well, that was three days ago, wasn't it?" Cowper mumbled. "I was here until closing – that's six o'clock – and then I called in at The Old Dun Cow for a quick pint, before heading to Gerald's for dinner."

"Gerald?" pressed Peter.

"Gerald Soames. He's my partner. I can give you his details if you need to speak with him to confirm anything. I've nothing to hide. I spent the night there and came straight to the shop in the morning."

"Thank you, Mr Cowper. It's just a formality. I'm sure you understand." Peter offered him a reassuring smile, and he seemed to relax a little. "How about the twelfth? Can you recall what you might have been doing that evening?"

Cowper tapped his chin. "Yes, as a matter of fact, I know precisely what I was doing. Here," he went to the counter and opened a cupboard, extracting a small display board, which he handed to Peter. Peter turned it so Elspeth could see. It showed a picture of a smiling woman in her sixties, along with an array of colourful book covers, all pastels and smiling women in nineteen-forties dress.

"I was hosting a signing event and talk at the shop, by Blythe Pettifer. She's a wonderful author from Oxford. She writes wartime sagas, and she's terribly underrated. All the bookshops over there are all too snobby to support her, of course, but we love her in Heighton. It's the third time she's visited, and she always commands a good audience."

"What time did your event finish, Mr Cowper?"

"Around eight thirty. Then we met up with Gerald and went on for dinner and drinks at Nightingale's, just up the street. We were there until gone eleven."

"Perfect," said Peter. He took out his notebook and jotted down the details. "I'm almost done with the questions, Mr Cowper. If you could just tell me whether you recognise either of these people?" He slid two photographs from inside his jacket and held them out for Cowper to see. "Geoffrey Altman, and Lucy Adams."

Cowper shook his head. "No, I'm sorry, I don't recognise either of them. They certainly weren't regulars at the shop."

Peter slipped the photographs back into his pocket. "Now, it would help us a great deal if you could think of anyone else who's shown a recent interest in the legend? Perhaps a customer who has wanted to talk to you about your book?"

"Well, there's plenty of *those*, DS Shaw," said Cowper. "I've sold nearly thirty copies since it launched in November."

"Do you keep records of who's bought them?"

"I fear not." He gestured to the counter. "As you can see, we prefer to do things the old-fashioned way here. I barely turn the computer on, except for answering emails or processing any orders we've received through the website."

"So no one in particular springs to mind?"

"Well, you might want to talk to Michael Williams. He's a novelist who lives locally. Writes garish thrillers with short chapters and lots of sex. You know the sort of thing."

"Unfortunately not," said Peter.

"Well, he's been in a few times. Even bought me a drink so he could 'pick my brains'. He's working on a new novel. His 'magnum opus', apparently. It's based on the legend of the Carrion King, and I know he's been reading a great deal around the subject."

Peter flipped open his notebook and jotted down the name. "Anyone else?"

Cowper tapped his bottom lip while he considered. "David Keel. He's the writer behind the new play they're debuting this week at Winthorpe."

"Yes, we've already spoken to Mr Keel," said Peter.

"Then that leaves Byron Miller," said Cowper. "He'd be the other expert in the region. He's an academic, a professor at the university. He lectures on ancient paganism and the occult, and the transition of history to legend through the passing of time. He gave a talk here last year, to a packed crowd. Fascinating stuff, actually." Cowper coughed. "Although I hope you'll find everything you need in my own modest tome."

Peter reached over and picked up a copy. "I'll take both copies, then, please," he said, reaching for his wallet.

"Oh, no, please," said Cowper, holding up a hand. "On me."

"Thank you, Mr Cowper. Very kind."

"Not at all," he said.

"Your discretion on the subject would be most appreciated, Mr Cowper," said Peter. "For the time being, at least. Now, if I could trouble you for Gerald's contact details?"

"Of course!" Cowper grabbed a scrap of paper from the counter, upon which he wrote out an address in neat print, along with a telephone number. He handed it to Peter, who folded it and slipped it into his notebook. "Do let him know not to worry, Detective. He gets awfully worked up."

"We'll be in touch," said Peter.

"Good hunting," said Cowper. He waved cheerily as they left the shop, each clutching a copy of his book.

"What now?" said Elspeth.

"I'll head back to the station to make some enquiries about these other names, see if I can track down the relevant addresses." He grinned. "Don't you have a woman to see about a photograph?"

Elspeth rolled her eyes. "I suppose I do," she said.

"Alright then, I'll call you later." He touched her arm, and then turned and ambled off down the street. Elspeth watched him go, and then checked her watch. There was just enough time to steel herself with some lunch before the big interview.

CHAPTER ELEVEN

Patricia Graves lived on Windsom Road, about fifteen minutes' walk from the centre of Heighton. It was a bright, clear afternoon, so after grabbing a quick sandwich at Lenny's, Elspeth decided to leave the car in town, using her phone's GPS to help her navigate the maze of unfamiliar residential streets.

It was an odd sensation, rekindling her association with the place. She wondered if she was just feeling a little morose, the result of her own situation, the fact she'd had to return like this, to the stomping ground of her youth. In many ways it felt as if she were taking a backwards step, returning not only to her parental home, but to a more naive time in her life, an era filled with teenage embarrassment, growing pains and childish missteps. While there was a certain comfort to be had, swaddling herself in the familiar, there were memories here she'd rather forget, too – mistakes she'd made, people she'd forgotten. To her, that's what life was supposed to be about – constant forward momentum. What she couldn't yet see with any clarity was whether she'd encountered a momentary bump in that road, or whether she'd been forced into making a U-turn.

Had London really all been for nothing? That was the question that kept going through her mind. Had she really wasted all that time she'd dedicated to Andrew and their future?

She cast the thought aside. Now wasn't the time. She was on her way to interview an elderly lady about winning an amateur photography competition, and she needed to remain upbeat, if only to put the woman at ease.

Meredith's receptionist, Carl, had forwarded Mrs Graves's address, along with a short, surprisingly formal note informing her that Mrs Graves was expecting her at one o'clock. Apparently the woman's hearing wasn't what it used to be, so she'd told Carl she'd leave the door on the latch, and that Elspeth should let herself in if she didn't get an answer after a couple of knocks.

She'd taken a few moments to look up the competition on the *Heighton Observer*'s website and located the photograph in question – a hedgehog snuffling around amongst some plant pots in the woman's back garden. It was sweet enough, but it was hardly going to win wildlife photo of the year. Still, it was money, and another credit with the paper. It would help to tide her over while she looked for other things.

Elspeth found the house easily enough. It was on a sweeping Victorian terrace, with a small but neat front yard, and bay windows on both the upper and lower floors. The door had been painted a bright pillar-box red, and the white gloss on the outer frames of the windows was starting to flake and peel.

She walked up the short path to the house and

rapped loudly on the door. She listened for any sounds from within, expecting to hear the shuffling of the older woman's footsteps in the hall. Nothing. She tried again, this time using the brass knocker, in the shape of a leaping fish.

She waited a few moments. Still nothing. With a shrug, she tried the handle. It turned, and the door opened after a slight shove.

"Hello? Mrs Graves? It's Elspeth Reeves from the *Heighton Observer*. I'm here about your interview."

She stepped inside, avoiding a slew of post, which must have been pushed through the letterbox earlier that morning and not yet been collected. Elspeth shut the door behind her, then stooped and picked them up, shuffling the envelopes and flyers into a neat pile and placing them on the telephone table in the narrow hall.

Inside, the house had the air of a home that had not been truly lived in for some time. It was too quiet, too solemn and sterile. Mrs Graves evidently kept the place in good order – it was clean and tidy, and the hall and stair carpet had been recently vacuumed. It was just that there was no sense of joy about the place. It lacked that aura of homeliness, that cosy feeling when you walked into a home and knew instantly that people laughed and loved and truly *lived* there, rather than simply existing.

That was the real story of this place, she decided – what had been lost, and what had become of the people left behind.

Elspeth shook her head. She wasn't here for that. This was meant to be a jolly, uplifting piece about a hedgehog and local woman who'd achieved something.

"Mrs Graves?" she called. "Are you home?" Elspeth supposed she had to be around somewhere – she'd left the door open as per the instructions. Feeling a little like a trespasser, Elspeth walked down the hall and into the dining room, wondering whether she should have taken her shoes off first. The room was empty and unused; a thin patina of dust covered the glass surface of the dining table, and the only sound came from the ticking of a small carriage clock on the mantel over the fireplace. The fire itself had long been removed from the cavity, replaced with a vase of dry flowers. In one of the recesses, crockery was displayed inside a wooden sideboard with glass-fronted doors, while the other contained a bookcase filled to bursting with cheap romance titles and puzzle books. Another door led through to the kitchen.

Like many of these Victorian terraces, the house had been extended to accommodate a narrow, flat-roofed gallery kitchen, with a small bathroom at the far end. This, too, was empty.

She wandered back through to the hallway, calling out again. She'd walked right past the living-room door – if the woman was in there, then she really *was* hard of hearing. Elspeth popped her head around the door. A sofa, two wingback leather armchairs, a small television set and a clutter of photographs in mismatched frames upon a dresser. But no Mrs Graves.

Elspeth was beginning to grow concerned. Was it a windup? Was this Meredith Stokes's way of testing her – sending her out to get an impossible interview to see how she coped? It didn't seem likely.

Elspeth walked to the bottom of the stairs. She couldn't hear anyone moving about up there. "Hello? Mrs Graves?"

Feeling more like an intruder than ever, Elspeth climbed the stairs. There was a small landing at the top, leading to an empty bathroom. She turned the corner and continued up the short flight of stairs to the upper landing. Here there were three further doors, leading to the bedrooms. Elspeth tried each of them in turn, knocking first to ensure she wasn't about to cause any embarrassment. The first was stacked high with boxes and assorted junk – the single bed was inaccessible for the maze of old television sets, books, clothes and – bizarrely – an old-fashioned rocking horse. It smelled of musty abandonment.

The second was the master bedroom, and light was streaming in through the bay window, picking out in extraordinary detail the vision of horror that awaited Elspeth as she entered: the horrifying, mutilated corpse of an elderly woman. Blood was everywhere, in dark crimson splashes – matted in her hair, sprayed up her face, drenching the front of her floral-patterned dress. It had spattered the walls and full-length mirror, stained the carpet in dark swathes.

The woman herself lay slumped on her side, her bloody fingers still clutching at the stainless steel handles of a pair of scissors. The blades were buried deep in her chest, but Elspeth could see where they'd been used to gouge her throat, her wrists; puncture her belly, slash her thighs. It had been a brutal and prolonged attack, and the woman had clearly suffered unimaginable pain.

There was a single, bloodied handprint on the surface of the mirror, as if she'd tried to lean against it for support in the moments before she'd collapsed and died.

Elspeth took a deep breath, steadying herself against the doorframe. The rich iron tang of the blood lodged in the back of her throat. She gagged, but managed to prevent herself from throwing up. There was no point checking for signs of life – it was obvious she was far too late for that. She staggered back onto the landing, her hands trembling. She felt suddenly cold and alone.

She grabbed hold of the banister and stood there for a moment, catching her breath. She wondered for a minute if there was a chance the killer was still in the house, but dismissed the idea. She'd been in every room on her way around. She would have discovered him before now if he were still lurking.

She swallowed, and then searched her bag for her phone. She almost dropped it as she thumbed the button, and then dialled 999.

"There's been a murder," she said, blankly. "Come quickly."

CHAPTER TWELVE

"Tell me again, Miss Reeves, why you were trespassing in the house of the victim?"

DCI Griffiths sat across from Elspeth, her expression unreadable. They were back at the station in Heighton, inside a small interview room. Elspeth had been brought over in a police car, once the scene had been secured and the SOCOs had descended, and was ostensibly there to give a statement, although Griffiths appeared to be treating it more as an interrogation.

"Like I said, I was there to interview her for the *Heighton Observer*. She'd won a photography competition, and the paper was supposed to be running a profile."

"Yes, but that still doesn't explain what you were doing in her bedroom," said Griffiths. She leaned forward, her hands on the table. She was wearing a gold wedding band, and she was tapping it unconsciously – or impatiently – upon the tabletop.

"I showed your constable the email instructions I'd been sent by the office. Mrs Graves was partially deaf, and I'd been told that if she didn't answer the door when I knocked, I should let myself in."

"Yes, but her *bedroom*," pressed Griffiths.

"Well, I was trying to find her," said Elspeth. She supposed it might seem a bit strange now that she'd explored the house as much as she had, but she'd been so intent on finding the woman. "I suppose I was concerned that something might be wrong. The front door was unlocked, but she wasn't in the living room or the kitchen. I called up the stairs and didn't get an answer, but knowing she might not be able to hear me properly, it seemed like the right thing to do, to make sure she was okay."

"But she wasn't okay, was she?" said Griffiths. There was no accusation in her voice, thankfully, but nevertheless, her stern manner was putting Elspeth on edge. Peter had said she had a tendency to jump to conclusions – Elspeth only hoped she wasn't going to jump to the *wrong* conclusion.

"No. She wasn't," said Elspeth. "I called the emergency services the moment I found her."

"And you didn't touch the body, or check for life signs?"

"No. It was pretty evident I was too late for that."

"You're not from around here, are you?" said Griffiths. She started tapping her wedding band on the table again. She was an attractive woman, with flawless brown skin and almond-coloured eyes. Her hair was tied back, and she was wearing only the slightest hint of make-up. Elspeth wished she could get away with such lightness of touch.

"What makes you say that?"

Griffiths shrugged. "You have the demeanour of a city girl."

What was that supposed to mean? She wondered if

it was really that obvious, if she'd really been so affected by her time in London.

"I grew up in Wilsby-under-Wychwood," said Elspeth. "I'm back to stay with my mum for a bit."

Griffiths smiled, as if to say 'I told you so'. "And you've already got a job on the local newspaper?"

"No," said Elspeth. "I'm doing a couple of freelance assignments, that's all. Look, I got made redundant recently, split up with my boyfriend – I came home to get away from it all."

Griffiths stared at her, as if weighing her up. "Alright, we're done here. PC Chambers will be along soon to help you write up your statement. Someone will see you home after that." They'd already taken her clothes for processing, leaving her dressed in a white paper suit. She'd had her fingerprints and DNA swabs taken too.

Griffiths pushed her chair back and got to her feet. "I'm sorry you've had to go through all of this, Miss Reeves. It's a hell of a thing, finding a body like that."

Elspeth nodded. Griffiths wasn't wrong – she kept having flashbacks to the moment she'd walked into the room: the glossy streaks of blood upon the woman's pale flesh, the ragged holes in her chest where the killer had forced the scissors in, the bloody handprint on the mirror. She shuddered again at the unbidden memory. "Do you think you'll catch them?"

"That's our job," said Griffiths.

Elspeth nodded, and Griffiths left the room.

She sat back in her chair, staring at the bare walls of the interview room. After a moment, she heard the door handle turn, and looked round to see Peter standing there, his face etched with concern. "Ellie? Oh my god, what happened?"

She painted on a smile. "Oh, you know, found another body. All in a day's work at the moment, it seems."

His shoulders dropped as he visibly relaxed. "Are you okay? Do you need anything?"

"In lieu of anything stronger, I could murder a coffee?" She realised what she'd said. "Sorry, that was an unfortunate phrase."

Peter smiled. "Coming up," he said. He disappeared for a couple of minutes, and then reappeared with a Styrofoam cup. He placed it on the table before her and dropped into the seat that had previously been occupied by Griffiths. "There you go. Tastes dreadful, but at least it's strong."

She picked it up and took a sip, nearly scalding her lips. Hastily, she put it down again. "And *hot.*"

"So, tell me."

Elspeth gave a weary sigh. "Forgive me for not wanting to go through it all again, but basically I turned up to do that interview with the elderly competition winner and found her dead. She'd been stabbed repeatedly with a pair of scissors. She was a real mess."

Peter winced. "God. I'm sorry you had to see that."

"Me too," she said. She reached out and touched the back of his hand. "But thanks for coming to check on me. I'm fine, really. It's been a miserable day, but I'm alright. I've got to give a formal statement in a minute, and then I'm going home for a long soak in the bath."

"I'll buy you a stiff drink later, if you want?"

She shook her head. "Not tonight. Thanks for

asking. I think I just want to curl up with a book."

He nodded. "Yeah, I can understand that. Another time."

"I'm counting on it."

Peter looked at his watch. "Look, I've got to run. I'm sorry. I've got a briefing…"

"Go," she said, waving him away. "You're working. Get out of here. I'm fine."

"I'll call you," he said, as he left the room.

Elspeth took a sip of her coffee, and hoped that PC Chambers wouldn't be too much longer. She wanted to get it all over and done with, and get back to Wilsby-under-Wychwood and her computer. She'd had a crappy day, and the very least she could do was turn it into a story.

The statement process had proved as laborious as she'd feared, but at least it was over with, and now she was back at home and curled up on the sofa reading Philip Cowper's book.

She'd told her mum all about it, of course – sparing her the grisliest of details – and Dorothy had listened intently, given her a hug, and made her a strong cup of tea. Now she was busy preparing some food in the kitchen. She wondered what her mum was making of all this. Elspeth had suddenly come roaring back into her life, invaded her home, and then gone and got herself involved in two murder enquiries, all in the space of a couple of days. And that was on top of all the problems with Andrew, and her job, and what the hell she was going to do in the future. If Dorothy was troubled by any of it, though, she was putting on a stoic face. Elspeth made a mental note to tell her mum how much she appreciated it.

She put the book down for a minute and checked her phone for any sign of email. The first thing she'd done after getting home was to dash off a piece for Meredith about the murder. She'd opted for a short account of what she'd discovered at the house on Windsom Road, how the police had responded, and her experience discovering the body – all the details the police were allowing her to give. She had no idea if the piece would ever see print, but she felt she needed to do *something*.

It wasn't exactly what Meredith was expecting – a puff piece about a local wildlife competition – but she had no intention of losing out on the freelance fee, so instead she'd delivered the story she *could* tell. It was late, she knew that, but it was *good*, and the circumstances were in her favour.

She'd delivered it over three hours ago, though, and she'd yet to hear anything back. She'd also fired off a bunch of emails to editors and former colleagues in London, telling them she was on the lookout for freelance work. Her inbox, though, was full of marketing spam, subscriptions, and messages from her London friends, asking after how she was doing. She'd have to respond to them sooner or later, but for now, she didn't want to get dragged back into that world. Not yet.

She placed her phone back on the arm of the sofa. She hadn't heard anything more from Peter, either.

"You know, that name, Patricia Graves. It's familiar for some reason. Was she well known?"

Dorothy shouted through from the kitchen.

"I don't think so. I asked around a bit in preparation for the interview. As far as I can tell she was a bit of a lonely old lady. She lost her husband some years ago. No kids, and no remaining family. She'd been a foster carer years ago, apparently, but gave it up when her husband died. Winning that photography competition was the only notable thing to happen to her for a decade."

Dorothy stuck her head around the doorframe. "Did you say foster kids?"

"Mmmm hmmm," murmured Elspeth, leafing through the pages of Cowper's book. There was very little detail in the text, barely more than she'd found in her old book on the mythology of Oxfordshire, but the illustrations were livid and grotesque, watercolours which looked as though they were based on the old woodcuts in her own book, along with depictions of the Carrion King carrying out rituals in the Wychwood, drawing circles in the soil with a staff, and peering into the shimmering surface of a mirror.

"That's it, then," said Dorothy, as she popped back in from the kitchen bearing another mug of tea.

Elspeth thanked her and accepted it with a smile, warming her hands on the ceramic. "What's that?"

"Tea, love."

"No, not the tea. You said 'that's it, then'."

"Oh, Patricia Graves. That's why I recognised her name."

"I'm sorry, Mum. You've lost me. I was looking at my book…"

"Don't worry. It's not important. It's probably thirty

or forty years ago now. Water under the bridge."

Elspeth folded the book shut on her lap. "Tell me."

"There's not much to tell. It's just... I seem to remember a story from the late seventies, about a foster child that went missing. A runaway. There was a big deal about it at the time, and for some reason that woman's name is lodged in my head. Patricia Graves. I could be wrong, it was all a long time ago, but it certainly sounds familiar." She shrugged. "Anyway, not that it matters now. Poor woman. It sounds as if she'd had a pretty miserable life."

Elspeth sipped at her tea. Perhaps she'd do a bit of digging, see if there was anything interesting in this foster kid story. It might form the basis of a longer piece.

"Ellie?"

"Sorry, Mum. Did you say something?"

Dorothy sighed ruefully. "You're miles away, aren't you? Only to be expected, really. I said do you mind if I turn the TV over? *EastEnders* is on in a minute. Only if you're not watching this..."

"You go ahead. I'm going to have a bath, and then chill out with my book."

"Good idea, love. You've had so much going on recently. You deserve some rest. Tea'll be ready soon."

Elspeth peeled herself off the sofa, stretched her weary limbs and kissed her mum on the top of her head. Her hair smelled of lavender. "Thanks, Mum."

She made it to the top of the stairs before her phone vibrated. She placed her mug on the windowsill on the landing, tucked the book under her arm, and checked the screen. It was an email from Meredith.

Nice piece. I'll run it on the website. Get me more on the murders, I'll run them too, same fee. Daily updates as things develop.
Meredith.

Elspeth grinned. Well, at least that was *something* positive to come out of the day's events.

CHAPTER THIRTEEN

"You look nice," said Peter. He was standing in the doorway of the cottage, dressed in his usual grey suit and looking a little windswept. He hastily brushed his hair with his fingers. It made little difference to his shaggy mop. "Are you off somewhere? I don't want to interrupt."

"Just into Heighton," said Elspeth, smoothing the front of her dress. She was running out of clean clothes, so had been forced to resort to a black dress that she usually reserved for evenings out. She was going to have to pick up some more jeans in town.

"Well, I'm heading that way," said Peter. "And there's news on the case. I thought you'd be interested." He kicked at the step with the side of his shoe – a habit he'd had since he was a boy.

Elspeth grinned. "Of course. Come on, you can tell me in the car." She grabbed her purse and bustled him out into the gusty morning. It was spitting rain, but warm, and they ran to the end of the garden path, where Peter had parked his blue Ford Focus up on the kerb.

"You know, when we were kids, I thought you'd end up with a bright red racing car or something," she said, as she opened the door. "This is all very… normal."

"Like I said, people grow up," said Peter. "Besides, it's a pool car from work." She waited until he'd finished his manoeuvre and they were pulling away down the road. "So, what news?"

"It's a bit grim," said Peter. "We've had the autopsy report on Lucy Adams."

"Let me guess – she was poisoned?" said Elspeth.

Peter nodded. "Yeah. Whoever killed her was sticking to the stories pretty closely. Even their choice of poison seems to reflect the mediaeval roots of the story – if you'll forgive my pun."

"I'm sorry?"

"She was injected with a concentrated extract of nightshade."

"How horrible."

Elspeth pictured the woman's slack-jawed face and shuddered. "And forensics? There must be something to go on, some evidence he left on her body?"

"He was careful," said Peter. "We found her clothes on the canal path. They'd been doused in lighter fluid and burned. Out there, in the woods, there's very little chance of picking up a stray hair or fingerprint, and the only identifiable fibres we could find on the body were from her own clothes, or strands torn from crow feathers. There was nothing of his on her handbag."

"So we're no closer to finding her killer," said Elspeth.

"Not necessarily. Uniform are appealing for any witnesses along the canal. It's a popular dog-walking spot." He reached for a mint from the packet in the cup holder and popped it into his mouth, passing them to her so she could help herself.

Elspeth nodded. "Thanks."

Peter turned the car down the road towards Heighton. "So, have you decided if you're sticking around, then?"

Elspeth considered her answer. She'd been ruminating on it all night, and after talking it over with her mum over breakfast, she'd decided to give it at least another week before heading back to London. This seemed to be where the story was at the moment, and she still couldn't face the idea of going back to the flat to collect her things. Besides, she didn't have anywhere to put them yet – she couldn't stay with Dorothy indefinitely, and if she was going to rent somewhere, she'd have to figure out where she wanted to be. "For now," she said. "You'll have to put up with me for another week or so, at least."

"Hmmm, when you put it like that…" said Peter.

Elspeth jabbed him with her elbow. "You were supposed to say something nice at that point."

"I was?" he said, with mock innocence. "How about, 'Do you want to come and help me interview that author, Michael Williams?' Is that nice enough?"

"It'll do," she said, laughing.

"He lives over in Ascott-under-Wychwood. I can drop you in Heighton first if you'd rather?"

"No, Heighton can wait," said Elspeth. "Provided, of course, we can stop for coffee on the way?"

The drive down to Ascott-under-Wychwood was quaint, sleepy, and picturesque. Sheep dotted the hillside like daisies run rampant across an unkempt lawn, and shafts of pale sunlight speared through broken clouds, searchlights sent to dispel the late morning mist.

Peter's playful banter had subsided during the drive over, and she suspected he was going through the mental equivalent of changing gears, preparing himself for the interview. She left him to it.

She was still feeling a little uncomfortable interfering with a police investigation, and potentially putting Peter in a difficult position in the process. Aside from her trespassing at the scene of Lucy Adams's murder, though, she supposed all she'd really done so far was help him question a bookshop owner about some ancient mythology. And now this. She wondered what to expect from Michael Williams.

She'd never read any of his books, although she'd seen them from time to time in bookshops and airports and he'd done well out of that sudden interest in historical conspiracy thrillers a few years earlier with a murder mystery about the spirits of dead Knights Templars in Lincolnshire, or something to that effect. And now, according to Philip Cowper, he was writing a novel about the Carrion King.

The satnav issued its polite command to turn left, and Peter swung the car along a narrow lane, and then on through the heart of the village. On the right she could see the spire of the old church, and a breaker's yard filled with the skeletal hulks of half a dozen old Beetles.

They turned left again, past a small shop, and then on out of the village down a narrow country lane. After a few minutes, the satnav warned them of a right turn approaching.

"So he lives on a farm?" she said.

"More that he lives in the farmhouse, I think," said Peter. "This hasn't been a working farm for some time. Look how overgrown the fields are."

She peered through the windscreen as the car jostled and bounced along the dirt track to the house. There were a couple of forlorn-looking horses in one of the fields, and the ruins of a barn in another, but Peter was right – the place looked more or less abandoned, desolate.

The farmhouse itself, however, was something else entirely. It was a grand Georgian affair, rectangular and slab-like, with rows of tall, symmetrical windows, and a portico over the door. They pulled up on the gravel driveway, tyres crunching across the stones.

A quick glance at the house told her a woman was peeking out of one of the downstairs windows. "Are we expected?"

"No," said Peter. "I usually find it's best to catch people off guard. That way they haven't had time to prepare in advance."

"Sneaky," said Elspeth.

"Standard practice, in these circumstances," said Peter. He opened the door and climbed out of the car. She followed suit.

It was windy and exposed, and she could feel rain beginning to spot on her arms and the back of her neck. "Come on," she said. "Let's get on with it."

Peter approached the grand entrance. The door was painted a rich navy blue, and looked as if it had received a fresh coat fairly recently. The fittings were brass, the knocker cast to resemble a lion's head with a sweeping mane. Not that these people were ostentatious in any way, Elspeth considered.

As Peter reached for the knocker, they heard the sound of footfalls stirring the gravel, and both looked around in unison to see a tall, slim woman coming around from the side of the house. She had shoulder-length dark hair that whipped up around her face in the cross-winds, causing her to try to control it with the back of her hand, brushing it behind her ears. She was strikingly beautiful, in tight jeans and a loose blouse, but the way she hugged herself suggested she lacked confidence. Elspeth guessed she was around forty-five.

"Can I help you?" she called. Her voice was thin and reedy.

"DS Shaw," said Peter, holding up his identification. "And Elspeth Reeves. We were hoping to speak with Michael Williams."

The woman cocked her head. "He's working," she said, flatly.

"Inside?" said Peter. "It really is important that we speak to him."

"Why, what's he done?" The venom practically dripped off her tongue.

"We just need to ask him a few questions. You are?"

"His wife," said the woman. She beckoned for them to follow her back the way she had come. "Much good that it does me. He's down in his 'summerhouse', working on his *magnum opus*."

Peter and Elspeth hurried after her. It was clear all wasn't well at the Williams residence.

The summerhouse, it transpired, was more of an

outbuilding, an old brick stable or storehouse that had been converted into a studio. It had been beautifully done, too; one whole wall had been replaced with tinted glass, and the flat roof with a pitched, modern affair, complete with vast shuttered skylights and solar panels.

The woman – who introduced herself haughtily as Rebecca – rapped loudly on the door, before shouldering it open and stomping in. "Mick? Mick?"

Elspeth and Peter waited patiently outside. She could hear the tinny rumbling of guitar feedback coming from somewhere within. It sounded like the tail end of a Ramones track, and it shut off abruptly.

"What is it? Can't you see I'm working?"

"So that's what you call it."

"We've been *through* this, Rebecca. It's research."

"Well, the police are here to see you."

"The *police*?" Elspeth heard a chair scrape back. "What do they want?"

"You'll have to ask them. They're outside." This was followed by more of Rebecca's stomping footsteps, before she erupted from the door in a sudden flurry, and stormed off across the courtyard without even a glance in their direction.

Peter looked at Elspeth, and then rapped on the studio door.

"Yes, yes, I'm coming," came the voice from within. He sounded tired more than angry. He opened the door and frowned. "Can I help you?"

"I certainly hope so," said Peter. He introduced them both again. "We're hoping you can assist us with some inquiries."

Williams furrowed his brow. He was a thickset man

in his early fifties, with a broad chest and ample stomach, and a full head of dark hair, going to grey. He had a neat, short beard, and reading glasses perched on the bridge of his nose, and a small star-shaped scar just beneath his left eye. He was wearing jeans and a rumpled plaid shirt, which hung loose at the waist. He looked like an ill-fitting companion to the slight, haughty woman they'd just encountered.

"I'm not sure how you think I can help you," he said, with obvious incomprehension.

"We're led to believe you're currently researching a novel about the Carrion King of Wychwood?" said Peter.

"That's right, yes. Who told you that?" Williams looked suddenly flustered.

"Philip Cowper," said Peter. "He seemed to think you were something of an expert on the subject."

Williams nodded. "Then you'd better come in."

The studio was large and well appointed, more like a small flat than an office. There was a heavy leather-topped desk in the far corner, hemmed in by a series of cupboards and bookcases to form a distinct work area. Behind this, three whiteboards had been mounted on the bare brick wall, and were covered in spidery multi-coloured scrawl.

To the left of the entrance was a display case, filled with a bizarre collection of oddments, including a stuffed eagle, an etched bowl, what appeared to be a rusted sword blade, and a couple of aged leather-bound tomes. A door led through to what Elspeth took to be a shower room and toilet.

Just inside the door on the right, a flight of narrow

steps led up to a mezzanine, upon which there was a mussed double bed and a scattering of abandoned clothes.

A battered old Chesterfield sofa and a coffee table, upon which a sheaf of papers and maps had been spread, finished off the décor of the unusual room. The whole place had an odour reminiscent of a dusty museum.

"Come in, take a seat," said Williams, indicating the sofa.

"It's an impressive workspace," said Peter, taking it all in. "Strange to think it was a farm building once."

"It's my pride and joy," said Williams. "I spend most of my days down here, contemplating the view through the glass partition and dreaming up new adventures." He glanced up at the mezzanine. "Sometimes, if things are going well on the book, I even sleep down here. It's peaceful, and means I can work late without disturbing Rebecca."

By which, Elspeth decided, he meant he could avoid arguments by keeping out of her way.

"Did you want a cup of tea?" said Williams. "There's a kettle around here somewhere, although I'm afraid I've learned to do without milk. Ironic, really, being on a farm."

"No, thank you," said Peter.

Williams looked expectantly at Elspeth, and she smiled and shook her head.

"So, why do the police want to know about the Carrion King?" said Williams.

"Let's just say we have our reasons," said Peter. "I wonder if you can tell me if you know either Geoffrey Altman or Lucy Adams?"

"Geoff Altman? Yes, I knew him." He looked up,

meeting Peter's gaze. "Dreadful what happened to him."

"Did you know him well?" said Peter.

"Not really," said Williams. "I'd met him in the pub a few times, and allowed him to shoot pheasants on the back fields. He'd also taken me out into the woods a couple of times."

"What do you mean, Mr Williams, that he'd taken you out into the woods?"

Williams cleared his throat. "Geoff was a gamekeeper, see. He knew the area like no one else. He'd hunted it for years. When I told him about the book I was writing, he offered to take me out, show me all the old pagan sites and the ancient perimeter of the Wychwood. We spent a couple of days trekking about so I could take reference shots and mark up a map." He pointed to a corkboard on the wall above his desk, where he'd pinned a messy assortment of photographs, all depicting trees.

"And you've no idea who might have wanted to kill him?"

Williams shook his head. "Like I said, we weren't friends. And besides, people like Geoff, they come and go like the seasons. Sometimes you wouldn't see him for months on end, and then other times he was there every time you went to the pub. He was that sort of man, kept his own counsel."

"And what about Lucy Adams?" said Peter.

Williams shook his head. "No. I have no idea who she is, I'm afraid. Has something happened to her, too? I saw something on the news about another murder."

Peter nodded. "Yes. I'm afraid so."

"I still can't quite see what this has to do with me and my book, I'm afraid," said Williams.

"Perhaps you can tell us where you were on the nights of the twelfth and twenty-third of this month," said Peter.

Williams looked as if Peter had slapped him in the face. "So, that's what this is about, is it?" He stalked over to his desk and pulled open a drawer. From inside he took out an old-fashioned planner and opened it, furiously turning the pages. "There. It's written here, in black and white. I was here, in the studio." He passed Peter the diary, tapping obstinately on the relevant entries. "You can see where I've marked off my daily word count on both days."

"Would your wife be able to confirm your whereabouts, Mr Williams?" said Elspeth. She kept her tone calm, in the hope that it might quell his sudden indignity. He was clearly a man with a hot temper.

"You'll have to ask *her*," said Williams. "Probably."

"So this novel you're writing," said Peter, deftly changing the subject. "Have you been working on it long?"

Williams took a deep breath. His cheeks were flushed. "Two years."

"Has there ever been a novel about the Carrion King before?"

"As far as I'm aware this will be the first."

"What do you make of Philip Cowper's work on the subject?" said Elspeth.

Williams laughed. "Shallow, riddled with assumptions, standing on the shoulders of his betters. Need I go on?"

"I think we get the point," said Peter. "He told us you'd had occasion to 'pick his brains' on the subject once or twice."

"Before I realised what a buffoon he is, yes," said Williams. "But it's been far more useful going back to the source material, reading the mediaeval accounts, and consulting with professionals."

"Professionals?" said Peter. "Such as Professor Byron Miller at the university? Cowper mentioned that he was an expert."

"Precisely. Now *there's* a man who really understands the symbolism inherent in the Carrion King's tale. They're moral tales, you see, similar in many ways to the parables in the Bible. Byron Miller has spent years decoding them. He's been a great help and inspiration."

"So you don't believe the stories are real?" said Elspeth.

Williams looked at her as if she were mad. "Wild magic and curses? Nymphs and shape-shifters? No, Miss Reeves, I think they are legends, myths, stories to terrify the young and give fair warning to the old."

"Then why go poking around the old pagan sites with Geoffrey Altman," said Peter, "if you believed the stories to be fictional?"

Williams frowned. "I didn't say the stories don't have *some* basis in truth. Think about all those familiar tales of King Arthur and Camelot, of Merlin and Tintagel, Robin Hood and his band of Merry Men, or Jesus of Nazareth, for that matter. Mythology is born from historical truth. That's what I'm trying to do, see? With my book, I'm aiming to peel back the layers, get at the origins of those stories. The Carrion King has been forgotten, but his cautionary tale still rings true today."

"And what cautionary tale is that, Mr Williams?" said Peter.

"That once we start down a dark path, once we allow the corruption in, it spreads like poison and takes root. That ultimately, power corrupts. Look at politicians today. Look at the mess they've made. Tell me that isn't an abject lesson for us all."

"Are you aware of a man named David Keel?" said Peter. "He's written a play about the Carrion King, and from talking to him, it sounds as if he's of a similar mind."

Williams rubbed at a spot on the centre of his forehead, just above the bridge of his nose, as if attempting to banish the sudden onset of a headache. "Yes, yes. I know David. I've read his play. It's not bad. It could never explore the real depths of the myths like a novel, of course, but it all helps to bring the Carrion King to people's attention."

"Have you had much to do with the Winthorpe Players?"

"No, not at all. To be honest, I rarely get out of here. I've been over once or twice to meet David, but he usually comes out here, if we're not corresponding by email."

"So you've never met Vanessa Eglington, the producer?"

"In passing, perhaps. I couldn't point her out in a room. I know they've got that young fella, Oscar something-or-other, playing the Carrion King. He seems quite good."

"Will you be going to see the play?" said Peter.

"Yes, David's already sent tickets, so I'll be there for opening night."

"Well, thank you," said Peter. "You've been most helpful." He got to his feet. "We'll leave you to get on with your work, Mr Williams."

"And good luck with your book," said Elspeth.

Williams nodded in appreciation, and shook their hands. He went back to his desk and started up his music again as they saw themselves out.

"Jump in the car, Ellie. I won't be a moment," said Peter. He started off across the courtyard.

"Where are you going?"

"I just want a quick word with Mrs Williams. Won't be a minute." She watched him disappear around the other side of the house. She didn't fancy his chances much.

A few minutes later she saw him heading across the gravel towards her. She leaned over and pushed open the driver's door for him. He clambered inside.

"Did she confirm his alibis?" she said, when he'd shut the door.

"In a manner of speaking," said Peter. "She said 'he was probably down in that bloody studio' both nights, but that she couldn't really care less. I don't know exactly what's going on there, but perhaps Michael Williams needs to pay a bit more attention to his own cautionary tales."

Elspeth laughed as Peter released the handbrake and brought the car around on the drive, heading back towards Heighton. She was glad to be leaving Michael Williams and his aggrieved wife behind them.

"I'm heading to Oxford now, to meet with Byron Miller," said Peter. "Do you want me to drop you back in Heighton, or do you want to tag along?"

"I'll tag along, if that's okay," said Elspeth. She settled back for the drive.

CHAPTER FOURTEEN

To Elspeth, Oxford had always seemed like a city trapped in a permanent state of dichotomy.

Walking through it now, it seemed to her like two Oxfords occupied the same space at once; a remembrance of the ancient city, where the streets of the long dead intersected with those of the living, and then the newer developments, the high street shops and fast food outlets, and glass- and chrome-fronted offices and Wi-Fi-enabled bistros.

She and Peter walked the narrow lanes, never far from the *ching ching* of veering bicycles, which, on this busy afternoon, seemed to have turned the streets into an inhospitable assault course. It was lunchtime, and students dashed hither and thither, refuelling on takeout coffee and sandwiches.

Elspeth loved the place, but felt wary of it, too, as if she were somehow out of place here, trespassing in a world of academic endeavour. She'd studied at university – at Middlesex – but Oxford had always seemed different, aloof.

Peter seemed more at ease, ambling along, his

auburn hair ruffled by the breeze, his hands jammed in his pockets. "Down here," he said, pointing her down a narrow lane. "We arranged for him to meet us at a café close to the college where he works."

Professor Byron Miller was sitting at a table on the street outside the café, a leather-bound notebook resting closed on the table before him, alongside a bottle of iced tea. He was smoking a cigarette, and the way he balanced it nonchalantly between his lips, along with his studied disinterest, made him look like a movie star in repose, lounging in his chair between takes. He had a neat head of sand-coloured hair, parted on the left. He was wearing navy chinos, a white shirt open at the collar, and a grey jacket. He took a long draw from his cigarette, blew the smoke out from the corner of his mouth, and smiled.

"Good afternoon." He looked her up and down with obvious interest, and then turned to Peter. "DS Shaw, I presume?"

Peter nodded and stuck out his hand, which Miller took, shaking it firmly. "And this is my colleague, Elspeth Reeves."

"Elspeth?" said Miller. "Now that's a name you don't hear very often. At least not anymore."

Elspeth smiled indulgently. "A family tradition," she said. She didn't shake his hand.

"Please, join me." He beckoned to the empty seats at the table, and then took another draw from his cigarette. Elspeth eyed it a little enviously; she'd given up over ten years earlier, but had never really lost the taste for it, to the extent that she still occasionally pinched one off her friends when she'd had too much to drink.

The waiter – a debonair man with a short, neat beard and floppy parting – circled the table almost before they'd finished arranging themselves, sweeping up some empty crockery and asking for their order in a lilting Eastern European accent. Elspeth ordered a black coffee and Peter a tea. The waiter buzzed off just as swiftly as he'd come, and a moment later she heard the whirring of the machine inside, churning the fresh beans.

"So, DS Shaw, you mentioned on the phone that you wished to discuss my work?"

"More that I have a few questions that I'm hoping you might be able to help me with," said Peter.

"Oh, interesting," said Miller, leaning forward. "*Questions*. How can I be of service?"

"We're hoping that you might be able to offer us some insight," said Peter, "into the myths of The King's Consort and The Master of the Hunt, and the stories behind these pictures." He reached into his jacket and withdrew two folded sheets of paper. He smoothed them out on the table and handed them to Miller. They were photocopies of the woodcuts from Ellie's book.

"Ah, yes," said Miller. "Two of the five sacrifices. These are taken from a fifteenth-century history of the region. The original is held in the Bodleian, although the woodcuts themselves have been reproduced any number of times. I think they probably sell postcards of them these days."

"We're aware of the basics of the mythology," said Peter, "from what we've been able to read online and in local books about the subject, but we were led to believe you might be able to elaborate a little for us, based on your research."

Miller unscrewed the cap from his bottle of iced tea and took a gulp. "Of course," he said. "So you're aware that the Carrion King had been cast out as a boy, and for years had lived in the wilds of the Wychwood, learning to temper his powers, but all the while harbouring a deep-seated hatred for the ealdorman who'd expelled him from his village?"

"Pretty much," said Peter. "And that eventually he would have his revenge through the use of a mirror."

"Precisely," said Miller. "Well, in the legends, The King's Consort was a fallen woman. A whore well known and well appreciated by the Saxon warriors of the region."

"Go on," said Elspeth.

"Her name was Hilde, and she's described as a creature of the purest heart, who had fallen upon difficult times, forced into a life of bleak oppression. Her mother had died during the birth of her sibling – who had also perished – and as a consequence she had been raised by her father, who forced her to be a whore, spending her days on her back, earning coin to swell his purse. As legends of the Carrion King grew, he became the talk of the entire region; whispered about before the fire at night, his reputation growing in stature with every telling. The notion of this heathen warrior-wizard, this dark man of the woods – it entranced people. You have to understand that in the stories, he's portrayed as a tragic figure, a man who had been cast out by those who'd claimed to love him. And so he'd retreated to the forest to build a kingdom of his own, apart from all the troubles of the land – a mythic realm where beauty and magic would flourish, where man might once again join with nature, and honesty and love would prevail.

"To women such as Hilde, the Carrion King represented a means of liberation, a new life, and so one day, after her father had promised use of her to a band of returning soldiers, she murdered him with his own dagger, stole a horse and fled for the woods."

Elspeth sipped at her coffee. As arrogant as he was, Miller was a rather excellent orator; she was utterly taken in by this new version of the story.

"Many had attempted to find the Carrion King before, of course, but he obfuscated, used his magic to divert their path and hide his growing kingdom from all whom he did not wish to find it. Hilde, though, he allowed to pass, for he could feel the longing in her heart. He took her in, and she swore fealty to him, forgoing all contact with the outside realm. In return, he promised to restore her purity, to remove all traces of her prior life, and he dressed her in a coat of white swan feathers to represent her rebirth. Soon enough, they fell deeply in love, and he made her his queen."

"That doesn't sound like a tragedy to me," said Peter, pouring his tea.

Miller smiled. "Ah, but just like all the best fairy tales, DS Shaw, there's a barb in the tale. For the Carrion King himself was not entirely pure of heart. As you know, he harboured a desire for revenge upon the ealdorman who had cast him out, and this darkness had taken root and grown. Like a disease, it had infected his very being, and when he lay with Hilde, it spread to her through his seed. Like a malaise, the poison ate at her soul, diminishing her, corrupting her. She grew desperately ill, and despite all efforts to save her – medicinal, magical, spiritual – she weakened and died.

"The Carrion King was distraught, but he had learned a valuable lesson – that the legacy of the man who had abandoned him was long-lived, and that he would never again find happiness until his hunger for revenge against the ealdorman was sated."

"And the image in the woodcut?" said Elspeth.

"As a tribute to his lost love, the Carrion King placed his Consort upon a shrine of leaves deep within the Wychwood, and charged seven crows with protecting her corpse, so that she might never be disturbed again." Miller sat back in his chair, flicking the ash from the tip of his cigarette.

"That's quite a tale," said Peter.

"Isn't it?" said Miller.

Elspeth drained the last of her coffee. "So what about The Master of the Hunt? How does his story fit?"

Miller smiled. "Oh, that's where things get *really* interesting. You see, that one's a terrible tale of love and betrayal to rival Judas and his thirty pieces of silver."

"Would you mind?" prompted Elspeth.

Miller laughed. "Not at all. I do enjoy an audience, although I will have to get back for a lecture before long." He scratched at his stubble-encrusted chin. "So, when the Carrion King was first cast out, he was a boy of only twelve. He found himself alone for the first time in his life, with burgeoning abilities that he could not understand. The Carrion King, you see, had been conceived during the Spring Equinox, and as such he had been imbued with the wild magic of the land, becoming a vessel of sorts. At the age of twelve, as he took his first steps towards manhood, this wild magic began to present itself in unusual ways; when he felt rage, the whole village shook; when he felt sadness, the water in the village well would sour. So it was that the ealdorman eventually ran him out, and even his parents did nothing to prevent it.

"The Carrion King fled into the woods. For seven days and nights he eked a living on berries and rainwater, but already he was growing weak from exposure, and delirium soon set in. He stumbled through the forests in search of shelter. Happenstance – or perhaps the work of his untamed magic – led him to a copse at the very heart of the Wychwood, where an old hermit had built himself a shelter amongst the boughs of an aged oak tree. Here, five boughs formed the shape of an enormous upturned hand," Miller paused while he held his own hand up demonstratively, "and it was in the palm of this hand that the hermit had taken up residence.

"Seeing the boy in such a terrible state, the hermit took pity on him and took him in. Over the days that followed, he nursed the boy back to health. The child had never experienced such kindness, and once he had regained his strength, he wished to repay the hermit for saving his life. He offered to serve the hermit, to fetch water, to run errands – in exchange for a place to lay his head.

"They became the strangest of companions, living side by side in the woods. The hermit schooled the boy in the ways of the natural world, teaching him to hunt and forage, to construct tools from the environs around him, to build fires and to fish. In turn the boy called upon his growing powers, his affinity with the land, to imbue the hermit with vitality and strength, and to grant him speed, foresight, and extended life.

"Over time the hermit underwent a deep and powerful change, falling deeper and deeper under the child's spell. He began to feel a new connection with the land around him, as the natural realm revealed itself to him properly for the first time. He became the greatest of hunters, and when he ran in the wild hunt, he ran with the spirit of Herne at his heels, and the fruits of his efforts were bountiful.

"For many years, until the boy had come of age, they existed in this way; but as the Carrion King's powers grew, along with the poison that had taken root in his soul, others flocked to his court. The Carrion King appointed four new apostles, but he had not forgotten the hermit's earlier kindness, and so granted the hermit a position at his side, The Master of the Hunt."

Miller paused, taking another swig from his drink. He was evidently enjoying himself, reciting stories for his captive audience. Even the waiter, Elspeth noticed, had come out to quietly wipe down the other tables while he listened to the tale.

"You mentioned a betrayal," said Elspeth.

Miller smiled. "Indeed. For all was not well in paradise. The Master of the Hunt, revitalised by the Carrion King's magic and grown preternaturally young, had found love amongst the fey folk of the forest. One night, during the hunt, he strayed too close to the uncharted regions of the Wychwood, where he encountered a sly nymph, who enchanted him and enslaved his heart. Unbeknownst to the hermit, the nymph's true goal was to lure the Carrion King from the safety of his kingdom, so that it might feast upon the shadow in his heart and imbue itself with his power."

"Nymphs have a terrible habit of doing that," said Peter, drawing a scowl from Miller.

"So it was that The Master of the Hunt arranged a feast in honour of the Carrion King, and raised a hunt so magnificent that all who might look upon it would marvel. For the first time in many years, the Carrion King would ride alongside the hermit, to lead the hunt together. Only, the hermit's head had been turned, and in his amorous fog, he had plotted to lead the Carrion King away from the rest of his party, to take him deep into the forest, where the nymph awaited them by the edge of a silver pool.

"By now, though, the Carrion King had grown bitter and wise, and had learned that even his closest allies might be corrupted by his power. Like a withering Midas, all whom he touched became rotten of heart, twisted with malcontent, and knowing not of the nymph's enchantment but suspicious still of the hermit's intent, he had come prepared.

"There, in the heart of the Wychwood, the Carrion King confronted his oldest friend, and found him wanting. Unable to give account of his actions – for the nymph's enchantment made it impossible for him to speak the truth of it – the hermit begged for forgiveness. The Carrion King knew, however, that in showing leniency, in demonstrating mercy, he would leave himself more vulnerable to betrayal in future, and so, with great remorse, he took his bow and struck down the hermit with an arrow to the heart, and left him there by the silver pool so that the nymphs might feed on what remained of his soul."

Elspeth realised she'd been gripping her empty coffee mug throughout the story, and placed it carefully on the table before her. "An impressive story," she said.

"And well practised," added Peter.

Miller laughed. "Guilty," he said. "I've told that one a few times during lectures. And to impress girls," he added, with a sly look at Elspeth. The attention made her feel uncomfortable, and she saw Peter bristle.

"I presume there are stories like this for all of the disciples?" he said.

"And others besides," said Miller. "Although I fear I'd be here all afternoon if I tried to elaborate, and as I mentioned, there's a lecture…"

Peter nodded. "Just a couple more questions. I understand that the Carrion King eventually enacted his revenge upon the ealdorman who had cast him out?"

"Yes. The stories read like a journey. First he must learn the necessary lessons that drive him towards the darkness. As I said, it's a tragedy, really. Faced with betrayal at every turn, the Carrion King's court soon sours, and his apostles are all lost. Meanwhile, he seeks revenge upon the ealdorman and smites him down, and with him, the final threads to his old life are cut. It's only after this that he gains his true power, and learns mastery over life and death itself. He uses it to walk in the netherworld, and is never seen or heard from again."

They were silent for a moment, as if taking this in.

"Are you aware of Philip Cowper, and his book about the Carrion King myths?" said Elspeth.

Miller laughed, and she sensed the streak of unkindness in his reaction. "Yes. I'm aware of him, and his book."

"Do I sense a hint of professional rivalry?" ventured Peter.

Miller raised an eyebrow. "Not a jot of it," he said. "Cowper's book is just a far too simplistic reading of the subject matter. He's a bit of a fool who misses the subtlety of the symbolism involved. It's surface-level stuff, like I said, aimed at tourists rather than anyone with a serious interest in the subject." He grinned. "There are some pretty pictures, though."

"What symbolism are you referring to?" said Peter. "It might help us."

Miller sighed. "The Carrion King is all of us. That's what the stories are really trying to say. He's a dark reflection of who we are, deep inside. He's unbridled passion, and sweet revenge. He's our darkest thoughts made manifest and given life. That's what's so beguiling about him. He could be any one of us."

That was entirely the problem, considered Elspeth. "Tell me about Michael Williams?" she said.

"Ah, now Mick's a different matter entirely." Miller's mood seemed suddenly to shift. He leaned forward, putting his elbows on the table, interested now. "Mick wants to get to the heart of the story. He's a *real* writer. An artist. Not like that Cowper idiot. Mick's not bothered about the sensationalist stuff. He's trying to key into the symbolism, the truth." He met Elspeth's gaze. His eyes seemed to burrow into her. "Have you read any of his novel?"

"No. He wasn't particularly forthcoming," she said.

Miller grinned. "Give him time, and he'll warm up," he said. "He just needs to learn to trust you first."

"You know him well, then?" said Peter.

"I know him as a fellow enthusiast," said Miller. "He came to me for advice, and when I saw what he was working on, I was only too glad to give it. I know he's written a few potboilers in his time, but this is different. It's good."

"What about David Keel? Are you aware of his play?"

Miller reached for his half-drunk bottle of iced tea. "Yes. The subject matter was my suggestion in the first place and I've been advising him. Like Mick, he's interested in getting the details of the story right, painting the very best portrait of the Carrion King that he can, and I can appreciate that. He's a bit of a sycophant, but he's a decent writer."

"You've been over to the theatre at Winthorpe a few times?"

Miller nodded. "A few. I've watched a couple of recent rehearsals and given David some feedback."

"So you know Lucy Adams?"

"Who?"

Peter rubbed his chin. "The owner and manager of the theatre."

"Ah, yes. The loud one. Always bickering with the producer."

"Vanessa Eglington," said Elspeth.

Miller smiled. "That's it. Vanessa. I've never known what to make of her, really."

"What makes you say that," said Peter.

"Oh, I don't know. I just get the sense that when you talk to her, you're only ever getting half the story. To be honest, I usually try to stay out of all that side of things, and confine my interactions to David. And Oscar, of course. He's always fishing for tips on how to portray the Carrion King during the different stages of his journey."

Peter nodded. "Last question. Can you tell me where you were on the nights of the twelfth and twenty-third of this month?"

Miller frowned. He leaned forward in his chair. "You asked if I could give you some insight into the Carrion King story, and now you're asking me to justify my movements?"

Peter held up a hand. "It's just standard procedure, Professor Miller. We're asking everyone who has any connection to the Winthorpe Theatre the same questions, just so we can eliminate them from our enquiries."

"I presume this is about the recent murders?"

Peter nodded.

"Well, last week is easy. You're talking about Thursday, aren't you? I was at the theatre, as I've just explained. I stayed until the end of the rehearsal, and then left when they all went off to the pub. I came straight back to Oxford."

"Can anyone vouch for you?"

"I imagine so," said Miller. "I went to the pub, The Daisy Chain. I'm there most evenings, to be honest. It's quiet and they're not averse to me sitting in the corner with a book."

"And what about the twelfth?" pressed Peter.

"I couldn't say," said Miller. "But I was most likely in the pub that night, too."

"You can't be more specific about your movements?"

Miller shrugged. "I don't keep a diary, DS Shaw, and I live alone. If I wasn't at home, I was in the pub, as I've explained. I don't really see how any of this is relevant. I certainly haven't killed anyone, if that's what you're insinuating." He grinned.

"As I said, we're just trying to eliminate people from our enquiries."

Miller got to his feet. "Well, if that's all, I really should be off." He glanced at Peter. "If you need anything, call my office. I'd be happy to help."

"Thank you for your time," said Peter.

They sat in silence for a moment, until Miller had disappeared down the other end of the lane and turned the corner.

"Well?" said Elspeth.

"Well what?"

"Well, I need a drink."

"Another coffee?" said Peter.

"No, a proper drink. Come on, pay the bill and we can get out of here. You'd better fill me in on what I can and can't print about all this. Then I'll need a lift back to Heighton. I want to pop into the office of the *Observer*, to check something out."

CHAPTER FIFTEEN

Meredith was sitting behind the desk in her office, peering wistfully out of the window at the alleyway when Elspeth rapped on the door.

"Sorry, didn't mean to startle you," said Elspeth, when Meredith looked around, peering at her in a dazed fashion as if surprised by her sudden appearance.

"No, not at all. I was just thinking." Meredith offered her a crooked smile. "What are you after? I don't have any more work I can throw your way just yet."

"No, it's not that," said Elspeth. "I suppose I'm just following a hunch."

"Alright…" said Meredith.

"When you bought this place, the *Heighton Observer* had been running for some time, hadn't it?"

Meredith nodded. "Since the early seventies, although it'd lost its way a bit since the early days. When I took it on, there was nothing but classified ads or stories about missing cats."

"Or local photograph competitions?" ventured Elspeth.

"Very droll. Why do you ask?"

"Patricia Graves. My mum mentioned the name

sounded familiar. She thought it had something to do with a story about a missing child in the late seventies. I couldn't find anything online but I wondered if you still had an archive I could check. It could help shed a bit of light."

Meredith smiled. "Well, you're welcome to go poking around down there. But you might wish you hadn't worn such a nice dress."

"You mean it's not all on microfiche or computer?" said Elspeth. She could feel her heart sinking.

Meredith laughed. "This is the *Heighton Observer*. Of *course* it's not on microfiche. There's a basement full of mouldering boxes. I can't even promise they're filed in the right order."

Elspeth sighed. "Well, in for a penny…"

"I admire your tenacity, Elspeth. I really do." Meredith pushed her chair back and got to her feet. "Come on, I'll show you."

They walked through the office. A small team of six people were sitting at a bank of desks, bathed in the light of their computer screens. The tinny radio was playing something god-awful by Justin Bieber, and the printer was churning out a constant raft of paper. No one bothered to look up.

"This way. Although be warned, it's deadline day for the print edition, so you'd better not get in anyone's way."

"I wouldn't dream of it," said Elspeth.

"How's the investigation going?" said Meredith, over her shoulder.

"Fascinating and disturbing in equal measure," said Elspeth. "I'll have an update for you soon."

They turned a corner at the far end of the office

– a corner that Elspeth hadn't even realised was there – to see a stone archway leading to a short, steep flight of steps. A heavyset woman with a twist of blue hair sat behind a battered desk that looked a little too small for her, tapping away noisily on a keyboard. Elspeth recognised her immediately from the theatre.

"This is Rose," said Meredith. "Our resident agony aunt. She only works a few hours a week, so she volunteered to take one for the team and sit back here so the others could be together."

"Hello again," said Rose, with a little wave. She peered over the top of her glasses.

"You two have met?" said Meredith.

"Yes, at Winthorpe Theatre," said Elspeth. "It's nice to see you again."

Elspeth had to admit, Rose didn't fit her stereotypical view of an agony aunt – for a start, she was far too young.

"You're not going down *there*, are you?" said Rose.

Elspeth shrugged. "Needs must."

Rose raised an eyebrow. "Well, I'd rather you than me. Just make sure you surface for a breather every now and then. It gets a bit… *musty* amongst the old stacks."

Elspeth laughed. "I'll bear that in mind. Thanks."

"Right, well, this is your mission, not mine," said Meredith. "The light switch is on the left inside the door. Good luck."

Elspeth wondered if this was how lion tamers felt the first time they were sent into the cage. "Alright, thanks, Meredith," she said.

She descended the steps, her heels clicking on the stone. The door at the bottom was wedged shut, warped through years of cold and damp. She gave it a shove, and it scraped noisily across the flagstones, jamming partially open. There was just enough room for her to squeeze through.

The dust tickled her nose as she fumbled through the cobwebs for the light switch. The wall was bare and cold, and thick with dust. She felt something touch the back of her hand and shuddered, before realising it was the tip of a dangling cord. She yanked it, and heard the start-up motors in the fluorescent tubes grind to life. She waited for a few seconds in the chill darkness while they slowly stirred, before the overhead strips stuttered suddenly, and then the basement was flooded with harsh yellow light.

Elspeth squinted while her eyes adjusted.

Meredith had been right – the place looked utterly abandoned. A series of freestanding metal storage shelves had been erected around the bare walls, with two further rows in the centre of the small room. All of them were piled high with cardboard boxes, many of them draped in gossamer blankets of cobwebs, or beginning to disintegrate, spilling their innards across the shelves like overripe fruit. There were no windows, and the two strip lights suspended from the ceiling were harsh and garish. A third hadn't come on when she'd pulled the cord.

For a moment she gaped, wondering how Meredith could allow things to get this bad. She supposed there wasn't much call for anyone to access the archive of a local newspaper, though – anything important would be held in archives at Oxford, or else at the British Library in London, and there was very little call for the journalists working on the paper to look back more than a few years.

Anything recent would be saved on the server.

She considered switching the light off and retreating back up the stairs. It wasn't as if anything hinged on her finding the old story – there could be nothing in it at all, even *if* her mum was right. Something about the look of abject horror she'd witnessed on the dead woman's face, though, made her want to push on. Mentally, she rolled up her sleeves.

She approached the nearest stack of shelves, unsure where else she should start. The boxes here seemed more recent, less faded, less caked in filth, and she walked slowly along the aisle of shelving units, reading the labels. They were all from the early part of the millennium. She needed to go back much further than that.

She turned, scanning the other central aisle behind her. The boxes here weren't so well labelled, but appeared to date back to the mid-nineties. She was going in the right direction, at least. She circled the stack, following the dates in descending order. Two units on the far wall held everything from the eighties, and beside them, rich with the odour of decay, was a dusty heap of boxes from the second half of the seventies.

"In for a penny," she muttered again, as she dusted off the front of a random box. It was from nineteen seventy-six. The one beside it was identical, and she guessed there'd be at least two or three boxes set aside for each year. Grimacing, she slid the box out, hacking and spluttering at the plume of dust, and placed it on the ground. Then, with a shrug of resignation, she dropped down beside it on the damp floor, crossed her legs, and began sifting through the contents.

* * *

"Fancy a cuppa?"

Elspeth looked up to see Rose hovering in the doorway, wrinkling her nose as if she was about to sneeze. She was brandishing two mugs, and trying to squeeze in through the narrow opening. Elspeth jumped to her aid, pulling herself to her feet and stumbling across on wonky legs to take the tea. She'd not sat on the floor for so long in quite some time, and now she was up again her thighs were protesting.

"You've got cobwebs in your hair," said Rose, as she shoved the door aside and pushed her way in.

"I've got cobwebs in places I didn't even know existed," countered Elspeth. She looked at the two mugs. One had a picture of a unicorn on it, the other an advert for a local printing firm. "I'm guessing the unicorn is yours?"

Rose grinned. "It was a silly present," she said. "From an old girlfriend. Reminds me of her."

Elspeth passed it over, and took a sip from her own mug. "Thanks for this," she said. "Much-needed sustenance."

Rose indicated the pile of boxes on the floor. Elspeth had just finished working through nineteen seventy-eight, and was about to start on seventy-nine. "You're really going for it, then?"

"I suppose I am," said Elspeth. "It sounds dreadfully American, but I've got a bit of a hunch."

"Nothing dreadful about sounding American," said Rose. "What are you looking for?"

"A story about a missing child. It's all very nebulous, really. It's just Mrs Graves. My mum recognised her name, and thought she'd been mixed up in some scandal during the late seventies." She shrugged. "I thought I'd take a look, see if there were any reports."

"I saw your piece on the website. Horrible story. Do you think they'll catch the killer?"

"I hope so," said Elspeth. "I know they're looking into it, running forensics and all that."

"And you're wondering if this old story might help get to the bottom of why someone killed her?" said Rose.

Elspeth nodded. "I suppose I am, yeah. It just feels a bit like unfinished business."

Rose crossed to the heap of boxes. "Where are you up to? I've got a few minutes. I'll give you a hand if you like?"

Elspeth smiled. "It's those boxes on the left. I've been through the others." She joined Rose. "Here, you take this box and I'll take that one." She slid one of the boxes across the floor, leaving a wad of trailing cobwebs. "And thanks."

Rose grinned. "I'm an agony aunt. I can't help but stick my nose into other people's business." She placed her mug of tea on the ground and sat down.

"An agony aunt and a stage manager at the theatre," said Elspeth. "They seem like strange bedfellows."

Rose shrugged. "They keep me happy. And just about off the breadline. They're a good crowd."

"Here?"

"Well, yes, but I meant at the theatre," said Rose. "We've been together for a while now, put on a few different productions, and I suppose we've become more like friends than colleagues." She laughed. "Or a strange, dysfunctional family."

"It must have been a real blow about Lucy," said Elspeth.

Rose shrugged. "She kept herself a little aloof from the gang, to be honest. But yeah, what happened to her is awful."

"Do you think anyone at the theatre was involved?"

"Oh, no," said Rose, emphatically. "I can't believe that for a minute. As I said, we're more like a family. Vanessa gets herself wound up far too often, David's a bit intense about the sanctity of his script, Oscar takes all the pagan stuff a bit too seriously... we've all got foibles that get on each other's nerves from time to time. But none of them would do something like that."

"I'm sure you're right," said Elspeth. She made a mental note to dig a little deeper into Oscar's fascination with the 'pagan stuff'.

Rose rubbed her hands together, as if anxious to get started. "Right. So what exactly am I looking for?"

"Front-page stuff, really – anything about a missing child from Heighton, or a reference to Patricia Graves."

"You mean like this?" Rose lifted a ragged newspaper from the box and passed it across to her. On the front was a blurry black and white photograph of a young boy, with the headline: YOUNG BOY, 8, MISSING FOR THREE DAYS.

Elspeth stared at the newspaper, and then at Rose. "How did you...?"

Rose grinned. "I don't know what took you so long," she said, laughing. "That wasn't very hard to find."

Elspeth shook her head in mock dismay. "I've been down here ages, and you just pop your head in for a couple of minutes and *voilá*!" She shuffled another box out of the way and dragged Rose's box closer. A quick rummage showed a series of news reports over the course of a number of weeks, detailing the search for the boy. It didn't appear that he'd been found, at least in the first couple of months. The stories seemed to peter out after that.

She scanned the first article quickly. The child, Thomas Stone, had been in foster care – with Patricia Graves, and her husband James – and was presumed to have run away. They'd reported it to the police, and were appealing to any who might have seen him. They were pictured, along with another boy of similar age, George Baker, also under their temporary care.

Elspeth felt a pang of regret; Patricia looked so young, and so worried for the child. She wondered what had happened, to the boy, and to this woman, for her to end up in the way she had, dead on her bedroom floor.

She decided she'd photocopy the articles and take them home for a more considered read. Maybe she could ask Peter to check in the police system to see if Thomas Stone had ever turned up. She hoped he'd been found safely.

"So, are those the answers you were looking for?" said Rose.

"Only more questions, I'm afraid," said Elspeth. "But it's a start. Thanks for your help."

"I hardly did anything," said Rose.

"You found the article. And you brought tea," countered Elspeth. "Anyone who does that is alright in my book."

Rose laughed. "Well, I'd better make a swift exit while the going's good. I'll leave you to deal with all of *this*." She indicated the boxes and slew of newspapers all around her as she got to her feet.

"I take it all back," said Elspeth. "Every word of it."

Rose chuckled as she made for the door, and then paused at the bottom of the stairs. "We're going for a drink later, after rehearsals, if you fancy coming along?"

Elspeth grinned. "Yeah, that would be lovely, thanks. I could do with a night out."

"Alright. Great," Rose beamed. "We'll be heading to The Horse and Cart in Winthorpe around nine thirty. See you there?"

"Great. I'll look forward to it."

Rose trundled off up the stairs, leaving Elspeth sitting there, surrounded by detritus, the newspaper from nineteen seventy-nine still unfolded on her knee.

Elspeth sighed. She was looking forward to a long, hot soak in the bath, just as soon as she'd finished up here. She looked again at the mess she'd created, and her heart sank. She hoped it was all going to be worth it.

CHAPTER SIXTEEN

Elspeth couldn't help but feel like an interloper as she stood at the bar in The Horse and Cart, reeling off a long list of drinks orders later that evening. The whole crowd from the theatre was there, with the noticeable exception of Vanessa, who had evidently declined to join them.

The mood amongst them all remained sombre – tense, even – and although Rose had dismissed it as a general nervousness about the impending opening night, Elspeth could tell immediately that there was a more serious undercurrent to their chatter. The rehearsals were going well, by all accounts but she suspected it had everything to do with Lucy Adams's murder and the continued police investigation into the missing costume. She'd been careful to keep it out of her reports for the *Heighton Observer* website and social media feeds, and the police hadn't yet released the information to any other news agencies or reporters, but she knew they had to suspect the missing costume was somehow involved – and with it, the implication that they were all potential suspects for the murder.

She smiled at Rose and Oscar as they came over to help her carry the drinks, and followed them back to the corner where the gang had assembled in their usual spot, pulling two small tables together so they could all fit around.

The pub was relatively quiet, aside from the theatre lot, with just a few older gents gathered around the bar and a couple of young men sitting in the opposite corner, deep in conversation. It had that rarefied, yet somewhat stereotypical air of a classic country pub, the sort of place she'd half missed down in London and half been glad to get away from – still mired in the décor of fifty years previous, cluttered with pictures of hunting dogs and men with shotguns, and rich with the scent of stale beer and waxed Barbour jackets.

Elspeth tentatively placed the drinks on the nearest table – now wishing she'd not attempted to carry so many at once – and then pulled out a stool and dropped down between Rose and David Keel. To Keel's left was Elizabeth Jones, the costume designer, who smiled warmly and thanked Elspeth for the drink.

Elspeth recognised all the other faces from the programme, having studied the cast list on Saturday evening, and again before coming out to meet them all tonight. The man who'd reminded her of Andrew – Graham Furnham, playing The Master of the Hunt – was sitting opposite her, and when he saw her looking he smiled nervously and reached for his pint, averting his eyes as he took a long swig. Elspeth did the same, sipping at her apple juice and wishing she were able to drink something stronger.

"So, Mr Keel – Vanessa tells me you're a bit of an expert on the old Wychwood myths?" she said, deciding her best course of action would be to just launch in.

Keel smiled at this, rubbing his ear as if mildly embarrassed. "David, please. And no, despite what our glorious leader might have to say on the subject, I'm far from an expert. It's more that I'm fascinated by the old stories, and what they can tell us about the modern day. That's what I'm trying to do with this play, you see – relate these ancient morality tales to modern life. There are lessons to be learned for us all." He grinned, and reached for his pint. This was a very different man than the one she'd seen at the theatre the other day. Here he seemed relatively relaxed and willing to talk. Perhaps the news of Lucy Adams's murder had affected him more deeply than she'd given him credit for, or more likely the opportunity to talk about his work had helped to soften him up.

"And what sort of lessons would those be?"

He sipped at his pint thoughtfully. "That the sins of the past always return to haunt us. That even if we think we've escaped, we'll be drawn back to the start of our story. That facing our fears is the only way to deal with them."

Elspeth glanced at Graham Furnham again. He was rubbing the back of his neck and looking longingly at Alice Turner, the young woman whose costume had gone missing. She turned her attention back to Keel. "I'm looking forward to seeing it," she said. "I met with Professor Byron Miller yesterday. He spoke very highly of the script. He mentioned he's been assisting you with your research?"

Keel laughed. "If by that you mean he's told me everything I needed to know about the original myths, then yes, he has. The subject was his idea in the first place. I couldn't have done it without him, to be honest. He's even attended a few of the rehearsals and given me notes, and advised Elizabeth on the costume designs. The man's a bit of a genius, at least in his chosen field."

Elspeth glanced at Elizabeth. "Where do you even start with costumes like that?"

Elizabeth laughed. "Well, half of it is made up, and the other half is taken from the only source we have – a bunch of mediaeval woodcuts. They're primitive, and were made five or six hundred years after the fact, but they've served us well as inspiration. I've done my best to marry it all up with the Saxon designs of the time, but really, it's complete fantasy."

"I've seen those woodcuts," said Elspeth. "They're quite…" she trailed off, looking for the right word.

"They're bloody horrible," said Keel, laughing. "Someone's imagined portraits of ritual death. But they help to show us how the myths developed. It's like religion, see – over the years the stories are twisted and added to, bent out of their original form to suit the expectations of the intended audience. They end up being riddled with anachronisms and strange asides. But as with all good morality tales, the central story, the heart of the lesson, rings true. Our play is just another step on the evolutionary ladder of the original stories."

"I like that idea," said Elspeth. "That stories are living things that change and evolve with the passing of the seasons."

"You should write that down," said Rose. "You can use that line in your review."

They all laughed. "So have you had much to do with Michael Williams, then? I gather he's writing a novel about the Carrion King and the Wychwood, too," said Elspeth.

David nodded. "Yeah, Mick's been another supporter. He doesn't have quite the same insight as Byron, but he's definitely helped to give the thing shape via email. I'm looking forward to his book. Whenever he manages to finish the bloody thing!" He took a long swig from his pint.

"So, Elizabeth – you're making a new costume for Alice, I presume?"

Elizabeth looked more than a little uncomfortable at the sudden change of topic. "Yes, yes. Bit of a rushed job, I'm afraid. But needs must."

"You don't really think that Vanessa took it, do you?" said Rose. This was clearly a thread from an earlier conversation Elspeth had missed.

Elizabeth was looking increasingly uncomfortable. "Well, how does it look? She's the only one who didn't come to the pub that night – which is strange enough, given how much she likes a drink. Especially after losing her cool like that with Lucy."

That was new. Neither Peter nor Vanessa had mentioned anything about a row. Vanessa had explained things between her and Lucy had been strained, but there'd been no talk of a recent row.

"But why would she sabotage her own play like that?" said Rose. "It doesn't make sense."

"Oh, I don't know," said Elizabeth. "Why does anyone do anything? But she's the only one who could have. We were all here, weren't we? And the costume was there when we left. I hung it up myself."

"Yes, but that could be nothing more than coincidence," said Rose. "Next you'll be saying she's the one who murdered Lucy."

"I didn't *say* that," said Elizabeth haughtily. "Although God knows Lucy gave her cause enough."

"This is *Vanessa* we're talking about," said Rose. "And besides, she was at the theatre all night, preparing for opening night."

"Well, not *all* night," said Oscar, leaning in. He had an unlit cigarette between his fingers, as if he were just about to head out for a smoke.

"What are you on about, Oscar?" said Keel.

"Nothing. It doesn't matter. I'm just saying she didn't stay at the theatre all night like she said."

"How do you know? You were here with us," said Keel.

"No, you left early, didn't you?" said Rose. "That's right. You went out for a smoke and didn't come back. I'd forgotten all about that. By the time someone noticed, you'd gone."

"Oscar?" pressed Keel.

"It was nothing. I'd forgotten my lighter. Left it back in the dressing room, so I went back to fetch it, that's all. The place was shut up and the lights were off. There was no sign of Vanessa."

"Have you told the police?" said Elspeth.

"I'd forgotten about it, to be honest. It was late

on, and I was drunk, so I'd walked there. It's probably nothing. She'll have finished up and gone home, that's all. I can't even be sure of the time. I only thought of it when you said she'd been there all night." He straightened up and placed the end of his cigarette between his lips. "Back in a mo."

Elspeth watched as he walked nonchalantly towards the front door and stepped out, as if completely ignorant of the bombshell he'd just dropped. Her mind was whirring. So Vanessa had argued with Lucy on the evening of Lucy's death, and hadn't mentioned it to the police. And there was a witness who could prove she wasn't where she said she'd been.

She had to talk to Peter.

She took a swig from her drink. Around her, the others had grown quiet.

Valiantly, Rose attempted to restart the conversation. "So when's your article going to run, Ellie? The one about the play."

"Umm, well, not sure yet," she said. "I'll probably tie it up with a review, if I can persuade my editor."

"So you're coming, for opening night?"

"If I can still get tickets," said Elspeth.

"Oh, don't worry about that," said Rose. "Leave it with me. I'll have a word with Vanessa."

"Great. Thanks." Elspeth downed the rest of her drink. "Look, thanks for inviting me along tonight, but I'm going to head off. I've got a deadline and an early start in the morning."

"Alright. Sure," said Rose. She looked a little crestfallen.

"Maybe we can do this again," said Elspeth.

"You're on," said Rose.

"Nice getting to know you," she said to Keel and Elizabeth as she got to her feet. All she could think about was calling Peter. "See you again."

She made a beeline for the door.

Outside, Oscar was pacing back and forth, sucking determinedly on his cigarette. "You off?" he said, when he saw her leaving the pub.

"Yeah. Work to do."

"They're alright, you know. That lot," he gestured towards the pub with a nod of his head. "They're like a family. Always bickering, but none of them would do anything to hurt the others. Not really."

Elspeth smiled. "That's exactly what Rose said."

There was a moment of awkward silence. She was just about to turn and walk away, when he spoke again. "So, do you want to go on somewhere? Grab something to eat, maybe? Get another drink? We could head into Heighton, or Oxford..."

Elspeth grinned. A few years ago she would have jumped at the chance for a wild night out with a man like him. But now... after everything that had happened recently, she just felt tired. She couldn't afford to make any more of a mess of her life, no matter how tempted she felt. And besides, she had no idea at all whether he could be trusted. "Sorry, deadlines. But I reckon there'll be plenty more willing victims in there."

"Nah. Family, remember." He grinned, backing away towards the pub entrance. "See you round, Ellie Reeves."

Shaking her head, Elspeth hurried back to her car. As soon as she'd fired up the engine and pulled away from the kerb, she thumbed the voice control on her steering wheel and waited for the beep.

"Call Peter Shaw," she said. Duly, the phone began to trill over the speakerphone. Peter answered after only three rings.

"Ellie? Are you okay?"

"Yeah, I'm fine. But I've just been for a drink with the theatre lot, and we really need to talk."

CHAPTER SEVENTEEN

He came here often to be alone with his memories. It was a peaceful place, unmolested by modernity, by the encroachment of houses and parks and cycle routes, by people walking their dogs, drinking cheap cider and abandoning cigarette ends in the undergrowth. It seemed to him as if it hadn't changed for centuries, a place captured in a single moment of time – one of the few truly wild places left around Heighton. He treasured it as a safe harbour, and for what resided here, hidden from the world.

Much of the ancient Wychwood had gone now, cut back over the centuries. What was left of it formed a few precious havens, like these small woods at the back of Heighton – left to grow wild because no one knew what else to do with them, and the council wouldn't allow the developers to move in.

That was the true beauty of the Wychwood – it was everywhere around them, always. No matter how much of it had been cleared away, it still exerted its influence. It was a wild place, imbued with wild magic. He'd known that as a child, sensed it as he gambolled around out here with Thomas, trying to forget about the rest of the world, to allow himself to be transported somewhere else.

To him, it had always been like stepping through the back of the wardrobe, entering this resplendent place, this relic of the ancient world. Here, he was invincible. Here he was at his best. If only Thomas could see him now. See how free he was, how unencumbered.

He sighed. Perhaps it wouldn't be too much longer.

Up ahead, he could see the tree that marked his destination. He trod carefully through the bed of moss and leaves towards it, unable to avoid crunching a fallen branch underfoot and startling a pigeon, which took off from the spindly upper branches of the nearest tree in a sudden excited flurry. He watched it go, sailing away over the treetops and out of view, back towards the real world. He continued on his way.

He liked the silence out here. He was only a few hundred yards from the nearest road, from the back gardens of the old Georgian terraces, and yet he could hear no cars, no squawking children. Just the slow tread of his own boots as he made his way to the hallowed place.

He reached the foot of the tree. It was a massive gnarled oak, its fat boughs sagging with the weight of centuries. Its bark formed a thick, brittle crust, broken in places where moss and beaks had worked their way into the cracks, prising it away from the softer wood beneath. Around it, leaves formed a soft, mouldering carpet.

He stood for a moment in its presence, listening to the gentle soughing of the breeze through its upper branches. Then, with a deep breath, he dropped to his knees, and reached for the small hollow at its base.

It was a small space, an aperture formed by the twisted roots, and as he reached in, he felt a shudder of anticipation. Carefully, he extracted a small bundle of filthy towels. He placed them on the ground before him. Then, with a quick glance around to ensure he wasn't being observed – for no one could know the secret of what was hidden here – he carefully unfolded the uppermost layer and sat back, peering down at the treasure he'd revealed.

It was the bones of a small child, bundled into a tidy heap. Slowly, his hands trembling, he reached down for the skull, cupping it in his palms, lifting it so that it was level with his own face.

"Soon. I promise. I'm coming for you. Just a little longer."

He stared at the hollow eye sockets for a few moments, as if anticipating a response, and then, silently, he returned the skull to the bundle, wrapped it carefully, and placed it back in its secret resting place.

Then, dusting his hands, he made his way back down the ancient track towards town. He had work to do, and Thomas was growing impatient.

CHAPTER EIGHTEEN

Peter was waiting for her when she emerged from the house at eight thirty the next morning, bleary-eyed and in dire need of more caffeine.

They'd made the arrangement the previous night on the phone, when Elspeth had outlined the conversations she'd heard in the pub. She'd then driven home, posted a quick update to the story on the *Heighton Observer*'s website, and then flopped onto her bed with her iPad to read more about the Carrion King and the other characters in his mythos. So far, everything appeared to tally with what Byron Miller had told them. She was particularly intrigued, though, by the end of the story, in which the Carrion King himself disappeared altogether from the Wychwood, having reached some kind of obscene transcendence following the death of all his apostles. She'd made a note to return to it that evening and do a bit more digging.

Peter was sitting behind the wheel of his car, tapping at the screen of his mobile. He looked up when he heard the front door close behind her, and then leaned over and opened the passenger door. She circled the car, climbed in, and pushed her handbag into the footwell between her feet. The car smelled of deodorant and stale takeaway.

"Morning."

"Mmmm hmmm," he mumbled. He'd returned to punching rapidly at the screen of his phone with both thumbs.

"Is that a game you're playing?" said Elspeth, trying to sound inquisitive rather than judgmental. This was something that had become a real bone of contention between her and Andrew towards the end – that he'd become addicted to some stupid game on his phone involving birds and gems, and spent hours with his face buried in it, grunting monosyllabic answers to her questions and refusing to engage in conversation. She realised now that he'd been purposefully disengaging, burying his head in the sand and avoiding her, but at the time it had just seemed like some infuriating new obsession.

"Emails," said Peter, without looking up. They sat in silence for a moment. Elspeth put her seatbelt on. A minute later he finished and tossed his phone into a plastic alcove in the dashboard. He shot her an apologetic look. "Sorry. All this is keeping me much busier than usual. Reports, statements, forensics…" He started the engine.

"Anything interesting?" she said.

"Nothing as interesting as what you told me last night." He slipped the car into gear and they started to crawl towards the end of the drive. "So let's just go over it again. One of the theatre lot invited you out for a drink last night."

"Yes, that's right. Rose Macauley, the stage manager. She works as an agony aunt at the *Heighton Observer* too, and I got chatting with her yesterday in the office archives. In fact, there's something I want to ask you later, about an old case I'm looking into related to the Patricia Graves murder."

Peter nodded. "Alright. We can talk about that later. I need to be crystal clear on what was said last night first. So while you were there, Oscar Waring told you he'd left the pub early on Thursday night to go and collect his lighter from the theatre, and when he got there, there was no sign of Vanessa?"

"Yeah. He just sort of announced it. He said all the lights were off and everything was locked up."

"But he still managed to retrieve his lighter?" said Peter.

Elspeth paused. "He didn't say."

Peter nodded. "And there was talk of a confrontation."

"Yes. That was something everyone seemed to agree on. There'd been a blow-up between Lucy Adams and Vanessa earlier that afternoon."

"Blow-up as in violent?"

"I can't be certain, but it sounded more like a stand-up row."

"Did they say what it was about?"

Elspeth sighed. Perhaps she should have done a bit more digging while she'd had the chance. Everything had just moved so quickly, though. "No. Sorry. But I got the impression they'd never really got along."

"Vanessa said as much. But then she told us she'd

been at the theatre until late, too, which was already a dubious alibi. So the question is: why is she lying to us?" Peter reached the junction at the end of the street and turned towards Heighton.

"Do you really think she could have done it?" said Elspeth.

"Do you?" deflected Peter.

"I…" she hesitated. What did she think? "Well, it sounds as if things were tense between them. And if what Oscar says is true, she's not told us everything about where she was that night. It's possible, I suppose. But I still think you're right – if she is involved, she can't have done it alone. A woman of her build couldn't have hoisted Lucy Adams's corpse like that on her own, let alone Geoff Altman."

"I think it's time we got to the bottom of what she was doing for all of that night," said Peter.

"So where are we going?" said Elspeth.

"The theatre. I've already called ahead, and Vanessa is working there all day. Time for a little chat."

"Do you think that's a good idea? Me coming along, I mean." It was one thing accompanying him to discuss the Carrion King mythology with a handful of experts, but interviewing an actual suspect…

Peter sighed. "Probably not. But I want you there. She might try to talk her way out of it, and you were the one who heard what the others were saying in the pub last night. Something might strike a chord."

"Alright," said Elspeth. "If you're sure."

They drove on through country lanes lined by bristling hedgerows and listing rows of trees, which seemed to crowd the car, leaning in to form a long, snaking tunnel through which only a scarce few shafts of morning sunlight were able to penetrate. Elspeth couldn't shake the impression that the trees were somehow conspiring, whispering to one another across the smooth river of tarmac that cut through their ancient heartland. She wondered what they were plotting.

They skirted Heighton, and fifteen minutes later were pulling up in the car park of Winthorpe Theatre. Elspeth wondered what Rose and the theatre lot would make of it when they heard she'd gone straight to Peter, and then worse – accompanied him to confront Vanessa. She somehow doubted she'd be invited out for drinks again.

Peter had been uncharacteristically quiet during the drive, both hands affixed to the wheel, eyes unwavering from the road. She guessed he must have been turning everything over in his mind, trying to extract sense and meaning from the new bits of data she'd presented him with. She knew he suspected Vanessa of hiding something – he'd said as much after his first interview with the woman – but there were troubling issues with her candidacy for the murderer, not least the fact they had no forensic evidence to link her to the murder scene, or the fact there was no apparent motive for why she might have killed Geoff Altman, or even if she knew him. Yet there remained that niggling doubt.

They climbed out of the car. It was a bracing morning, and out here, on the edge of the Winthorpe estate, they were exposed to the elements. She wished she'd brought more than a light jacket over her blouse.

"I'm going to leave this to you," she said.

Peter nodded, preoccupied, as he led the way down towards the auditorium.

It wasn't yet nine o'clock, and the grass was still damp and dewy. She kept to the path, following behind Peter as he hurried down the auditorium steps and around behind the stage area, towards the small office and dressing rooms. He was clearly anxious to get this over with.

As he approached the door he glanced over his shoulder to ensure she was behind him, and then rapped three times before trying the handle. It was unlocked, and the door swung open easily on creaking hinges. She hurried in behind him, keen to get out of the cold.

Vanessa was in the kitchenette with her back to them, pondering over an empty mug. The kettle was noisily reaching its climax and she clearly hadn't heard them enter. Peter motioned for Elspeth to stay back, and cleared his throat. Vanessa, startled, looked up, stared at them both for a moment as if trying to register who they were, and then the kettle clicked and seemed to break her reverie, and she smiled. "Just in time," she said. "Tea?"

Peter shook his head. "No, thank you."

Elspeth was about to ask for a coffee, then thought better of it.

Vanessa nodded, and splashed some water into her own mug. She was wearing black leggings and a loose-fitting shirt, and Elspeth couldn't help thinking how slight the woman looked. Tired, too – which wasn't surprising, given how hard she'd been working in the run up to opening night. The others all appeared to be part time or volunteers, working around their day jobs. Vanessa had the unenviable task of holding it all together. Particularly now Lucy was gone, too.

Vanessa took up her mug and walked through into the communal room where, the other night, Elspeth had met the gathered cast and crew. "So, what can I do for you?"

"I have a couple of follow-up questions," said Peter. "A few things from your statement that don't seem to agree with the run of events set out by one or two others."

Vanessa sipped her tea. She looked over at Elspeth, her manner accusing. "And you're working with the police now?"

"I'm just trying to help," said Elspeth.

Vanessa turned back to Peter. "Go on, then. What's everyone been saying?"

"You were seen having a stand-up row with Lucy Adams on the day she died. A row you failed to mention."

Vanessa sighed. "I didn't think it was relevant. We were always rowing. As I said, the relationship between us had become strained. She wouldn't let me do my job. She wanted to pick over every little detail."

"Did that annoy you enough to want her dead?" said Peter. The sheer brutality of the words was shocking.

Vanessa looked appalled. "No. Of course not. Look, we might have had our disagreements, but I would never have wished that on her. On anyone."

"But you lied to us about your whereabouts that night, didn't you?" pressed Peter.

"I…" She seemed to falter. The flash of defiance she'd shown just moments before had gone. Now, she just looked tired and vulnerable. "I was here, working just like I said."

"All night?" said Peter.

Vanessa looked like a deer caught in headlights.

"You realise how this looks?" said Peter. "We have a witness who returned to the theatre later that evening. We know you weren't here. So I think you'd better start explaining where you *were* at that time."

Very deliberately, Vanessa set her mug down on the table. Elspeth could see that her hand was shaking. "I *didn't* kill her."

"Then help me out," said Peter, his tone level, reasonable. "Tell me what you were really doing."

Vanessa took a deep breath. "I was with my brother," she said.

"Your *brother*?" said Elspeth, unable to prevent herself from chiming in at this unexpected revelation. "Why would you want to keep that from the police?"

"Because he's a heroin addict," said Vanessa, "and I'm trying to help him. I didn't want him anywhere near the police. I was trying to keep him out of all this. If he gets spooked, he might run again. It took me six months to find him last time, living rough in Manchester, stealing to get enough money to buy drugs..." she trailed off, unable to look either of them in the eye. "It's been going on for so long, I can hardly remember a time when I didn't worry that I'd go home each night to find him dead on the sofa from an overdose."

"Do any of the others know about this?" said Peter.

"No. Lucy found out, but..." She hung her head.

"Is that what you argued about on the day she died?"

Vanessa nodded. "She'd been going through the accounts. She found a few discrepancies in the petty cash."

"Money you'd stolen for your brother to buy drugs," said Peter.

Elspeth couldn't stand it anymore. She went to Vanessa's side, slipped her arm around her shoulders.

"I didn't steal it," said Vanessa. "I borrowed it. I was going to put it back. Once we got paid, after opening night, I'd have the money to replace it. It was nothing. No money at all to a woman like her. I'd never have stolen from her. I tried to tell her."

"But she didn't understand," said Peter. "She wouldn't listen. She threatened to expose you."

Vanessa raised her head, and there was another flash of that innate defiance. This was the real Vanessa, Elspeth knew. She'd fought to protect her brother for so long that it had begun to erode her, to define her – but beneath it all, there was an edge of steel. "I didn't kill her," she said. "How would I be able to help Robbie then? If I were in prison? It would be the end of him."

"We'll have to speak to him," said Peter. "To corroborate your story."

Vanessa nodded. "Alright. But please – can *you* do it? I couldn't bear it if he did another runner. Don't just send another faceless policeman around who won't understand."

"Of course," said Peter. "I'll see to it. But you're going to have to come back to the station to give another formal statement. And if John Adams wants to press charges about the missing money, he's quite within his rights. He'll have to be informed. You should have told us, Ms Eglington. The chief inspector could have you up on charges of withholding evidence."

"Yes. I understand," said Vanessa. "Can we go now? I'd rather get it over and done with."

Peter nodded. "We'll wait outside while you lock everything up." He gestured to Elspeth, and she followed him out.

"So we're no closer to finding your killer," she said. She had to admit – she'd been relieved to hear Vanessa's story. She hadn't wanted to believe that the woman had been capable of the horrors she'd seen in the woods behind her mum's house. "And we're quickly running out of leads."

"Not just yet," said Peter. "There are two sides to every story. If Vanessa wasn't here when Oscar Waring came back for his lighter…"

"Then he had the opportunity to take the costume too," finished Elspeth. "I hadn't considered that. I mean… he seems too…"

"Stoned?" said Peter.

Elspeth grinned. "Yeah. I guess. I was going to say impulsive. Too spontaneous to plan anything so well orchestrated. But Rose did say he'd developed a bit of an obsession with the whole Carrion King thing. She thought he might be taking his role a little too seriously."

"We'll head there next. His home address will be logged in the system. I'll drop Ms Eglington at the station and Patel can see to her statement."

The door opened and Vanessa stepped out, wearing a short denim jacket over her shirt. She pulled the door shut behind her. "Don't you need to lock up?" said Elspeth.

"No. It's all done on a key code." Vanessa indicated a small panel of push buttons on the door. "As I told DC

163

Patel the other day, only me, Lucy and Rose know the pass code. Oh, and Oscar, I suppose, because he's always locking himself out when he goes for a smoke."

Elspeth and Peter exchanged glances.

"Right then," said Peter. "Let's get you to the station, Ms Eglington. This way."

CHAPTER NINETEEN

Oscar Waring, it seemed, was living up to every cliché of the struggling actor's journey.

His flat was on the ground floor of a large mid-terrace Victorian house, and the buzzer plate by the front door suggested there were three further apartments in the same building – two on the floors above and one in the basement. Elspeth peered down into the murky depths at the bottom of the steps, where empty crisp packets, dry leaves and cigarette butts had gathered, swirled around by the wind. The pillar-box red paint on the front door was peeling, and net curtains – yellowed with age and tobacco – had been pulled across the front bay windows.

Peter pressed the buzzer for a second time.

There was a shuffling sound from the other side of the door. "Alright, alright," came the response. Elspeth recognised the voice immediately. She was glad she hadn't succumbed to the man's charms the previous evening, if this was what had awaited her.

The door opened and Oscar's face appeared in the gap. His eyes were red-rimmed, and he was unshaven, his long hair lank. He was wearing a black T-shirt and skinny black jeans, and for the first time, Elspeth noticed he had a run of tattoos up the inside of both arms, of unfamiliar symbols and whorls.

"Oh, hello," he said, catching sight of Peter and opening the door a little wider. He peered over Peter's shoulder at Elspeth. "Couldn't keep away, eh?"

Peter turned to catch her eye with a flash of wry amusement, and she looked away, her cheeks burning.

"I have some follow-up questions for you," said Peter. "May we come in?"

"Of course." Oscar stood aside and ushered them in, and they followed him to a flat which opened directly into the living room, from which another door led off, presumably towards the kitchen, bedroom and bathroom. The flat seemed better maintained inside than out, although Oscar was obviously a slob: a greasy pizza box had been dumped on the floor by the fireplace, ashtrays overflowed on the coffee table, and mugs and wine glasses, stained from abandoned dregs, littered almost every available surface.

There was a large gilt-framed mirror propped against the wall behind the door, which looked as if it should have been mounted somewhere. An electric guitar with a missing string was resting on one of two sofas, and there were posters plastered over the walls, one depicting Baphomet, another a skeleton rising from its grave, its bony fingers protruding through the soil. The rest appeared to be garish artwork from album covers or pictures of bands she wasn't familiar with. The whole place had the air of a student's bedroom about it – as if Oscar was resolutely attempting to staunch the oncoming tide of adulthood, and winning.

The one exception to this was a sextet of framed watercolours, which held pride of place in the alcove to the left of the fireplace – a depiction of the five apostles, mirroring the poses from the mediaeval woodcuts. Above them, the Carrion King stood in a wooded grove, his arms held aloft, five crows circling above his head. He was wearing a cape of downy black feathers, and a crown of thorns upon his head.

Beneath the framed prints was a small bookcase, along with a shelf holding what appeared to be fragments of animal bones, a decidedly creepy-looking wax doll, and a hazel branch.

Peter crossed the room to take a closer look, while Elspeth took a seat beside the guitar, trying to ignore the stink of ingrained smoke.

"Interesting pictures," said Peter.

"Yeah, I love all that 'five sacrifices' stuff. I picked them up at a local craft fair," said Oscar, wandering around to stand beside him. "Good, aren't they?" He pointed to the uppermost picture. "The Carrion King, you see. Thought it was appropriate."

"And all of this," asked Peter, indicting the paraphernalia on the shelf.

Oscar laughed. "Well, it's all a bit silly really, isn't it? It doesn't mean anything, but I thought it would help get me in the mood. You know, a bit of method acting."

"And how far do you take those methods?" said Peter. His tone was level, but firm. "How involved in this particular role have you become?"

Oscar looked a little taken aback. "Now hold on a

minute. What's going on here?" He glanced at Elspeth, as if willing her to explain.

"I see you have copies of books about the Carrion King here, too," said Peter, studying the bookcase.

"Of course. As I said – I like to do my research." Oscar's tone had altered. The carefully studied, laissez-faire attitude had all but disappeared. "Now if you'd kindly tell me what you're doing here…"

"Very well," said Peter. "I have cause to believe you haven't been entirely truthful with us, Mr Waring. That you weren't, in fact, in the pub all night with your colleagues last Thursday, but left early to return to the theatre."

Oscar fumbled in his shirt pocket for his tobacco pouch. He took it out and started rolling a cigarette, but his fingers were shaking. "That's right, yeah. I went out for a smoke and realised I'd left my lighter in the dressing room. It was nothing. I'd forgotten all about it until last night, when they were talking about Vanessa being at the theatre all night."

"So you can confirm that when you went back, you found the theatre had been closed up for the night and there was no one else around."

"That's right. Vanessa was supposed to be there, but she wasn't. That's what I told Ellie last night in the pub." He licked the edge of his cigarette paper and carefully rolled the tobacco into a thin tube, which he placed between his lips. "I was only there for five minutes. I took my lighter and went home."

"How did you get into the theatre if it was locked?" said Peter.

"Vanessa told me the pass code a while back. I'm the

only one who smokes, see, and I kept getting locked out."

Peter nodded. "And what about the costume? Why did you take that?"

Elspeth studied Oscar's face. He was chewing his bottom lip, and nervously picking at the pocket of his jeans. He was still holding something back. Peter had seen it, and was pressing him. "Look, I've got *nothing* to do with what happened to Lucy. I don't even know *what* happened, really. The first I heard about it was on Friday afternoon, when Vanessa called."

"That wasn't what I asked, Oscar," said Peter.

"It was nothing. A silly game. A bit of kinky role play, that's all. I promise, it's got nothing to do with any murder."

"I think you'd better start from the beginning," said Peter. "And make sure you tell us *everything* this time."

Oscar lit his cigarette and took a long, desperate draw. He was still shaking. "It's Sasha," he said. "She's missing."

"Sasha?" said Elspeth. This was the first she'd heard of anyone called Sasha.

"My girlfriend, I suppose," said Oscar. He shrugged. "Or perhaps not anymore."

"Start with the pub," said Peter. "What happened when you left?"

Oscar nodded. He crossed to the window and stood with his back to them, as if peering out through the filthy net curtains. "It's just like I said. I went out for a smoke and realised I'd left my lighter. It's precious, see?" He turned, holding out a battered old bronze Zippo. "It used to belong to my granddad."

"So you decided to go back and fetch it," said Peter.

"Yeah. I took a walk down to the theatre. I expected to find Vanessa there, but everything was quiet. So I let myself in and found the lighter where I'd left it."

"And…"

"And that's when I saw the costumes on the rail. Like I said, it was just a bit of silly fun. Me and Sasha, dressing up as the Carrion King and his Consort. We'd messed around like that before, having a laugh. It was a way of celebrating me getting the gig, really. I didn't think it would do any harm. You know…" he trailed off, embarrassed. He wouldn't make eye contact with Elspeth.

"So you took both costumes home?" said Peter.

Oscar nodded. "Yeah. I was going to put them back the next day. No harm done. I brought them back here. Sasha was waiting for me. She was really into it, couldn't wait to try it on."

"And?"

"And what do you think? We had a few drinks, and whiled away a few hours."

"So why didn't you put the costume back the next morning with the other one? Where is it now?"

Oscar shook his head. "I don't know. We had a blazing row. It was the most stupid thing. Something about some bloody party she wanted me to go to, but I had rehearsals and said I couldn't go. She stormed out, and she took the costume with her. She was still wearing it."

Peter sighed. "So you put your costume back the next morning before anyone noticed, and feigned ignorance when we realised that Alice's was missing. Is that it?"

Oscar nodded. "I tried to get it back, but Sasha won't answer her phone. She's not at her flat. I think she's trying to punish me or something." He sucked at his cigarette again, causing ash to spill over his T-shirt. He brushed it onto the floor. "But then you lot came to the theatre and started asking questions, and I panicked. I didn't want to lose the gig. It's the best role I've had in years, a real platform. So I couldn't let on that I'd taken the costume. Vanessa would have fired me there and then."

"So you lied to the police," said Peter, his tone brimming with disapproval.

"It was only a bloody costume. It's hardly the end of the world." Oscar blew smoke out of the corner of his mouth. "What is it that you haven't told us? What's the costume got to do with Lucy?"

"We'll save that for down at the station," said Peter. "I'm going to need Sasha's details, phone numbers, addresses. And you're going to have to hope we can find her to corroborate your story."

Oscar crossed the room and shakily stubbed his cigarette out in the nearest ashtray, spilling a load of spent butts upon the tabletop and dusting his fingers with ash. He wiped them on his jeans. "I'd never do anything to hurt Lucy. I kinda liked her, the way she stood up for herself and took no bull from Vanessa."

"And just to clarify – you didn't see Lucy again that night?"

"No. Not after she left with that writer bloke she's always hanging around with."

Peter glanced at Elspeth, who shrugged. "David Keel?"

"No, not him. That novelist. I can't remember his name, now. He's writing a book about the Carrion King. Professor Miller seems to think quite highly of him, but he's always seemed a bit up himself to me."

"Michael Williams," said Elspeth.

Oscar nodded. "That's him. He was waiting for her in the car park. I was out having a smoke and saw them leave together. That was the last time I saw her."

Peter frowned. "You should have said that in the interview."

He pulled out his phone and thumbed the screen. He held it to his ear. "Yes. It's DS Shaw. I need you to send a squad car for Michael Williams right away." A pause. "Yes, *now*. Bring him in for questioning. And tell DC Patel I've got a missing witness I need him to find." He slipped the phone back into his pocket and beckoned to Oscar. "You're coming down to the station with me."

Oscar nodded but didn't say anything. He looked utterly forlorn.

"Ellie…" Peter shot her an apologetic look.

Elspeth held up her hand as she got to her feet. "It's okay. I know when I'm not needed. I'll take a taxi."

"Thanks. I think I'm going to be tied up for a while."

CHAPTER TWENTY

"You're pacing like a caged animal, Ellie. Can't you sit down for a minute?"

"I'm sorry, Mum." She was standing by the window, peering at her phone screen in frustration. It had been six hours. She'd been through all of the newspaper reports she'd brought back from the *Heighton Observer*, and now she was growing impatient for an update. "It's just I'm expecting a call."

"From Peter?"

"Yeah. He's been interviewing a suspect and I'm waiting to hear what's happened."

Dorothy paused the TV. "Have you tried calling him?"

"I left him a message. But he's busy. He knows to call when he gets done."

Dorothy rolled her eyes. "Well, there you are, then. Sit yourself down. He'll call you when he can."

Elspeth walked through to the kitchen and poked around in the cupboards, looking for something to distract her. She finally settled on a teabag she found behind the tea caddy, a sample wrapped in a foil envelope that purported to be blended with rose petals. Intrigued, she put the kettle on.

"If you're making one, love," came Dorothy's voice from the other room, almost as soon as she'd flicked the switch.

She checked her phone again. There was another message from Abigail, asking if she fancied going to see a band the following Friday. She clicked the link and listened to half a song online. She'd never heard of them – a northern band called Urban Myths – but they sounded decent enough. She texted back a quick thumbs up, deciding that it was about time she made reparations to Abigail. A night out would do her good, and she could get the train in and crash on Abigail's sofa. The text pinged back immediately with an icon of a smiling face.

The kettle boiled. She put her phone on the table and grabbed another mug from the cupboard, then nearly jumped out of her skin at a sudden rap on the door. She placed the mug on the counter and ran through to the hallway, stubbing her toe on the telephone table. Cursing, she rubbed it for a moment, and then hurried over to the door, still wincing. "Coming!"

She flicked the chain on – just to be sure – and then opened the door.

Peter stood on the step, looking tired and drawn. He smiled when he saw her, but she could see it took supreme effort. The afternoon had evidently been longer than even he had imagined. At least it had stopped raining.

"Perfect timing," she said. "I've just boiled the kettle."

He held up a hand. "No, I can't, as much as the idea appeals. I've only come to give you this." He reached into his pocket and pulled out a small box, which he handed to her.

"What's this?"

"A recording of the interview with Michael Williams," he said.

She looked at the box more closely. "A *cassette* tape?" she said. "Really?"

"Never let it be said that the police force isn't the last bastion of defence against those who would abolish outmoded technology."

Elspeth turned it over in her hand. She hadn't even *held* one for over a decade. "*Really?*" she repeated.

Peter looked exasperated. "Yes. *Really*. We still use them to record interviews. It's a tried and tested format, gives us a physical copy as evidence, and we've already got all the relevant equipment."

Elspeth shook her head. "Thankfully, so do I. I just hope it works."

"I'll need it back first thing in the morning," he said. "It's a copy, but all the same, I'm taking a big risk."

"I know. Thank you. I feel terrible. I don't want to get you into trouble. Did he mention our visit to his studio?"

"Not in any way that's going to raise questions. We've just got to tread carefully, that's all. I know I can trust you."

"I'll listen to this tonight," she said.

"Just make sure I get it back. It makes for interesting listening."

She opened the door a little wider, stepping aside to give him room. "Aren't you coming in? I thought you could give me the salient points. You look like you could do with a rest."

He shook his head. "No. Griffiths is pulling everyone

back to the station. We can't hold Williams for very long without any forensic evidence. Everything we've got is circumstantial. She's trying to find an angle to buy us more time."

Elspeth nodded. Clearly Williams hadn't admitted to Lucy Adams's murder, then.

"Not even for five minutes? You look dead on your feet."

He shook his head. "Sorry. Duty calls. Remember what I told you about the life of a policeman. We don't always make good company."

"Maybe not," said Elspeth, "but you make good friends. Thanks for this."

"Least I could do for my girl wonder." He turned to leave but paused. "Oh, I nearly forgot. Sasha Reid – Oscar Waring's girlfriend."

"Yes?"

"Oscar was right. She's missing. Or, at least, she's not been back to her house, and she's not answering her phone. Her car has gone. We've put an alert out and we've got uniforms searching for her."

"You don't think Oscar…?"

"It's possible," said Peter. "But then it's also possible that *she's* got something to do with it. They could be working together. Or she might just have driven off in a huff, and she'll turn up in a couple of days wondering what all the fuss is about. We won't know until we find her."

"What about Vanessa, and her brother?"

"Her alibi seems to check out. Her brother has confirmed she was with him that night. Although, to be honest, he was so stoned that it was hard getting any sense out of him. If he was that out of it on Thursday night, too, I have my doubts he'd even have noticed if she was there or not. It's tenuous at best."

She nodded. "I don't know how you do this all the time, juggling everything, knowing what to prioritise."

"Practice," said Peter. "And luck."

There was a long pause. "Oh, before I forget, there's something else, about Thomas Stone," she said.

"Thomas Stone?"

She outlined everything she'd discovered so far from the newspaper reports. "I'm trying to find out what happened to him. Whether he was ever found. And George Baker, too – where did he end up? There might be some connection there. Or maybe just another angle for a story."

"I'll take a look tomorrow for you, if you like? There's bound to be some old records on the system somewhere. If he didn't turn up, there's even a chance the case might still be open."

She nodded. "Thanks. Busy night ahead, then."

He sighed. "Yeah. See you tomorrow? Lunch at Lenny's, one thirty?"

"Perfect."

The old cassette deck in her bedroom had been unplugged, but the wires were all still there, dangling from the back of the machine, tangled and matted in dust. She plugged it in and switched it on, relieved to hear the speakers crackle to life. One of the cassette decks was missing its 'play' button, so she tried the tape in the other one first, crossing her fingers that it wouldn't catch and unspool. She had a biro at the ready, just in case.

To her amazement, the reels began to turn, and a moment later she heard a voice she recognised immediately as belonging to Inspector Griffiths. The woman introduced herself to the suspect, reeled off some preliminaries for the recording – the time, date, and those present – and then asked Williams to state his name for the record.

He did so, begrudgingly.

The cassette hissed. "Do you know why you're here?" said Griffiths.

"No. I do not," said Williams. Even on the cassette, Elspeth could sense the bubbling undercurrent of anger. "I've already spoken to your sergeant, who's checked my alibis with my wife. I've nothing to add to what I've already said to him. I'm not involved in any murders."

"Let's just go back to what you told DS Shaw, shall we, Mr Williams? For the benefit of the tape, I'm showing Mr Williams a photograph of Geoffrey Altman. You explained that you were acquainted with Mr Altman, and that he had, on occasion, hunted on your land and helped with the research of your novel."

"That's right," said Williams, impatiently.

"I'm now showing Mr Williams a photograph of Lucy Adams. You told DS Shaw that you have never met Mrs Adams. Is that correct, Mr Williams?"

"That's correct."

"Then can you explain why we have a witness that places you leaving the theatre at Winthorpe with her, no more than a few hours before she died?"

"What? They must be mistaken. I've never met the woman!"

Elspeth could hear the crack in his voice. He was panicked. The arrogance had evaporated and been replaced by bluster.

"Then I'm sure you'll have no problem providing us with a DNA sample, Mr Williams, so we can confirm that you weren't with Mrs Adams that night?"

"I... I..." he stumbled for a moment, as if trying to find his words. "I think I need to speak to my solicitor," he said.

"Very well, Mr Williams. Interview suspended." The recording stopped abruptly.

Elspeth paused it for a moment, sipping her tea. Peter was right, it certainly made interesting listening. They'd take DNA evidence from him regardless, no doubt, and she guessed it would be a simple matter to confirm he'd slept with Lucy Adams, but Peter had said they'd found no other DNA evidence at the crime scene.

She started the tape again.

"Interview recommencing at five eighteen pm." Griffiths cleared her throat. "So, Mr Williams, I'm going to ask you again – did you know the deceased, Mrs Lucy Adams?"

"Yes," said Williams. He sounded like a different man. The fight had gone out of him.

"And did you have a sexual relationship with Mrs Lucy Adams?"

"I did."

"How long had you known her?"

"About six months. I met her at the theatre one night, after calling in to see David Keel. We got chatting, carried on talking online, and then met one night in Heighton. It was a bit awkward at first, but... well, you know..."

"Did you murder Lucy Adams, Mr Williams?"

There was a brief pause, followed by some barely audible mumbling, as Williams, she presumed, consulted his solicitor.

"No. As I've already stated, I didn't murder Lucy, or Geoff, or anyone else for that matter."

"Then why did you lie to my detective sergeant when he asked you if you knew the victim?"

"Because I'm a married man, Inspector. I hardly want to go broadcasting my infidelity. You must understand that?"

"I understand that you might have been the last person to see Mrs Adams alive, and that your lies might have impeded a murder investigation."

"Look, I love my wife," said Williams. "Really, I do. But things have been... difficult. You saw that," he was obviously talking to Peter, "you saw what's she's been like. We're going through a bit of a rough patch. It's not that I didn't care for Lucy, but it was just sex. We both knew what we were getting into. She was married too."

"Walk us through what happened that night, Mr Williams, the evening of the twenty-third of June."

"I left my studio at around six thirty. Rebecca was up at the house, and I knew she wouldn't even realise I'd gone. She never does. I left the lights on in the studio, locked up, and drove to Winthorpe. I met Lucy in the car park. She was already there when I arrived."

"What was she wearing?"

"A black dress and black stockings," he said. "We

drove into Heighton, ate dinner at a little restaurant called Mitsou, then left about nine. We went to a little hotel around the corner. They knew us in there. I think she'd probably taken men there before, to be honest. We paid for the room and went upstairs. Then... well..."

"You had sexual intercourse," said Griffiths.

"It sounds so cold when you put it like that, but yes, that's what happened."

"Then what? You drove her out to the woods and killed her?"

"What? No! Why would I do that? Look, I was onto a good thing with Lucy. She gave me what I wanted, and she wasn't about to go blurting it out to my wife. We saw each other every couple of weeks, let off a bit of steam, and went our way. Why would I want to kill her?"

"Tell us what happened after you'd had sex."

"I took a shower, then we had a cup of tea, and then left. It all sounds so sordid when you lay it out like that, but it wasn't. It was nice. We both understood what it was."

"You drove her back to Winthorpe Manor?"

"To the theatre car park, yes. I never dropped her by the house in case her husband saw."

"So you left her there in the car park and drove off?"

"To my shame. I wanted to get back to my studio. Earlier, in the restaurant, we'd been talking about the book, you see, and a thought had occurred to me, a plot point. I wanted to get it down."

"And you drove straight home to Ascott-under-Wychwood?"

"I did."

"Can anyone confirm this? We'll be speaking with

the staff at the restaurant and hotel, of course, but did anyone see you arrive home? Your wife, Mr Williams?"

There was another pause.

"Please speak for the tape, Mr Williams."

"No. No one saw me arrive home. I didn't see Rebecca until the next morning, when I went up to the house for breakfast. I spent the night alone in the studio."

"What time did you arrive back at the studio?"

"I didn't check, but it must have been around ten thirty."

"So you claim your liaison with Mrs Adams at the hotel only lasted an hour?"

"If that," said Williams. "As I explained, we were only there for one thing."

"Alright. Interview terminated at five twenty-three." The recording stopped.

Elspeth allowed the tape to run for a few moments to ensure there was nothing else to follow, then shut it off and pressed 'rewind'.

So, Williams admitted to sleeping with Lucy Adams that night, but claimed to have left her in the theatre car park around ten o'clock. What had happened to her after that, before she ended up dead in the Wychwood? Elspeth was beginning to wonder if they'd ever know. If Williams was to be believed, she never made it back from the theatre car park to her house.

Griffiths clearly thought Williams was lying. It was evident in her tone and the manner of her questions, and from what Peter had said on the doorstep, about her trying to find a means to retain him in custody. The police clearly didn't have enough to charge him with.

Nor did they have a motive, or any evidence, to link him to Geoffrey Altman's death. He'd seemed genuinely disturbed by the news when she'd questioned him with Peter. She could understand Griffiths' desperation to draw a line under the case, but it felt as if she was pushing a little too hard to make the circumstances fit.

The cassette had finished rewinding. Elspeth popped it out of the player and slipped it back into the box. She'd talk it through with Peter in the morning, but she was beginning to suspect that Williams was innocent. There was no doubt he was a fool, that he'd treated his wife appallingly, but Elspeth was yet to be convinced he was the killer. Just like he'd said on the tape – what did he have to gain?

She needed to get some rest. She was tired, and her mind was working overtime, still processing everything that had happened in London, her feelings about returning home, meeting Peter again after all this time, the murders…

She climbed onto the bed, placed the folder carefully on the floor by the nightstand, and dialled up some Chairlift on her phone. Then, with the speaker on low, she closed her eyes and slowly drifted off to sleep.

CHAPTER TWENTY-ONE

"Y ou're uncharacteristically quiet," said Peter.
They were sitting in Lenny's, sipping coffee after lunch. Elspeth was peering out of the window at the high street, watching the world go by. It was spitting with rain, and people were weaving in and out of shops, carrier bags clutched tight, umbrellas threatening to decapitate the unwary.

"I'm sorry?" she said.

Peter laughed. "I said you're quiet today."

She gestured dismissively. "Just thoughtful. Mulling over the details of the case."

"So it's a 'case' now, is it?" said Peter, amused. "I mean, let's not split hairs, but technically I thought, to you, it was a 'story'."

Elspeth laughed. "I thought you were enjoying letting me do all of your work for you?"

"Oh, it's like *that*, is it?" said Peter. "Game on."

They both laughed.

"So, what did you think of the tape?" Peter asked. He'd insisted she hand it over as soon as she arrived, muttering about how he never should have given it to her anyway, but how he thought she ought to listen.

"You were right. It made interesting listening. He sounds genuinely regretful about everything."

"You think he's innocent?"

She nodded. "Of the murders, yes. Like he said, what did he have to gain?"

"Maybe she was threatening to tell his wife."

"And what if she had? You've seen the state of the relationship between those two. There's little love lost there. Let's face it: he was already looking elsewhere. I'm not condoning what he was doing with Lucy Adams, but I don't believe he killed her because of it. And if he *was* responsible, why dress her up like that? That makes no sense, if his motive was simply to silence her. Then there's Geoffrey Altman… I get the sense this goes beyond a lovers' tiff."

Peter held up his hand. "I get it. And I agree. I can't claim to like the man very much, but I don't believe he's a killer. I don't think he's got the balls for it, for a start. If he did he'd have left his wife years ago and there'd be no need for all that subterfuge in the first place."

"I suppose you're right," she said.

"Anyway, we had to let him go this morning. There's no way we could keep him in custody, not without any evidence. He'll probably be on his way home now, working out what he's going to say to his wife."

"I don't know which of them to feel sorry for," said Elspeth.

"Neither." He sipped his coffee, and then reached for a carrier bag under the table. From it, he produced a thick file filled with paper. It was yellowed and brittle, tied with string. "The file on the Thomas Stone case," he said, handing it to her.

"Thanks. Did they ever find him?"

"No. Either he's still out there somewhere, or something more sinister happened. Unfortunately, we'll probably never know."

"Well, it's got to be worth a look, just in case it sheds any light. You need this back tomorrow, too?"

"Sorry…" He shrugged. "Before anyone realises it's missing. You're not the only one reading up on Patricia Graves, after what happened. We had the autopsy and forensic reports back yesterday, too."

"And?"

"There's very little to tell. No DNA evidence at the scene. Other than you and Patricia Graves herself, we can't find any evidence that a third party had been in her bedroom in the recent past."

"Nothing at all?"

"No, the killer must have been extraordinarily careful. There's something else, too – the pathologist says that the angle of the wounds suggests they were self-inflicted." He took another sip of his coffee.

"What, they think it was *suicide*?" said Elspeth. She found it hard to believe that the woman could have done that to herself.

"We haven't ruled it out," said Peter, "although I grant you, it does seem a pretty extreme way to kill yourself. Toxicology suggests she wasn't acting under the influence of alcohol or any substances – there was nothing but aspirin in her bloodstream. So we're still assuming murder, for now. We've got uniforms doing another round of door-to-door enquiries to see if anyone in the area saw anything suspicious."

"Was anything missing from her house? Could it have been a botched robbery?"

Peter shook his head. "I don't think so. Nothing obvious had been taken. There was cash and jewellery that hadn't been touched."

"Then it looks as though she was targeted," said Elspeth. "Which would make sense, given the ferocity of the attack. I can't stop thinking about the mess they'd made of her."

Peter offered her a sad smile. "I know. I guess it's not the welcome home you were expecting."

Elspeth shrugged. "It's not all bad," she said.

"Look, I'd better be going. There's tons still to do at the station." He put the lid back on his coffee. "Do you fancy a drink later? At The White Hart?"

"Why not," said Elspeth.

"Great. I'll give you a call this evening when I get done. What's the rest of your day looking like?"

Elspeth tapped the folder on the table. "I imagine this will keep me busy."

Elspeth put the kettle on again, and dumped the uneaten remnants of her toast in the bin. Dorothy would be home from work soon, and she'd have to clear everything off the kitchen table.

Murphy was snaking around her ankles, angling for a treat. She grabbed the packet from the cupboard and sprinkled a few in his bowl, then made her coffee and returned to her reading.

So far, she'd learned little that she hadn't already known or suspected. Thomas Stone had run away from the home of his foster carers, Patricia and James Graves, in late 1979. He'd been eight years old. He'd disappeared in the night, along with a sports bag full of his paltry belongings, and when the Graves had discovered him missing the next morning, they'd called the police immediately. A countywide call was put out, but there were no reported sightings. The following day his photograph was circulated to the national media, along with police forces up and down the country, but despite all of this, the boy had never been found.

Patricia and James Graves had clearly been beside themselves – the transcripts in the folder talked of how Patricia blamed herself, bemoaning that she should have done a better job of looking after the boy, and how James had sat in stony silence throughout, distant and occasionally distraught.

The thing that interested Elspeth most, however, was the response of the *other* foster child, George Baker, also eight years old. When questioned he'd first claimed that Thomas had had a disagreement with the Graves earlier that night, and that it was this that had led to his disappearance. He also said he was worried they were going to send him back to a care home with all the other rowdy kids, who would push him around and bully him.

Within a couple of days, though, he'd altered his story, saying he must have been mistaken. The policeman in charge of the investigation – Detective Inspector Paul Somersby – had berated the child for telling tales and scratched his earlier testimony from the record. It had remained in the file all the same, however, and Elspeth found herself wondering what had caused the boy to lie. Had he really been that fearful that the Graves would give him back?

She made a note of the boy's name, along with his date of birth – 21 March 1971 – and a few pertinent details from his two conflicting statements.

There was little else of note in the file, really: a description of Thomas Stone, along with two photographs, now yellowing with age; a handful of potential sightings from around the country, none of which had been substantiated; a statement by the constable who'd carried out door-to-door questioning of the Graves's neighbours, during which no one had provided any useful information, and an official-looking form from the Thames Valley Police, reviewing the contents of the file ten years on from the boy's disappearance, and declaring the case 'unresolved'.

The only other useful fact she'd managed to glean was that the social worker who had placed the boys in the care of the Graves had been called Millicent Brown. The forms gave an address in Chipping Norton. She jotted that down, too.

The woman had probably retired now, maybe even moved house or area, but the address was worth a visit and Elspeth wondered if she might be encouraged to give an interview if she was still there. It had been a long time, and there was no reason to suspect she'd have anything new to add, but Elspeth was trying to construct a picture of Patricia's life, and it was possible

Brown had remained in contact with the family after Thomas had fled and the police had given up on the search. She might know what had become of George Baker, for a start, and whether the Graves really had been quite so terrifying as foster parents. But should she really go disturbing an old woman about something that happened nearly forty years ago?

She heard a car pulling up on the driveway. Dorothy was home. Maybe she'd talk it through with her over dinner, before heading out for her drink with Peter that evening – assuming he managed to get away. Dorothy had always been a good sounding board.

She'd only just begun reassembling the file when her phone buzzed.

CHAPTER TWENTY-TWO

The White Hart was busy and clamorous, the jukebox blaring out an eclectic mix of old Supergrass, Def Leppard and Rick Astley songs, but they found a small table close to the door, where they could sit opposite one another and just about hear each other over the din. Elspeth bought the first round, and decided to stick with the gin and tonic she'd sampled the other night.

"So, you decided to stay in Wilsby-under-Wychwood?" she said, after she'd made herself comfortable on the rickety old chair. "Never thought about travelling the world, seeing the sights, living it up amongst the bright lights of the big city?"

"I like it here," said Peter. "It's quiet, serene, and it's nice to come home to."

She smiled. He had a point.

"I know it must seem boring to you after all those years away, but I can't imagine living anywhere else. Better the devil you know and all that."

When she'd lived here before, all Elspeth had wanted to do was get away, explore the world and meet new people, find adventure. Yet she was beginning to see the attraction of the place, now that she was appraising it with fresh eyes. It was sleepy, but it was beautiful. She supposed that at the moment it represented a kind of haven, a place to hide away from the distractions of her real life. From Andrew, and everything she was going to have to sort out when she eventually plucked up the courage to go back. "I can understand that."

"Will you miss London, you think? If you decide to stay."

"Of course, but probably not in the way you think. I love the bustle of people on the way to work each morning. There's something about being surrounded by all those individuals that makes me feel alive." She didn't know how to explain it any other way. That had always been the attraction for her, the notion that she was living at the heart of things; that something momentous might happen at any moment.

Peter shuddered. "For me it's like being swallowed up and forgotten, like your identity is subsumed by the weight of people pressing in from all sides, and you've become just another face amongst the seething masses. I can't stand that feeling of being lost. I need room to breathe."

"I've never thought of it like that," she said. It was a melancholy notion, the idea of enforced anonymity, of somehow ceasing to exist.

They lapsed into silence for a moment.

"What about your friends? Have you got many down there?"

Elspeth shrugged. "A few. Just now, though, I could do without the sympathy. I know that sounds cruel and unappreciative, but all they want to do is deconstruct what's happened and offer me unsolicited advice." She took a sip of her gin and tonic. It was strong, and on an empty stomach, she knew it would go straight to her head. "God, I sound like a heartless bitch. I don't mean it like that. I just need a break, that's all. A bit of time. They'll understand."

Peter gulped at his pint, taking half of it down in one go.

"What about you?" she said.

"Me?"

"No girlfriends, boyfriends?"

He gave a crooked smile. "There have been a few. It's hard work, though, going out with a copper. Things don't tend to end well."

"The punishing hours?"

"Not really. People can learn to live with that. It's just… it's hard to leave it behind sometimes, you know? You see all these things, the very worst of humanity, and then you're expected to go home and smile and walk the dog and empty the bins. Sometimes it's hard to go back to being normal again. Especially when you're preoccupied with a case. People think policing is a job, but it's not, really. It's a life. It rules you. After a while, you only keep doing it because you can't stop. That makes it sound like I'm unhappy, but I'm not." He rubbed his chin. "I guess it must be a bit like being a writer, really."

Elspeth frowned. The door behind her opened and she felt a sudden draught as three young men came in, stamping their feet and laughing. She waited until they'd joined the queue for the bar before continuing.

"How do you mean?"

"Not the work, of course, but more what it does to you. Look at Michael Williams. When he's working on a book, that's *all* he's doing. There's no room for other people. He's living down there in that summerhouse, thinking about nothing else. It's like he's on a train, hurtling through a tunnel, and he can't get off until the end of the line. It's a tortured metaphor, I know, but I can understand it, in a way. It's like everything else just falls away, nothing else matters, and the world is on hold for a while, until it's all over. That's what it's like when you're working a case. Life stops. That can be hard for a person to live with. Look at Rebecca Williams. Look what it's done to her."

"You sound as though you're talking from experience."

Peter took another swig from his beer. "She was called Sarah. We lived together for nearly three years. She moved out just before Christmas."

"I'm sorry."

Peter shrugged. "So am I. But that's what it's like. That's what happens. I've seen it so many times. The job gets in the way."

"You sound so certain," said Elspeth. "But nothing's that black and white. You don't have to make the choice between a life and a career."

"That's just it," said Peter. "That's what I mean. There *is* no choice. It's about who you are."

"Then it's also about finding the right person," said Elspeth. "Someone who understands, who appreciates you for who you are, and the time that you *can* spend with them."

"Ah," said Peter, leaning back in his chair with a

smirk on his lips. "You always did have a thing about the Holy Grail."

Elspeth grinned. "Anyway, that's enough talk about lost love and misery."

Peter laughed. He downed the rest of his beer, and then glanced at the bar. The queue was three people deep, and the poor barmaid looked frantic as she hurriedly splashed beer into glasses and fetched packets of crisps from under the counter. "Listen, do you want to get out of here?"

Elspeth nodded. "Yeah. I think I do."

"I was thinking we could grab some food. Maybe order a takeaway? I know it's not particularly glamorous, but I've got a bottle of gin back at my place, and we could send for pizza or Chinese or something?" He looked awkward, embarrassed, as if he was worried she would take it the wrong way or reject him.

"Sounds great," she said. "Junk food is exactly what I need. It has to be pizza, though. Preferably with extra pepperoni."

He grinned. "Perfect."

Peter's house was just as she remembered it from childhood, as if his parents had simply upped and left, leaving all of their furniture and knick-knacks behind. Which, she supposed, was exactly what people probably did when they moved to a different country. They'd upped sticks to Portugal a few years ago, Peter had explained, signing the house over to him as they left. She wondered whether Peter got out there very often to visit.

Peter had added a few touches of his own, of course

– pop art on the walls in the living room, a model car on the mantelpiece, a widescreen TV and gaming console, a heap of old *Top Gear* DVDs, and a couple of bookcases filled with paperback crime novels and policing manuals. The dining room, too – once a small room reached from the hallway but long ago knocked through to form a single, larger space off the living room – had been given over to Peter's belongings. Gone was the dining table, replaced instead by a series of squat self-assembly shelving units housing row upon row of identical cardboard boxes.

While he put a call in to the pizza place in Heighton, she went through to the kitchen and poured them both another drink. He didn't appear to have any tonic, so she searched around in the kitchen cupboards for an alternative, eventually settling on a bottle of still lemonade and a few ice cubes from the freezer. He seemed to keep the place clean enough – the dishes were stacked neatly on the surface, ready to put away, and a pile of ironing sat folded in a laundry basket. There were three empty whisky bottles in the recycling.

"Cheers," she said, handing him a glass as she wandered back through to the living room.

He clinked glasses with her, took a sip, and raised an appreciative eyebrow. "Pizza's on the way," he said.

"Great." She took a sip of her drink, and then walked through to the dining room. "I remember sitting here with your mum and dad, eating roast lamb on a Sunday afternoon after we'd finished playing in the paddling pool in the garden," she said.

"Your hair was all damp and spiky," said Peter.

"And Mum wrapped it up in a towel."

Elspeth laughed. "That's right. And she gave us raspberry trifle for dessert."

"It was all a long time ago," said Peter. "Another life."

"It doesn't feel like that to me," said Elspeth. "Long ago, yes, but not forgotten."

"You didn't visit," he said, and then looked immediately apologetic, as if he realised the undercurrent of accusation in the statement.

"No, I didn't," she said. "I suppose I was trying to look forward, to focus on the future. I was happy to escape. I'd always wanted to get away. Now I feel foolish for ever wanting that. Look at what happened. None of it worked out as I'd planned."

"You shouldn't feel foolish, Ellie. It's not a bad thing to want to make something of yourself."

"I know. But I realise now what I left behind. I didn't just move away. I moved on. People like you and Helen and Benedict – you were friends, and I let you drift away. I got too wrapped up in what *I* was doing that I didn't stop to think about any of you until it was too late, and too much time had already passed."

"You're too hard on yourself," said Peter. "And you're here now. You can't change the past, any more than you can predict the future. The best thing you can do now is take some time, and be a little kinder to yourself. Things will work themselves out."

"I hope so." She wandered along the row of shelving units. "So what's in all these boxes?" They were long and thin, and lidded, and there were dozens of them slotted neatly into individual cubby holes, like a massive rectangular beehive. She'd never seen anything like it. "Case files?"

Peter looked a little sheepish. "No, not case files," he said. "Nothing, really."

"They take up a lot of space for nothing," said Elspeth. She narrowed her eyes. "What is it? What are you trying to hide?"

Peter sighed. "Comic books. The boxes are full of American comic books. I collect them."

"What, all of these boxes?"

"Yes."

Elspeth laughed.

"See, I knew you'd laugh. You probably think they're childish."

"No, it's not that," she said. "It's the look on your face, the fact you felt you had to keep them from me." She smiled. "You don't have to worry about trying to impress me, you know."

"Now you're just patronising me," he said. He looked a little crestfallen.

"So, which do you prefer – Gail Simone's darker, sexier Batgirl, or Batgirl of Burnside?"

He stared at her. "Really? You've read those?"

Elspeth shrugged. "I'm not a complete heathen, you know. Books are books, irrespective of whether they've got pictures in them. Do you still like poetry?"

He pointed at the bookshelves beside the TV. There, above the serried ranks of crime novels, was a shelf of thin poetry books. "Pride of place," he said.

"And do you still write it, too?"

"Oh, God, you remember that, do you? No, I

haven't done anything like that for years."

"You *should*. You were good."

"I was a teenager, and preoccupied with teenage things: life, death, and wanting to impress girls, mostly. It was all very immature."

"Maturity is overrated," said Elspeth. "Like most things." She held out her empty glass. "Another drink?"

"I'll fetch them," he said. He jumped up from the sofa and took her glass. Their eyes met, and he lingered there for just a few seconds too long. She wondered for a moment if he might try to kiss her. Then the moment passed, and he was heading for the kitchen, mumbling something about finding some crockery.

It was probably for the best, thought Elspeth. It would only complicate things. She had enough on her plate to deal with, both practically and emotionally. And besides, she had to focus on the story.

The pizza came and went, and they sat together on the sofa, laughing – only a little ironically – at reruns of old episodes of *Friends*, which appeared to be showing non-stop on one of the satellite channels.

The bottle of gin soon disappeared, and around eleven the soporific effects began to manifest, and Elspeth decided it was time to head home. She placed her empty glass on the coffee table and fetched her boots.

"You off?" said Peter.

She nodded. "I think you've had the best of me tonight. Time to sleep." She slipped her boots on. "Thanks, though. I needed it."

"Well at least I made you laugh, and after everything that's been going on recently, that's not a bad result, is it?"

"Not at all. I still can't get over what the pathologist said about Patricia Graves, though."

Peter leaned his head back against the lip of the sofa. "They're releasing the body. The funeral's on Monday afternoon, I believe."

"It still feels as if a piece of the puzzle is missing. Does that make sense?"

"Of course. But that's how deaths like this always feel, especially if there's no obvious reason for it. You and I spend our lives trying to unpick other people's stories, and it's the not knowing that's the hardest part."

"Perhaps. But it's not too late to *understand*. The thing is, Peter, this is what I do. This is who I am. It's like you were saying earlier, about being a policeman, about not being able to stop. I've tried. But I *need* to understand. I pick and pick until the scab comes off and I can get to the story underneath. Sometimes it's not pretty, and sometimes I'm the only one who cares, but it doesn't change anything. I know that doesn't make much sense, but it's how I feel."

She tied her laces, fumbling drunkenly. "Some reporters are there to do a job. They turn up every day and write the news, or they sit at their desk and write what they're *told* to write, and then when five thirty rolls around, they go home, kiss their partners and get on with their lives. I don't work like that. I've never been able to work like that. Half the time it gets me into terrible trouble, but I won't engage with that sort of corporate bull. I want to get to the truth."

Peter was grinning, clearly enjoying her inebriated rant.

"So yes, you're right, it's too late to help Patricia Graves. And I'm not sure I ever would have been able to help her anyway. But I do want to understand why she did what she did. I want to know why I found her like that on her bedroom floor."

"But how? Where do you even start?"

"I start by paying a visit to the Graves's old social worker to see if she can shed any light."

"The police interviewed her extensively at the time," said Peter. "I saw that in the file."

"Yes," said Elspeth, "but I'll be asking different sorts of questions. When you're working on a 'story' and not a 'case'," she smiled pointedly, eliciting a grin from Peter, "you're interested in different things. Sometimes you can find out more about what went on, just by taking a more personal approach."

Peter laughed. "Consider me thoroughly schooled," he said. "And by the way – you're drunk."

She got to her feet. "You're right, and I'm going. Goodnight."

"Hang on." He prised himself out of the pit of the sofa. "I'll walk you home."

She waved him back to his seat. "Don't be daft. It's only over the road."

He shook his head. "No. I'm coming." He walked out into the hall, jammed his feet into a pair of shoes, and opened the door. The cold breeze hit her like a slap in the face. He ushered her out into the still night. Somewhere in the distance, a car rolled by. "Come on."

She took his arm as they crossed the road and ambled along the pavement to the cul-de-sac. "I have two tickets to see the opening night of *Corvus* tomorrow, if you fancy it?"

"I think it would be churlish not to," said Peter, with a smile.

"Alright. You can pick me up at six. I'm going to get my head down tomorrow, reading through that file and putting feelers out for more work."

"Great," he said. "I'll be here."

CHAPTER TWENTY-THREE

The theatre was packed.

As Elspeth took her seat on the front row – reserved for her by Rose – she felt a sudden stab of guilt for not bringing her mother along to see the performance. Dorothy had hinted, too, telling Elspeth that she'd met David Keel a few times, that he only lived a few doors down from them at the end of the road. Elspeth had told herself it was a work thing; that it was important for Peter to see the play, for the background it might offer on the Carrion King myths. Now, though, she was wondering if all that had just been a way of rationalising it to herself.

She'd spent the day firing off more enquiries about freelance work, and had even had a quick look online at rental property for Heighton and the surrounding area. She'd told herself she was just looking – just getting a measure of her options – but increasingly, she was wondering about whether the best thing to do would be to relocate more permanently back here, near home. Or perhaps that just meant she'd be running away. There was so much swirling around in her head.

Whatever the case, she definitely wasn't ready to start seeing anyone again. And yet, despite all of that, there was something there, with Peter. Perhaps it was just the spark of an old friendship reignited. Perhaps it was simply due to their proximity, working together on the Carrion King case. Or perhaps she should just stop worrying about it and try to enjoy the show.

She leaned back in her seat, glancing at Peter as he settled in beside her. He was studying the stage area, and looking suitably impressed. She had to admit, they'd done a great job. The stage furniture was minimal – just the stump of a tree and a pretty effective bonfire made with streamers, fans and electric lights. Lamps had been placed strategically amongst the trees on the outer edges of the copse, creating an atmospheric glow, seemingly emanating from deep within the Wychwood. Sinister music was tinkling somewhere in the background, and smoke curled around the edges of the stage like creeping mist.

"Have you ever been to one of these?" she said, leaning forward again as people bustled past on the row behind, laughing as they made their way to their seats.

"No. Never." Peter looked sheepish. "It's terrible to admit this, especially here, but I've always had the impression that am-dram was something to be avoided. I think Mum and Dad were the same. They never mentioned this place. But it doesn't look as if there's very much amateur about it."

Elspeth grinned. "Yeah. It's a far cry from the village hall on a Sunday afternoon."

She had to admit, she was surprised the show was still going ahead, after everything that had come out regarding Vanessa Eglington and Oscar Waring. John Adams had apparently decided not to press charges over the missing petty cash – so Peter had told her – and although Rose had mentioned that tensions were running high between the cast and crew, they were all intent on putting on a good show.

The atmosphere amongst the audience was subdued and expectant. It was near enough a full house, with just a few empty seats, and as the latecomers made their apologies and the lights dipped, she caught sight of Michael Williams, sitting two rows back on the other side of the steps. Rebecca Williams sat beside him, looking decidedly unhappy to be there.

All eyes turned to the stage, and a hush settled over the gathered crowd. A figure was emerging from amongst the trees, backlit by the ethereal glow. As they approached the back of the stage area, they stopped perfectly still for a moment in stark silhouette. The music had grown in intensity and volume, until it was nothing but the tribal beating of drums, louder and louder, faster and faster. And then they stopped, dead, and the figure raised its arms, revealing stunning feathery wings. It threw back its head, and then the stage was plunged into darkness.

Elspeth sat forward, enraptured. She sensed movement in the dark as the players took their positions for the first scene.

Slowly, the light returned, softer this time, to reveal a small boy, sitting at a roughly hewn wooden table, staring at a dead crow. He poked it with the end of his finger. A man came in, dressed in the garb of a Saxon peasant – she knew from the programme that this was

Graham Furnham, doubling up his roles – and began to berate the boy, bellowing so loudly that the entire auditorium rang with the sound of his voice. The boy cringed, dashing off into the woods to escape the brutal backhanded swipes of his father.

From here the play followed the journey of the Carrion King, from his roots as a peasant boy in the late ninth century, to a young man cast out by the ealdorman of his village, to whom his family was in service. From there it explored the creation of his 'kingdom' in the wilds of the mysterious Wychwood, and the slow gathering of his apostles.

The play seemed to follow the progression of the stories told by Byron Miller almost exactly, which had been reinforced by the material she'd gleaned from the Internet and the books she'd been able to skim in the last few days. David Keel had done an impressive job of drawing the Carrion King as a sympathetic character, however – tragically flawed, damaged, and betrayed by those who loved him. And she had to hand it to Oscar – for all of his otherworldliness in real life, it was a subtle, well-considered performance. She'd found herself rooting for him, right up until the point he plunged the knife into the Consort's chest, and the lights went out for the interval.

She turned to Peter, trying to read his expression. "Well, what do you think?"

"They're good, aren't they? It makes it seem so much more real, seeing the stories brought to life like that. Although, that last scene was a little too close for comfort." He frowned. "Anyway, I need a drink. You want anything?"

"I'll come with you," she said. "I could do with stretching my legs." He held out his hand and pulled her up.

The rest of the audience had clearly had the same idea, and while Peter queued for teas at the catering tent, she made a beeline for the portable toilets, mentally making notes for her review while she stood in line. Nearby, Vanessa was doing the rounds, dressed in a glamorous blue dress, weaving amongst the theatregoers and merrily basking in their compliments. She was clearly very good at her job – both in terms of the quality of the production and in the way in which she was able to schmooze so effortlessly.

Nearby, she saw David Keel standing with Byron Miller, both of them holding champagne flutes. Keel was dressed in a dinner suit, and was furiously bending Miller's ear, no doubt fawning over him again. Miller's input to the play would be obvious to anyone who'd heard him speak about the Carrion King, but despite that, he'd barely received a mention in the programme – just a small 'with thanks to' in the acknowledgements at the end. She suspected Keel wouldn't have been happy with anything more. Although she recognised his talent, Elspeth didn't much like the man. He was all too happy to talk about Miller's mentorship in person, but when it came to taking the glory, she couldn't see him giving any ground.

Michael Williams was roaming about on the lawn, looking tired, while Rebecca was nowhere to be seen. It seemed all of the great and the good had turned out for opening night. She even caught the eye of Philip Cowper, who smiled and looked as if he were about to come over, until he realised where she was, and gave her a little wave instead, before turning his attention back to the two old gents he was standing with.

Vaguely embarrassed, she ducked into the next available loo and closed the door.

She couldn't scream.

If only she could scream, she could alert someone to the horror, the nightmare that was taking place right there, so close to where they were milling about, sipping champagne. She could hear their chatter, although it was growing distant now, as the rope tightened around her throat, and she gasped desperately for air that wouldn't come. Her hands were bound behind her back, and she fought ineffectually at the twine, bloodying her wrists. It was no use. She was going to die, here in the woods, and there was nothing she could do to stop it. Tears coursed down her face. Her cheeks burned. Her lungs felt as if they were going to burst.

"It's alright," said the voice, so close that she could feel his warm breath against her ear. "Just let go. It's easier when you don't fight." He stroked her hair tenderly. "Just slip away. You haven't done anything wrong. I'm not here to punish you. You're giving me a gift, is all. A precious gift."

He'd been whispering to her like this as he'd trussed her up, telling her about his plans, his sick scheme to recreate the work of the Carrion King, to transcend 'beyond the veil' so that he might rescue the soul of his long dead friend. She'd known then he was utterly insane, and also that it made him dangerous. She'd only half listened as she'd fought frantically to get away, but then he had looped the rope around her neck and drawn it taut, and she knew all hope was lost.

"Time to say goodbye," he said, and gave the noose one final tug, so that it constricted violently around her throat. The last thing she felt as the blackness swarmed in was something sharp and painful piercing her lips.

Peter was already back at their seats by the time Elspeth returned to the auditorium, and he handed her a Styrofoam cup as she settled in for the second half, wrapping herself in a woollen throw. The temperature had dropped considerably with the fading light, and the audience were huddling together against the chill. She leaned against Peter, and he pulled the edges of the throw over his lap, too, sipping quietly at his tea.

The stage had been re-dressed during the interval, and now two enormous mirrors had been brought out, placed at either end of the stage. This, she presumed, was the scene in which the Carrion King enacted his revenge against the ealdorman that had cast him out, using an arcane ritual to seize control of the other man's reflection.

In the stories, the Carrion King had reserved this torturous death for those who had wronged him in his previous life. The murder of his apostles had been a morose affair, a matter of necessity from which he derived little pleasure, whereas the death of the ealdorman represented the setting right of old wrongs and the Carrion King's terrible vengeance.

A hush settled over the audience. Two figures emerged from the trees – Oscar, in his role as the Carrion King, and a man named Ash Farley as the ealdorman. Elspeth had been introduced to him briefly at the pub, but hadn't had chance to talk to him. He was also portraying The Fool, the last of the apostles to die.

The two actors took up their positions before the mirrors. The ealdorman stripped to his waist and leaned close to the mirror, trimming his beard with a dagger. Meanwhile, the Carrion King used the end of his staff to mark out a circle upon the ground, and then within the circle scraped a series of symbols or runes with a stick, which might or might not have been intended to represent some form of magical wand.

Following this, the Carrion King appeared to study his mirror for a few moments, as if watching something unfolding deep within the reflection. Music drifted in, choral and otherworldly, as he lifted his arm – and to a gasp of surprise from the audience, the ealdorman mirrored his action.

With a cry of consternation, the ealdorman continued to mirror the actions of the Carrion King as the Carrion King toyed with him, puppeting him, laughing obscenely as the ealdorman fought this strange, arcane influence from which he could not break free.

Then, in a move that caused Elspeth to draw a sharp intake of breath, despite knowing what was coming, the Carrion King made a series of violent, juddering gestures, and the ealdorman followed suit, thrusting his dagger repeatedly into his chest. Fake blood spurted, and the ealdorman reached out and touched the mirror, before collapsing in a bloodied heap upon the ground.

There was silence from the audience as the Carrion King turned and stared up at them, triumphant. The horror of the moment was tangible.

Elspeth turned to look at Peter, to see he was leaning forward, peering at the stage. He glanced at her, as if in sudden recognition. He'd seen it too. This was exactly how Patricia Graves had been found.

There was a shrill scream from somewhere in the trees, just off-stage. Elspeth peered into the gloaming, trying to make out what was happening. Was this part of the show, the ealdorman's wife running on stage to weep over his fallen remains?

A woman emerged from the trees. She was wearing a blue dress. She ran onto the centre of the stage, so that the floodlights picked out her harrowed expression, the way she was wringing her hands, the tears flooding down her cheeks. It was Vanessa Eglington.

"H… help," she stuttered. "Please, someone help. Something terrible has happened. It's Rose."

Peter was already up out of his seat, running towards the stage. As a rumble of concern spread throughout the audience behind her, Elspeth – heart lurching – threw her tea on the ground and hurried after him, hoping beyond all hope that what she feared would not – *could* not – be true.

CHAPTER TWENTY-FOUR

As Elspeth crashed through the trees behind the stage area, the full extent of the situation became horribly, brutally clear.

Up ahead, Peter had skidded to a halt in a small clearing, and before him, a woman was on her knees, stark and statuesque in the twilight.

At first, Elspeth couldn't even make out who it was. She'd been hoping there'd been an accident; that they could send for an ambulance and everything would be okay... but then realisation dawned, and she knew that it was too late for any of that.

Rose had been positioned on her knees, slumped forward, but restrained by her wrists, which had been tied behind her back and attached to a wooden stake. It was roughly hewn, and had been hammered deep into the soft loam. She was wearing jeans – now caked with mud – but her blouse had been removed, and she'd been dressed in a long woollen garment which looked primitive and uncomfortable.

Her face was contorted into a kind of desperate, inhuman snarl, tinged with purple, and there was a thin, puckered slit around her throat that looked like the mark left behind by a ligature. Blood had seeped from the wound, dribbling down her chest like some obscene scarf. Most disturbingly, her lips had been sewn shut with thick black twine, and her swollen tongue had burst through the gaps between the stitches, jutting and pink and bloody.

It was one of the most horrendous things Elspeth had ever seen. She sensed bile rising in her throat, and turned away, hacking, her hand clamped over her mouth. She fought down the vomit, her eyes streaming.

"Oh God... oh no..." she stammered, stumbling forward, her hand to her mouth. She hadn't known the woman for more than a few days, but Rose's kindness at the office... The ground seemed to suddenly yawn open beneath her.

People were streaming into the clearing behind her, members of the audience come to offer their assistance, or else to ogle at the terrible scene.

Peter was bellowing at people to get back, to keep away from the crime scene, and Vanessa was leaning against a nearby tree, trembling in shock. She watched Peter make a quick call on his phone. It wouldn't be long before the place was swarming with police, ambulance crews, SOCOs and more.

She couldn't take her eyes off the nightmarish scene before her. Her hands were shaking. The last few days had presented her with more horrors than she'd ever imagined she'd see, but despite it all, she'd managed to maintain some level of detachment – even after stumbling on the harrowing scene of Patricia Graves's death.

This, though, was different. This was someone she knew. Someone who might have become a friend.

Elspeth heard someone walking towards her, and turned to see David Keel. He looked as white as a sheet, and kept running his hands through his hair. "The Confessor," he said.

Elspeth chewed her bottom lip. She felt sluggish – not through lethargy, but through a kind of spreading numbness, a growing sense of dissonance and unreality.

Keel drew a deep breath. "Are you okay?"

She stared at him. "No. But that's beside the point. Rose…"

He nodded. "I know. Come on. Let's go back to the auditorium and wait for the police. I think your friend is going to be busy for a while."

She glanced at Peter, who was busy shepherding people away, trying to set up a makeshift perimeter around the body. Keel was right – she'd have to leave Peter to work.

A little while later she was back in her seat, curled underneath her throw and sipping hot tea, which the catering staff had valiantly been dishing out on trays – the stereotypical British response to a crisis. The sirens had come and gone, and what seemed like scores of uniformed men and women were now milling about amongst the audience members, taking down names and contact details, trying to piece together a picture of what had happened. She'd told them what she could – who she'd seen where during the interval, what had happened when she'd heard the scream, how David Keel had accompanied her back to her seat.

She was frustrated with herself for her reaction, and grateful that, now, she was finally beginning to regain her composure. Nevertheless, her mind was still back in the clearing with Rose, trying to make sense of everything she'd seen. Who could have done it? They must have acted during the interval, while everyone else was milling about, chatting and drinking and smiling. Just the thought that someone had been doing *that* to Rose, just a short way from where she'd been sitting laughing with Peter… the thought made her nauseous. She glanced around the auditorium. It was likely that one of the faces here, or one of the cast and crew, was responsible. And that also meant they were likely involved in the murders of Geoffrey Altman and Lucy Adams, too. But who? There were over two hundred people here, including all the people that Peter had interviewed as potential suspects so far. The thought that the culprit might be looking at her now, and smiling, made her shudder.

She felt a hand on her shoulder and nearly jumped out of her skin, slopping tea across the floor.

"Whoa, whoa, I'm sorry." It was Peter, looking weary and flustered. "I didn't mean to startle you."

She shook her head. "No, it's fine."

He looked as if he were about to ask her if she was okay. She held up a hand. "Don't."

"I didn't say a thing." He waited for her to catch her breath.

"What was that thing she was wearing?" she said, after a moment.

"We'll know more later," he said. "Once the SOCOs have finished. I think I'm going to be here for a while."

"I guessed as much. You were great back then, taking charge like that. I… I kind of fell to pieces."

"You're too hard on yourself," said Peter. "I know you weren't great friends or anything, but you knew her, and she was nice. She didn't deserve that. It's no surprise that you reacted how you did."

"*No one* deserves that," said Elspeth. "I saw her lips. They were straight out of the woodcuts in my book."

"Yeah, I know. It has all the hallmarks of being related to the other murders."

"Which means the killer is most likely here," said Elspeth.

Peter shrugged. "It doesn't help us narrow things down much, I'm afraid, unless we can track everyone's movements. It'll take a while to piece everything together."

"She was throttled?"

Peter nodded his confirmation. "Looks that way. Choked with a ligature. The autopsy will tell us more."

Elspeth realised she was clenching her fist in her lap, and relaxed it. "We're going to catch them," she said. Her queasiness was already giving way to an upwelling of burning, ferocious anger. "We're going to find them before they can do this to anyone else."

"We're doing all we can," said Peter. He sounded a little defensive.

"Well, we're going to do more," she said.

He nodded. "I'm sorry. It must be difficult."

"I hardly knew her," said Elspeth. "But she was kind,

and funny, and this has happened to her just because of her part-time job at the paper."

"We can't jump to conclusions yet," said Peter.

"It's obvious!" said Elspeth. "The killer picked her because she's an agony aunt. What do agony aunts do? They listen to people's secrets, just like The Confessor in the myths."

"I know. And you're probably right. But we need to look at *everything*. Trust me, I'm not going to let this rest."

CHAPTER TWENTY-FIVE

He felt the weariness in his bones: a deep, dull ache. It had been a long, difficult night, but his work was not yet done. From now until the end, he would not find rest. He had started along this lonely path, and he had no choice now but to see it to its conclusion. Only then could he be free from the pain, from the hatred that clouded his vision, from the shackles of morality and flesh that still bound him. Only then could he be reunited with his one true companion; the only one who had ever truly understood.

Thomas waited beyond that veil, impatient and alone. He would find him, and return him to the light. That was his only goal. All of it – all of this – was simply the means to that end. Even his vengeance meant nothing when compared to that.

The theatre had been predictably tiresome, the preening fools acting out the story – *his* story – without ever truly understanding its subtleties, its true meaning. The vacant cretins in the audience had showered them with praise, all the while ignorant of the man who sat in their midst – the true heir of the Carrion King, the only one of them who truly understood.

Well, he had shown them what it meant to be the Carrion King. Now, The Confessor would be silent for eternity, her lips finally shut, his secrets safe. It had felt good to unburden himself to her as he did his work; to share with another person the horrors he had faced in his quest, the things he had been forced to do. He thought that, towards the end, as the needle slipped through her puckered lips and the twine pulled taut, she might even have begun to understand.

The darkness here was near absolute. Dawn was still an hour away, and yet he knew she would be awake. He'd studied her routine, just as he had studied them all. The woman was so brimming with vanity that she would rise each morning before the break of day to fulfil her own little ritual, taking to her private gym to work her body with weights and machines, to attempt to stave off the inevitable toll of the years.

Today, though, that would end. Today she would pay for her abandonment.

She was the only one who might have understood, who might have helped him. He remembered her pretty face, the way she had laughed as she'd kicked about in the dry leaves of autumn, the day she had hosed him down with her water pistol, squealing in triumph as he lay on the ground, wet and breathless and laughing. Together, the three of them had been strong and brave, able to face the world and all its many trials.

After Thomas was lost she had retreated from him, though, and when he thought of her now, he thought only of her silent, brooding expression, of her refusal to meet his eye, of the way in which she had turned her back on him in his hour of need.

And now she had turned her back on her husband, too.

After today, she would never turn her back on anyone again.

He scanned the torch along the ground, keeping the beam low. He barely needed it; so long had he been walking these woods, so long had he prepared. The Wychwood, too, willed him on. He could sense it, whispering all around him, anxious and encouraging. It knew of his pain, of his journey; it recognised one of its own. Here, history was repeating itself, just like the turning of the seasons. The Carrion King would once again rise to power, and all would be right.

Ahead, he spied the stump. He approached it and set down the torch. Then, taking up his staff, he scored a circle in the soft loam, disturbing roots and leaves. The ground seemed to recognise him, though, parting easily as it had before.

He set the mirror upon the stump and lit a candle before it, its flame dancing in the gentle breeze. He extinguished the torch. Around him, the woods seemed reverentially silent.

With the tip of a stick he made the sacred symbols in the earth just within the circle, careful to remain within the bounds of its power, to keep the circle unbroken.

Then, discarding the stick, he adopted the correct pose, peered into the mirror, and waited.

Five minutes later he was rewarded with the sight of the woman. She was wearing tight leggings and a white T-shirt, and for a moment he felt the stirring of voycuristic arousal. He breathed deeply, clearing his mind of such things. He watched the woman throw a towel over the handlebars of her exercise bike, and then stand before the mirrored wall, stretching as she warmed her muscles and ligaments. He remained still and silent, patiently awaiting his opportunity.

A few moments later she went to collect her dumbbells and brought them back before the mirror, planting her feet firmly on the mat. She began her routine, holding them before her chest, then thrusting out to the sides, before bringing them back again and repeating the motion. He allowed her to continue with this for a moment. Then, deciding the moment had arrived, he moved his hand, at first mirroring her motion, and then arresting it, the dumbbell in her right hand held outstretched, her arm locked into position.

He saw the familiar look of confusion cross her face, swiftly replaced by panic as she tried, unsuccessfully, to move her arm. She dropped the other dumbbell on the floor.

He moved his other arm, twisting and raising it, so that both of his hands were clasped together. The woman followed suit, grabbing onto the dumbbell with both hands. She was screaming now, but he knew that no one could hear her – her husband had long ago taken to sleeping elsewhere, away from this harridan of a wife.

He considered taunting her, drawing it out, but then dismissed the idea. Better that it was done. Raising his outstretched arms, he held them above his head for a moment, and then brought them down, swiftly and violently, towards his head.

In the mirror, the woman brought the dumbbell crashing down into her skull with a force that cracked it open like a fragile egg. She tumbled to the floor before the mirror, blood pooling on the mat. The dumbbell rolled away, catching on the edge of the exercise bike.

He cocked his head to one side, staring for a moment, fascinated by the look in her still-open eyes. It was as if he could see the light going out in them.

Then he leaned over, breaking the circle, and blew the candle out with a single sharp breath.

CHAPTER TWENTY-SIX

"Ellie?"

"Ungh. What is it?"

"It's Peter. Are you there?"

Elspeth rolled onto her back, squinted up at the screen on her phone – which seemed exceptionally bright – and then pressed it to her ear. "I'm here," she croaked. "What's the matter?"

"I'm sorry to call. I know it's early. I wanted to check if you were okay."

Elspeth propped herself up on one elbow and rubbed blearily at her eyes. "Yeah. I'm okay. It was just the shock, you know?"

"I know. So you got home alright?"

"In the end. It was late, but it was fine. Can't say I got much sleep. How about you?"

"No. We were working through the night. I'm on my way home now to try to get a couple of hours in."

"Any developments?"

"No, the SOCO report is going to take a while. There's a lot to be done." Peter's voice sounded tired on the other end of the phone. "But I've arranged to meet with Byron Miller again this afternoon, to see what he can tell us about The Confessor, and the other apostles, too."

"You're heading back to Oxford, then?" said Elspeth. She felt dog-tired. After getting home a few hours earlier, she'd undressed and lain on her bed, trying to go to sleep, but her wandering mind fought her at every juncture. No matter what she tried to focus on, every time she closed her eyes she saw only Rose, dead and on her knees, her lips stitched shut with coarse twine. The image made her stomach churn.

"No, not Oxford," said Peter. "He's coming to Heighton."

"To the station?" asked Elspeth.

"No. I'm meeting him at The Reading Stop, the book café on Postgate." He paused, as though unsure whether to continue. "Do you want to come?"

Elspeth heaved a mental sigh of relief. She'd wondered, after the previous night, whether he'd grown cold on the idea of involving her in the investigation. If Byron Miller's strange, fable-like stories could help to shed any light on what had happened to Rose, or why, then she wanted to hear it. "Yes," she said. "I'd like to come."

"Are you sure you're up to it?"

"Don't mollycoddle me, Peter. I'm sure."

"Alright, then. Let's meet beforehand outside Lenny's. Say, one o'clock?"

She glanced at the time on her phone. It was only just after nine. "Perfect," she said. "It'll give me a chance to finish up with the file you loaned me."

"Yeah. You'd better bring that with you, too."

"Okay."

"I'll be glad when all this is over, Ellie. I really will." He cut the connection.

Elspeth dropped her phone on the bed and fell back onto her pillow, but she knew she wouldn't be able to get back to sleep.

Dorothy would already be out at work.

Still feeling sluggish and wishing she could escape from the terrible feeling of inertia that had set upon her after seeing Rose's corpse, she climbed off the bed, pulled a dressing gown on and wandered down to the living room, where she flopped in front of the television to watch a rerun of *Antiques Road Trip* before she had to worry about making herself look presentable again.

"Did you find anything else useful?"

Peter took the proffered folder and slipped it into a bag.

"Not really," said Elspeth. "But I'm seeing Millicent Brown on Monday afternoon. She's not free until then. Took a bit of digging to find her current address, but she sounded happy enough to chat. I'm interested to find out what became of the other foster child, George Baker. He sounds so scared in those interview transcripts, and the way he suddenly changed his story – I can't help wondering whether someone was applying pressure to make him fall in line. It's nothing more than a niggling feeling, really, but I'd like to find George Baker and see what he has to say about it all now. I can't help feeling that whatever went on back then is somehow linked to what happened to

Patricia Graves the other day. It's the one momentous event in what appeared to have been a pretty mundane existence. It's got to have some bearing."

"Well, just be careful. People can take exception when you go digging up the past. Trust me, I know from experience."

"Duly noted."

They were queuing in Lenny's for coffee. She'd managed to make herself look half human, at least – after concealing the rings beneath her eyes with make-up – but Peter was looking a little worse for the wear.

They reached the front of the queue, and the barista took their order for two filter coffees with a fixed grin and forced jollity that, to Elspeth, was like nails being drawn across a chalkboard. They collected their drinks and then stepped out into the brisk afternoon.

"So we're back to square one," said Elspeth. "And worse, we have another victim."

"Not entirely," said Peter. "As dreadful as it sounds, a new victim opens up new avenues of investigation. Our job now – or *my* job, at least – is to deconstruct every aspect of Rose's life, to contrast it with the lives of Geoffrey Altman and Lucy Adams, and try to find any correlations."

"What did DCI Griffiths make of our theory, about how the victims were being selected?"

Peter took a sip from his coffee, and almost spat it over himself as it burned his lips. "Bloody thing," he said, wiping his mouth with the back of his hand.

Elspeth smiled.

"She agrees that we could be on to something. Or rather, she agrees that *I* could be on to something. Sorry."

"No need." She waved her hand airily. "As long as I'm right too."

"That's why I've asked Miller to come over, to be honest. It might help us to understand what happened to Rose, but perhaps more importantly, I want to see if we can build a profile of who the killer might be targeting next. If Miller can tell us about The Master of the Pentacle and The Fool, not to mention The Confessor, then perhaps we'll be able to make the link in time to stop them. I can't see them stopping now. We have to assume they're aiming for a complete set."

"It's got to be worth a go," said Elspeth. She glanced at her watch. "What time are we meeting him?"

"Two," said Peter. They were approaching the market square as they ambled slowly through the town towards Postgate, and he stopped, sat on a low wall. "Which might *just* give us time for this infernal coffee to cool down to sub-stellar levels."

Elspeth laughed. "Budge up," she said, sitting down beside him. Pigeons were scrabbling about amongst the detritus of the previous day's market, pecking at cabbage leaves and cigarette ends amongst the cobblestones. She sipped at her coffee. "I still can't quite believe it's real. It all feels like some horrible dream."

He put his arm around her, and they sat in companionable silence until it was time to go.

CHAPTER TWENTY-SEVEN

They found Miller inside The Reading Stop, ensconced in the corner in a deep leather armchair, sipping a coffee and reading – somewhat ironically – a Michael Williams thriller called *The Fate Caller*. He placed it back on the shelf when he saw them approaching.

"Not one of his best," he said.

The Reading Stop was a recent addition to Heighton's burgeoning art scene – to all intents and purposes a café like any other, peddling the usual ostentatious array of flat whites, mocha chocolate brownies and fruit-flavoured frappés, but with the novel addition that the seating booths had all been created out of bowing cases of second-hand paperbacks. The books were all for sale, but also free to browse for anyone purchasing food or drink. The café also had an upper floor for evening events, where guest authors could give readings or submit themselves to question and answer sessions with their reading public. It had a nice vibe, Elspeth felt. She had too much of a loyalty to Lenny's to truly defect, but she could see herself attending a few events here in the future.

They joined Miller, taking seats opposite him.

Elspeth felt herself wishing she didn't feel quite so weary.

"Thank you for making the time to talk to us again," said Peter. "It's good of you to drive over."

Miller shrugged. "I have no lectures today, and besides, it gave me the perfect excuse to look up a friend in the area."

"It wouldn't happen to be Michael Williams or Philip Cowper, would it?" said Peter.

Miller waved a dismissive hand. "Hardly," he said, but didn't elaborate. He reached inside his jacket and withdrew a small black case. "I hope you don't mind. I know it's a terrible habit, but I can't go too long without one. Since it's regarded as a little uncouth these days, I've finally submitted myself to the ritual humiliation of one of these." He opened the case and took out a vaporizer.

Peter smiled. "I hear they're all the rage these days."

Miller inclined his head. "So, how can I be of service?"

"What can you tell us about the Carrion King's other apostles?" said Peter. "And in particular the woman known as The Confessor?"

Miller rolled his device between his lips. "Ah, yes. I understand a little more now, about why you requested my assistance. I take it this isn't the first?"

The news of Rose's death had spread like wildfire, including – of course – the details of how her body had been dressed in what looked like a costume from the play. With so many people in attendance, it would have been impossible to attempt to contain it, and subsequently news vans had been crawling all over the area that morning. Elspeth herself had drafted a short piece for the *Heighton Observer* website, with a promise to Meredith that she'd provide another, longer update later that afternoon.

Elspeth sensed Peter bristle. "I'm afraid I can't confirm that. But as you can imagine, we'd appreciate any help you might be able to offer."

Miller nodded. He plumed vapour from the corner of his mouth. Elspeth found herself annoyed by his affected nonchalance. It didn't suit him.

"The Confessor was a witch who inveigled her way into the Carrion King's inner circle," he said. "It was said that in the age before the Carrion King's coming, she had discovered the rites through which one might commune with the spirits of the dead; a medium, of sorts, who could pierce the veil between worlds both corporeal and ethereal."

He downed the last of his espresso as if it were a shot of tequila, and then held his empty cup aloft to the waitress, beckoning for another. "And anything for my friends, too," he called, but both Peter and Elspeth shook their heads.

"She had not always been this way," continued Miller. "Once, she'd been a simple slave girl of a farmer from the nearby village. She was a striking young woman, however, imbued with a preternatural beauty that turned the heads of all the men who were lucky enough to cross her path. For this reason, the farmer confined her to a life of servitude upon the farm, away from the wandering eyes of those who might do the young girl wrong.

"The girl, Esme, was content enough with her lot.

She knew little of life beyond the farm, and the dark ways of men. In protecting her innocence, however, the farmer had done her a devastating wrong, for she had learned nothing of distrust or deception, and therefore could not recognise it in others. When the ealdorman's tax collector – an arrogant, wayward young man – called upon the farm to demand Danegeld of the farmer, he spied Esme drawing water from the well, and became utterly bewitched.

"Day and night, the tax collector could think of nothing else. He claimed the woman came to him in his dreams, and, like a siren of old, beckoned him to her bed.

"Driven mad by desire, the man arranged for the farmer to be summoned to the ealdorman's home one morning. Then, knowing the farmer's wife would be visiting the market and the girl was home alone, he forced his way into the farmhouse and raped her.

"Confused, alone, and unable to comprehend what had happened to her, Esme fled. She had nowhere to go, and no money, and for days she stumbled through the wilderness, her strength ebbing with every passing moment. Unknown to her, the youth's seed had taken root, and already, a child was beginning to grow inside of her.

"Eventually, Esme stumbled upon a small hut in the woods, and in her desperation, she fell upon the mercy of the two witches who had made the place their home. The witches took her in and gave her bread and water and a place to sleep, but there was little to be done, and the girl wavered near the brink of death. The witches sensed the goodness in Esme, however, and so, at great risk to their own wellbeing, they performed a forbidden rite that would perpetuate her life. She was saved, but at great cost. The life of her child was forfeit, and Esme herself would never again age, for she was no longer truly alive. Instead, she awoke to find herself trapped in an interstitial state between life and death, able to exist on both sides of the veil simultaneously. She had become 'hinterkind', a walker between worlds.

"While she was grateful to the witches for all they had done, for the first time in her life, Esme felt unsatisfied; incomplete. For now she knew the dark ways of men, and her innocence had been lost, stolen by the youth who had raped her.

"Time no longer had any meaning to her, however, and so for twenty years she remained in the company of the two witches, learning all she could of their dark arts. The witches grew to love her as a daughter, and she them, as mothers in darkness. Her talents grew, and she regularly communed with the spirits, seeking consolation for all she had lost.

"When the time eventually came that she had absorbed all of the knowledge the witches could offer, she bid them farewell, for she understood that the next part of her journey could only be undertaken alone. She crossed the veil and delved deep into the heart of the underworld. For six full years she searched the dark realm, until, finally, she found what she was looking for: the cacodemon, a demon that kept her living spirit bound in a gilded cage.

"The cacodemon had the power to restore her life, to make her whole again. But it would only do so in exchange for something of equal or greater value – the secrets of a man named the Carrion King, whom it had encountered before, and greatly feared. Esme agreed, and formed a pact with the cacodemon – she would obtain for it the Carrion King's innermost thoughts in exchange for the restoration of her living spirit.

"So it was that Esme returned from the underworld and sought out the Carrion King, to whom she pledged her allegiance. Remember, time was of no consequence to Esme, so for many years she served the Carrion King faithfully, earning his trust, eventually being elevated to the role of apostle. She became The Confessor, keeper of his innermost secrets, his greatest confidante. But the Carrion King was a man, and she knew the truth of men, and all the while she plotted to return to the underworld and the cacodemon to bargain for her soul.

"But the demons of the underworld are wily and duplicitous, and another had fathomed the plans of the cacodemon, and wished to retain Esme's soul in the underworld for its own amusement. It appeared to the Carrion King in a feverish dream to warn him of Esme's ploy. In exchange, it asked only that it might retain her living soul. The Carrion King readily agreed, and while Esme slept, he stole into her chamber and throttled her.

"However, the Carrion King knew of Esme's transitory condition, and so to prevent her from sharing his secrets with the creatures of the underworld, he stitched her lips with twine and bound her hands behind her back so she could never seek her freedom. He dressed her in the garb of a slave and tied her body to a stake in the centre of the kingdom as a warning to all who might betray their king, while her spirit was left to wander the underworld for eternity in silence."

Miller smiled and took another drag from his e-cigarette. He glanced from Peter to Elspeth. "I'm sorry. I'm afraid I've gone on too long. I tend to get carried away by these stories, you see. I've lived with them for so long."

"Not at all," said Peter. "In fact, if you'll forgive me, I'm going to ask you to carry on, and tell us a little about The Master of the Pentacle, and The Fool, if you would? I'm hoping it might help us to identify any potential targets."

Miller raised an eyebrow. "An encore?" he said. The waitress was approaching with his espresso. He smiled his thanks as she placed it on the table.

All Elspeth could think about was poor Rose, silenced like the woman in the story for all the secrets she had known, and all the people she had helped.

Miller cleared his throat. "The Master of the Pentacle was the Carrion King's right-hand man, so to speak. He was not, in and of himself, a magician, lacking the natural ability for the realisation of such things. But he understood well the rites of magic, and guided the Carrion King in all his many rituals and spells. Where The Confessor bore the burden of her master's secrets, The Master of the Pentacle was charged with guarding the ancient lore, and protecting it from falling into the hands of the Carrion King's enemies – for there were many who would use such knowledge against him.

"It is thought The Master of the Pentacle had once been a Christian monk named Edmund, who, along with his brothers, had amassed a great library of spiritual works, a collection so valuable, so learned, that it was guarded by a garrison from the local town."

"The abbot of this monastery believed that, in gathering all the accumulated knowledge of Him, he might prove once and for all the existence of the Christian God, for he knew that in the face of darkness, he needed evidence of light.

"Edmund believed wholeheartedly in this crusade, and for decades he toiled, transcribing all the great Christian works, many of them now forgotten. Dutifully he pored over every word of the old texts, some so ancient that they originated from the time of Christ himself. Edmund's belief in the Christian myth blossomed, and his heart swelled in wonder as he sought meaning in their symbolism.

"Yet try as he might, he could not complete the abbot's task, for the evidence they sought was not to be found in words alone. The Christian myth is founded on faith, as you know, and no matter how many books the abbot collated in his library, the empirical truths he longed for could never be found.

"Edmund, though, was persistent, and in his hubris believed the key to the abbot's quest might lie in the forbidden texts; those of pagan origin, which the abbot had censured and locked away from the pure hearts and uncorrupted minds of his followers. These were the dark tomes, the books that spoke of the wild magic, the spirits of the land and sea, and the ancient traditions of the time before man. Here, Edmund was certain that he would find what he so desperately craved, for if he could not find evidence of God in the works of Christian scholars, perhaps he could find it in the works of the heathen primitives.

"The abbot, of course, would hear none of it, proclaiming the heathen texts heretical, but Edmund was not to be dissuaded, and despite the abbot's warnings to the contrary, began to pay secret, nightly visits to the lowest level, where he familiarised himself with all the pagan works of man."

Miller took another draw on his vaporizer, and allowed the smoke to escape from his nostrils. "Of course, in doing so, Edmund realised his error, for rather than prove the existence of the Christian God, he convinced himself only of the existence of the ancient, heathen gods. He took his findings to the abbot, and was cast out for his blasphemy."

"How sad," said Elspeth.

Miller smiled. "The Carrion King, though, had long sought access to the knowledge contained in those ancient tomes, and so welcomed Edmund with open arms, and took his knowledge upon himself, sharing in his understanding of the ancient traditions and the power such knowledge and rituals could offer.

"In Edmund he saw a repository of all that was right and honest, a truly enlightened soul, who had stared into the light and seen only darkness. Edmund was brought into the fold as The Master of the Pentacle, and remained by the Carrion King's side in all things."

"I'm guessing he also came to something of a sticky end?" said Peter.

Miller nodded. "Edmund had spent too long in the company of men, repressing his true desires. Now, set free, and understanding at last that beauty was not a sin, and that the natural world might be worshipped through congress with another, he sought the love of a beautiful woman. This woman was a raven-haired follower of the Carrion King named Catherine, whose heart was faithful to her king in every way.

"Edmund, however, had learned many things from the pagan tomes, and he brewed a draught from rose petals and hawthorn, which he administered to Catherine one night after a great feast. Catherine was overcome by an uncontrollable lust, and Edmund had his way with her in her chambers. Afterwards, exhausted, they fell together into a deep slumber.

"When, awakening in the night and seeking solace from his dreams, the Carrion King came in search of Catherine, he discovered her in Edmund's arms. Finding the empty cup and realising what Edmund had done, the Carrion King dragged him howling from Catherine's bed. He staked Edmund to the ground and, taking a single crow's feather, etched an incantation into the man's naked back. It was a spell of binding, taught to the Carrion King by Edmund himself, which anchored the soul to the dying body. Now, even in death, Edmund would never gain the solace of a life in the underworld. His spirit would remain tied to his decomposing corpse for all eternity, howling in torment and repentance for the crime he had committed."

"That's quite a punishment," said Peter.

"The Carrion King was not known for his mercy," said Miller.

Elspeth rubbed her temples, attempting to stave off the tiredness. "Have you ever considered setting these stories, as you tell them, down in a book, Professor Miller?"

Miller laughed. "Oh, no. That sounds far too much like hard work. I'd much rather leave that to people like Mick Williams. He's much better qualified."

"So, that leaves us with The Fool," said Peter. "I presume he, too, has a tale of woe?"

"The Fool is an interesting case apart," said Miller. "He was a simple man, drawn from the Carrion King's adoring flock. He was nothing but a farmer, with no occult knowledge or supernatural insights to his name. Yet the Carrion King elevated him regardless, and kept him close as a kind of warning, a reminder of the credulous idiots who had plagued his existence. The Fool was his barometer, you see, and by his standard the Carrion King judged all other men, and found them wanting."

"So he, too, had to die?" said Elspeth.

"They all did," said Miller. "The Fool was the very last of them, and while the Carrion King saw that he was naive and innocent – the only one of the apostles not to betray him – he nevertheless remained a shackle, the fifth sacrifice. For the Carrion King could not rise to true prominence until he had set himself free of all of his apostles; until he had made the supreme sacrifice and abandoned his humanity. Only then could he transcend and claim his true power.

"The Fool, then, went willingly to his own death, so convinced was he in the altruism of his master. He was blindfolded and hung from a tree by his neck."

"And what became of the Carrion King?"

"Ah, now, there's a question," said Miller. He downed his second coffee. "Having freed himself from the shackles of his past by taking revenge upon the ealdorman through the use of his mirror, the death of The Fool became his final sacrifice. He had finally freed himself from the kingdom of men, from the physicality of the flesh, and in doing so gained power over life and death itself. He completed his transcendence and became one with the forest, wild and free. Much like Esme, he walked the underworld, protected by his magic, able to manipulate the souls of others, to raise spirits from the grave and cast others down at a whim. Some say he is still out there today, watching over all who dare step foot within the bounds of the Wychwood."

"And do you believe that, Professor Miller?" said Elspeth.

"They're romantic stories, Miss Reeves, rich in symbolism but not in historical fact. There's no archaeological evidence to support any of the parables. Believe me, I've checked."

"Then what is it about these stories that's led you to devote so much of your life to studying them?"

Miller looked thoughtful. "Like Edmund, I suppose I'm seeking the truth. Not in a base, historical sense, but in a philosophical one." He shrugged. "That's the luxury of academia."

"Alright, Professor Miller, we'll let you get back to your studies." Peter nodded to Elspeth, and they both got to their feet. "Thanks again for your time."

"My pleasure," he said. "And good luck with your enquiries."

Outside, it had started to spit with rain, and Elspeth could sense that a storm was brewing. She pulled her jacket a little tighter around her shoulders. "What did you make of all that?" she said.

"I think he's very full of himself," said Peter, "but it could be useful. I'm going to head back to the station and try to get some of it down, mull it over for a bit. All that stuff about 'hinterkind' and the underworld – I can't quite see how any of that relates to what happened to Rose."

"I think a lot of it is just window dressing," said Elspeth. "The key is trying to decipher the stories to work out who the killer might choose as The Master of the Pentacle and The Fool. Is there anyone from the theatre who's particularly religious?"

"No," said Peter. "But we know Oscar Waring has a juvenile fascination with pagan mythology." His phone buzzed, and he took it from his pocket and held it to his ear. "Shaw." He frowned, and then looked suddenly pleased with himself. "Alright. Thanks. I'll be there shortly."

"News?"

"Sasha Reid's just turned up, alive and well and a little indignant." He gestured over his shoulder with his thumb. "The car's only round the corner?"

"Come on, then," she said. "Let's find out if Oscar Waring's been telling the truth." They turned and ran as the heavens opened, feet splashing through the flash puddles that formed upon the glistening paving slabs.

CHAPTER TWENTY-EIGHT

A police car was already parked outside Sasha Reid's house when Peter pulled his car to a stop a little way further down the road, tucking it in behind a sporty red Mazda. It was a busy street with little or no off-road parking, and neat rows of small terraced houses lining both sides of the road, probably dating back to the early Edwardian era.

It was a far cry from the impoverished neighbourhood of Oscar Waring, with neatly manicured borders, gleaming front doors and windows, and a general lack of abandoned waste clogging up the front yards. Elspeth wondered what the woman made of Oscar's living arrangements. It certainly didn't appear to be what she was used to.

Peter cut the engine and climbed out, clearly anxious to get to the bottom of whatever had been going on with Sasha Reid. One way or another, this was the breakthrough he'd been waiting for. The woman's testimony would either corroborate Oscar's alibi or reinforce the police case against him – which at present remained entirely circumstantial, despite his being the apparent best fit for Lucy's murder.

Elspeth hurried to keep up as Peter made a beeline for the house, slamming the car door behind her. He bleeped it locked without looking back.

As they approached the house she saw DC Patel coming out to greet them. He looked pleased with himself.

"She's inside, sir," he said. "She only arrived today. Says she's been staying with a friend in Sheffield for a few days and left her phone charger at home. She didn't bother finding another as she didn't want any calls from Oscar Waring while she was away."

"Alright, good work, Patel." Peter turned to Elspeth. "You'd better wait out here, Ellie. Patel will keep you company for a minute while I have a word with Ms Reid."

Elspeth nodded, trying to hide her disappointment. She watched as Peter ducked inside the house, pushing the door shut behind him.

"So," said Patel. "You and Shaw, eh?"

Elspeth sighed. "We're old friends," she said. "Nothing more." She knew this wasn't entirely true – that Peter, at least, had rather obvious ambitions for something more – but she was still working out how she felt about the breakup, and still trying to decide what to do with her life. She certainly didn't want to go reinforcing gossip at the police station, or giving anybody the wrong idea.

Patel gave the sort of nod that suggested he'd heard it all before.

"What about you," said Elspeth. "Married, kids?"

"Yeah, yeah. We have two kids. Anita is seven and Rohan is three. They're a right handful." He beamed.

"Wouldn't be without them, though."

Elspeth smiled. Patel must have been around thirty, and seemed cheery in the sort of way that policemen – in her experience – rarely did. She wondered if it was simply that he hadn't had it knocked out of him yet. Or perhaps she was just being cynical.

"Have you worked with him for long? Peter, I mean."

"A couple of years," said Patel. "He's good. A little unorthodox sometimes, but he gets results, and that's really all the DCI seems interested in. You met her, didn't you?"

Elspeth nodded. "Yeah, the other day, when I found the body."

Patel smiled, as if to say 'then you know exactly what I'm getting at'.

They both laughed.

Elspeth nodded towards the house. "Did she say whether she'd been with Oscar Waring that night?"

Patel seemed to weigh up whether or not to say anything, then shrugged. "Yeah. I think Griffiths is going to be disappointed. She said she was with him until the early hours. She got up to make a drink, put the costume on to keep warm, and when she went back to bed they had a blazing row. She stormed out, got in the car and drove off. Later the next day she called in sick to work, made arrangements with her friend and drove up to Sheffield. That's her car, there. The grey Corsa."

Elspeth rolled this over in her mind. So if Oscar had been telling the truth, who *had* done for Lucy Adams that night? Not to mention Rose? They'd obviously been at the theatre the previous night, but then so had a couple of hundred other people, not to mention the rest of the cast and crew. Could it have been Michael Williams? That still seemed like a possibility.

They couldn't yet rule out Vanessa Eglington, either. Her brother had given her an alibi, but it was tenuous at best, and judging by what Peter had said, Robbie Eglington was so out of it on heroin that he probably wouldn't even have noticed if his sister had slipped out for a couple of hours in the middle of the night. She was still a possible candidate, although Elspeth was having a hard time trying to work out what reason either of them would have to kill Rose, unless it was simply the fact she was an agony aunt.

If someone was recreating the Carrion King myths, they might simply have chosen her because of her suitability for the role of The Confessor, just as Lucy Adams could have been picked because of her promiscuity, and Geoff Altman because of his occupation as a gamekeeper. Somehow, the thought of that was even more horrifying than the idea that they'd been murdered because of something they'd done, or something they knew.

Elspeth looked round at the sound of the front door opening, and Peter emerged, closely followed by a stunningly beautiful young woman in her early twenties. She had coffee-coloured skin, with thick, dark hair that tumbled down to her shoulders in loose ringlets. She was wearing a loose-fitting yellow dress that fell to her ankles, and she was nodding as she listened to whatever Peter was saying to her.

Elspeth and Patel stood back as they stepped out

onto the street and Sasha led Peter over to her car. She took out her keys and blipped the lock, then opened up the boot. They both stood there for a moment, peering down into the car. Then Peter reached over, and when he came back up, he was holding the crumpled remains of a white feather cloak in both hands. Elspeth could see the disappointment on his face. Just like the clothes they'd found on Rose, the costume Lucy Adams had been wearing out in the woods had not come from the wardrobe of the play. They'd been chasing a dead end.

Sasha Reid asked Peter a question, and he nodded. She closed the boot behind them as they walked back towards the house. Peter stopped by the police car, handing the costume to Patel. "Get this bagged and over to the station with Ms Reid. I'll follow behind. She'll give a formal statement, but it seems that whatever else Mr Waring has been up to, he's not responsible for the death of Lucy Adams – at least directly."

"Right you are, sir," said Patel. Sasha had disappeared back into the house, presumably to collect her coat and bag.

"Ellie, do you need a lift into town?"

"If you can drop me off on the way?"

He blipped the lock on the car. "Jump in. I'll just see Ms Reid off with Patel, and I'll be with you."

CHAPTER TWENTY-NINE

The drive back into town was abruptly interrupted by a crackling voice from the police radio, as Peter turned the car out of the end of the street.

"DS Shaw? Are you there?"

"Welcome to my life," said Peter. He put a finger to his lips to indicate she should stay quiet, then reached over and thumbed the button on the receiver, yanking it free from its cradle.

"Shaw here."

"Ah, sir, there's been a reported disturbance at the Williams residence. I thought you should know. We're despatching a squad car."

"What sort of disturbance?"

"The caller reported the place has been turned over and the residents aren't present on the scene."

Peter glanced at Elspeth, concern evident in his eyes. "Do you have a name for the caller?"

"Yes." There was a brief hiss of static. "David Keel, sir."

"Thanks, Cooper. I'm heading over there now." He dropped the handset into the cradle and swung the car left at a T-junction. "Sorry, Ellie," he said. "Duty calls." He put his foot down, and they roared off down the street.

Three cars were parked on the gravel driveway as they pulled up outside the Williams residence: a small red sports car, a more sober silver-grey saloon, and a white Audi, splashed up the side with streaks of dried mud. There was no sign of the squad car yet, but it couldn't be that far behind.

It'd taken them only fifteen minutes to get across from Heighton. Peter had driven at a speed that left Elspeth feeling queasy, as if she'd just stepped off a rollercoaster and was no longer certain of her centre of gravity. She climbed out, and leaned against the car roof with one hand while she steadied herself, taking slow, measured breaths. Clearly he hadn't given up on *all* his youthful ambitions to become a rally driver.

Peter was already marching across the gravel, his boots crunching with every step. Elspeth hurried to catch up. There was an air of foreboding about the place today that she hadn't noticed the last time they'd visited. She knew she was probably imagining it, but she had the eerie notion that something was seriously wrong.

They trudged down the path and across the small courtyard to the converted outbuilding. David Keel was already coming up the path to meet them. He was wearing a brown leather coat and jeans. He looked nervous, a bit like he had at the theatre, when he'd comforted Elspeth about Rose. He kept scratching the back of his neck and looking over his shoulder. "Oh, thank God," he said.

"Mr Keel," said Peter. "You reported a disturbance?"

"If that's what you want to call it," said Keel. "But something's gone on. And given everything that's been happening recently... I don't know what to think."

"Alright," said Peter. "You'd better show me."

"This way, down at Mick's office," said Keel. He started to retrace his steps, leading them down towards the summerhouse.

"I take it that's your car on the drive, Mr Keel," said Peter.

"Yeah, yeah, the white one," said Keel.

"And what exactly are you doing here?"

"I had a meeting arranged with Mick. After everything that happened with the play... well, I was trying to work out if there's anything I could salvage from it."

"But Mr Williams wasn't here when you arrived?" said Peter.

"No. No sign of Mick, or Rebecca. But their cars are both there on the drive. I got here about twenty minutes ago, tried the house, then came down here when I got no answer."

They'd reached the door to the summerhouse. Raindrops had beaded on its slick surface. It was hanging ajar.

"And what did you find?" said Peter.

"See for yourself," said Keel. "It was like this when I found it."

Peter ducked inside, and Elspeth followed behind him, feeling a mounting sense of disquiet.

All the windows were covered, and inside it was difficult to discern anything amongst the pooling shadows. They flowed like liquid, cloaking the room, making sinister, unfamiliar shapes from the everyday; a plant pot became a looming assassin, a ruffled rug became a body on the floor. Elspeth stood just inside the doorway, waiting for her eyes to adjust.

"Hello?" called Peter. "Mr Williams? It's DS Shaw." He was on her left, fumbling on the wall for a light switch. He found it a moment later, and with a click, the entire space was flooded with brilliant yellow light. Elspeth narrowed her stinging eyes as they adjusted to the sudden glare, glancing from left to right.

There'd been a disturbance, alright. A chair was overturned, a picture frame was shattered and there were sheets of paper all over the floor, shed from a stack on the desk to form a mismatched carpet. This, she presumed, was Michael Williams's magnum opus, the manuscript for his novel about the Carrion King. Each of them was covered in neat black typeface, and worse, spattered across them in a long line towards the door was a streak of vivid red blood.

"Stay back," said Peter. "Don't come any further inside." His training had obviously kicked in; his expression was stern and calculating as he read the crime scene for evidence, for any hint at what might have gone on here. "Did you touch anything, Mr Keel?" he called over his shoulder.

"No," said Keel, from the doorway. "The door was ajar when I arrived. I went in, calling for Mick, and noticed the mess. I put the light on, saw the blood, and then went straight back up to the house. I still couldn't get an answer, so I called the police."

Peter walked back to the door. "Why did you put the light out again?"

Keel shrugged. "I don't really know. Habit, I guess. I wasn't thinking straight. Do you think something's happened to Mick?"

"I don't know," said Peter, his voice level. "Have you tried his mobile?"

Keel nodded. "Several times. It's ringing out."

"I think I should check the house," said Peter.

Keel gave him a quizzical look. "But I already did. There's no one home."

"*Inside* the house." He led Elspeth back outside. "Mr Keel, would you be so good as to remain here in case the squad car arrives before I'm back?"

Keel looked like a deer in headlights. "Of course."

"Ellie, come with me."

She followed him back up towards the house. "Shouldn't I wait with Mr Keel?" she said.

Peter shook his head. "I want you where I can see you. Stick with me." He approached the front door and rapped loudly with the knocker. He waited for a moment, but no one stirred inside the house, and no one came to the door. He knocked again, then stepped back and looked up at the windows.

"Do you think they've had a fight, and done a runner?" said Elspeth. She leaned in, cupped her hands around her eyes and peered through the living-room window. She couldn't make out much, other than the hulking silhouette of a sofa and the slanting reflection of the sunlight in the TV screen, but there didn't appear to be any signs of life.

"God, I hope not," said Peter. "We had him in custody earlier." The inference was obvious. It wouldn't reflect well on the police if they had to mount a national manhunt for a suspect they'd set loose that same day. "We'll put a call out to the hospitals once we've checked the house, just in case it was an accident."

"But their cars are still here. And surely if they'd called for an ambulance it would have been logged by the emergency services who took the call from Mr Keel?"

"Yeah," said Peter. "That's what's worrying me." He was circling the house now, looking for an alternative way in. Elspeth reasoned there had to be a side entrance or rear door, because Rebecca had come out that way to find them the last time they'd visited. He'd obviously had the same idea.

"Round here," he called, a moment later. She hurried after him, her boots sinking in the loose gravel. She thought she could hear a dog barking, somewhere deep inside the house.

Peter was standing by a white stable door that presumably led to the kitchen or scullery. He knocked again, and then tried the handle. It was locked.

"How do you propose to get in?" said Elspeth.

"Let's try a good old-fashioned shoulder barge," he said. He approached the side door, rattled it in the frame as if trying to figure out where to apply the most pressure, and then stepped back, dipped his shoulder, and ran at it. He struck it with a thunderous *crunch*, but rebounded almost immediately, his face creased in pain. The door remained resolutely shut. He glanced at Elspeth, looking rueful.

"Are you hurt?" she said.

"Only my pride."

"Look, are you sure this is necessary?"

Peter ignored her. He sidled up to the door, raised his foot, and kicked it. It bowed in the frame but didn't break. "One more…" said Peter. He repeated the motion, jamming his boot hard against the lock, and this time, with a splinter of cracking wood, the door shuddered and swung open.

Elspeth had been right in her assumption that the door would lead into the kitchen. It was glorious, too; expensive and modern, with a central island, an American-style fridge, pan racks, an Aga range, and a marble floor with matching work surfaces. It was just a shame, she thought, that the couple had been too unhappy in each other's company to enjoy it.

Peter flicked the lights on as they went. In the dining room, the place was decorated with an expensive heritage taste; as if the Williams had enjoyed the pretence of restoring their Georgian home to its former glory, along with elaborate plaster florettes and chandeliers, replica furniture and antique carriage clocks – but also updating it, too, with an expensive array of modern gadgets.

"Mrs Williams?" Peter had moved through to the living room. For a moment Elspeth thought he had found her, but it had just been a precautionary question, spoken into the darkness, and she found him alone. This room was at the front of the house, and adorned with a massive curved-screen television, sofas and chairs, magazine racks and fireplace, and a couple of bookcases filled with what looked like romantic fiction. None of

Michael's books were in evidence here – he must have kept them all down in the studio.

"Upstairs?" she said. She had a sharp sense of déjà vu, and she thought about the way she'd wandered from room to room in another house recently, one far less grandiose – and what she had found on the floor in the bedroom.

Peter shook his head. "Out there, first. There's another room across the hall." Elspeth nodded and followed. The hall was as grand as she'd imagined, with a ticking grandfather clock and a galleried staircase, swirling banisters smooth and enticing. The walls had been painted a bright, clean white, and hung with photographs in mismatched wooden frames. The Williams had no children – so far as Elspeth knew – but the photographs reflected upon the happier times in their lives: portraits in the garden, early book signings, holidays together in the sun, their wedding day. Rebecca looked so young and happy.

Peter opened the door to the other room and they both stepped inside. It was almost precisely the same size and shape as the living room, a mirror image, in fact, on the other side of the house. Rather than a sitting room, though, the room had been kitted out as a gym, with a treadmill, a weight-lifting rig, a bench press and an exercise bike. The back wall was mirrored, with a rail running across it at waist height, and the floor was polished boards, lacquered with glossy varnish.

Rebecca Williams was on her back before the mirrored wall, surrounded by a large congealing pool of her own blood. Her skull had been viciously caved in, so that her once-beautiful face was grotesquely distorted, one eye rolled back in a shattered orbit. Bone fragments, clumps of hair and brain matter had spilled across the floorboards, like obscene islands in a sea of oily blood. Close by, a dumbbell lay on the ground, sticky with blood. She was still dressed in the clothes she'd been working out in. This wasn't another ritual killing. Something else had happened here – something brutal and awful.

Elspeth felt an upwelling of anger, frustration, and intense sadness. Something dreadful had happened here on the farm, and it wasn't yet clear how it all connected. Had Michael Williams done this to his wife, before fleeing? And the spilled blood in the summerhouse – was it his, hers, or someone else's?

"I'm going to call for backup now, Ellie," said Peter. She realised he was standing in front of her. He put his hands on her shoulders, and then hugged her close. She put her cheek on his shoulder and hugged him back, but felt nothing at all – nothing but a horrifying, empty numbness.

"I think you should wait in the car." He paused for a moment. "Ellie?"

"Sorry, what did you say?"

"I said I think you should wait in the car. I'm sorry, I'm going to be here for a while, and I imagine DCI Griffiths is going to have some questions for you, but I think it's best if you keep a low profile while the SOCOs come in."

Elspeth nodded and took the keys he was proffering. She'd seen enough. Peter was already dialling the station, his grim expression under-lit by the light from his phone. With a weak smile, Elspeth turned and left the room.

* * *

She sat in the passenger seat of Peter's car while the police cars, ambulances and SOCOs came and went, lights winking, sirens wailing. David Keel was sitting in the back of a police car at the bottom of the drive, presumably giving a statement, and she supposed she'd probably be next.

She'd tried making notes on her phone, tried sleeping, but she couldn't settle to anything. She'd called her mum, feigning light-heartedness, and explained that she was out with Peter, so not to worry, and not to wait up.

It was late now, gone eleven, and she hadn't seen Peter for over an hour. She was cold, and she'd considered turning the keys in the engine and starting the heater, but she didn't want to draw any attention to herself. Nor did she want to go looking for him.

She heard a rap on the window and turned to see Inspector Griffiths peering in through the passenger window, her fingers pressed against the glass. She stood back when she saw that Elspeth had noticed her.

Elspeth pressed the button but the electric window refused to activate without the keys in the ignition, so she popped the door open instead and slipped out. Griffiths was wearing a disconcerting expression, somewhere between contained fury and admiration.

"I'm beginning to wonder if I'm going to find you at all of my crime scenes, Ms Reeves."

Elspeth's mouth felt dry. She moistened her lips. "I'm sorry," was all she could muster. "I was trying to help."

Griffiths nodded. "DS Shaw explained the situation," she said.

Elspeth wondered what he'd said. "What'll happen now?"

"We'll take the body back to the morgue and get it all written up. And we'll mount a search for the husband. He's the most likely suspect." She chewed her bottom lip, as if she were about to say more, and then clearly changed her mind. "Do you need anything?" said Griffiths. "There's a flask of tea doing the rounds?"

"You know what, a hot tea would be just about perfect right now."

"Alright. I'll see what I can rustle up. You sit tight. It's going to be a long night. We'll need a statement from you before it's all over."

"I'm not going anywhere," said Elspeth.

"No, I can see that," said Griffiths. She stomped off across the driveway, barking something into her radio. The only part of it Elspeth understood was: "Shaw? You'd better get your girlfriend some tea."

Elspeth climbed back into the car, closed the door, and decided to find something cheerful to listen to on her phone. She thumbed through her selection, and in the end settled for David Bowie's *Scary Monsters*.

She propped the phone on the dashboard and leaned back, closed her eyes and tried to forget about everything going on around her.

CHAPTER THIRTY

Consciousness returned slowly, light stuttering in sudden, erratic bursts. He had no idea where he was. His eyes felt gummy. He was cold and wet, uncomfortable. Someone had removed his shirt.

And then everything erupted in pain – horrific, agonising, blinding pain. He swooned, close to passing out again. Then the light returned, and he sucked at the air, fighting panic. His heart was thrumming wildly.

Michael Williams moaned and tried to move, but this just elicited further stabbing pain in his arms and wrists. The muscles in his back were cramping, and he couldn't feel his legs.

Everything went dark again. He thought he sensed someone moving nearby.

He swallowed, but his throat felt dry. He tried to speak. "H... h... help." It was nothing but a dry, broken croak. His mind was racing. What was happening? Where was he? He couldn't remember what had happened, how he'd got here. Why was his mind so sluggish? "Rebecca?"

The light flashed over him again, causing him to

wince. The other person was holding a torch. Slowly his eyes adjusted to the glare. He realised he was outside. He was kneeling in the mud, amongst the mulch of fallen leaves. Trees rustled all around him in the breeze. He was hunched over, his feet bound beneath him. His wrists had been staked to the ground with huge iron nails, splintering the bones. The sight of the bloody, mangled mess caused him to wail pathetically. Dark blood was oozing out of the wounds with every thud of his heart, mingling with the damp soil. Then and there, he knew he was already dead.

The light blinked off again.

"I can pay," he said, through gritted teeth. "I have money. Name your price."

Silence.

"Just tell me what you want!"

Still nothing.

He heard footsteps behind him. His captor was moving around in the darkness. He fought another rising tide of panic. "Please…"

"It's not personal. Please don't think it's that. It's just a necessary evil, nothing more. I don't have any choice, you see. I'm recreating his great works, and everything has to be the same. Otherwise none of it will work."

The voice sounded fleetingly familiar, but disguised somehow, and Michael's mind was whirling, unable to hold onto a single thought for more than a few moments. And the pain, the pain…

The torch again, this time from behind. He sensed his captor leaning close, then felt the press of hands upon his back. His skin crawled, and he tried to twist around, to look back over his shoulder, but the pain in his wrists was searing, and he was forced to bow his head, unable to strain against his bonds.

He felt the bite of the incision as something sharp sliced into his flesh, and screamed. He willed unconsciousness to come and swallow him again, but it wasn't to be.

More cutting. More pain. With a dawning sense of horror, he realised what was happening, what this all meant. He'd been staked to the ground, and his captor was carving ancient pagan sigils into his back. A spell of binding, just like The Master of the Pentacle from the Carrion King myths. Was this how it had been for the others, for Geoff and Lucy and that girl from the theatre?

"Oh God, no. No!"

"I'm so sorry," said the man. "But know that your sacrifice will not be in vain. With your death, I take one step closer to the veil. Soon I shall walk amongst the living and the dead, and have power over both."

CHAPTER THIRTY-ONE

"Ellie?"

Elspeth groaned and peeled open her eyes. It was bright in her bedroom – brighter than it should have been. She looked round to see Dorothy standing by the window, wreathed in a halo of sunlight and dust motes. She'd opened the curtains, and was holding what smelled enticingly like a hot mug of coffee.

"What are you doing, Mum?"

"It's almost midday. I thought you might appreciate a wake-up call. I've made coffee, and I'm doing some bacon and eggs."

Elspeth groaned, and tried to fold herself into her pillow. She was weary, right down to her very bones. "Thanks, Mum. That's lovely. I'll be down in a minute."

"Right, I'll leave this on the nightstand," said Dorothy.

Elspeth watched through bleary eyes as Dorothy left the room, closing the door behind her.

She'd only had a few hours' sleep. After sitting in the car until the early hours, she'd been accompanied into the house by a young constable who'd introduced himself as PC Blake. He'd sat with her in the kitchen – having first made her a fresh mug of coffee – while she wrote out her statement, going over everything that had happened at the Williams's house that night. Then, when she'd finished, he'd walked her back to the car, where she'd found Peter waiting for her. The SOCOs had all packed up, and the body had been carted away to the morgue, and so DCI Griffiths had called it a night, making arrangements with her team to reconvene in the morning to go over everything.

Peter had driven her home, barely saying a word as he continued to process everything they'd seen. She'd been so certain that Michael Williams was innocent of the murders of Lucy Adams and Geoffrey Altman, but now she wasn't so sure. He'd been in the audience for the play, too, so he might have had the opportunity to slip backstage during the interval and kill Rose. It had seemed unlikely – she'd seen him pacing the lawn – but she couldn't discount anything now. If he *was* capable of doing that to his wife… Then again, it might prove to be entirely unrelated. Perhaps he and Rebecca had fallen out after news of his relationship with Lucy Adams had come to light, and it had escalated from there. And then there was the spilled blood in the summerhouse. Could Rebecca have attacked him first?

She wondered if she'd hear from Peter today, and what the continued investigations at the Williams's house were yielding.

She rolled over and reached for her phone. There was a message from Meredith that read simply: '???'. It had come through just after nine that morning.

Clearly, news had broken about Rebecca's murder. She was going to have to pull something together quickly that morning.

Elspeth rubbed her gritty eyes, propped herself up on her pillow, and then fired off a quick response, explaining that she'd have an update for the website shortly.

Elspeth stretched, yawning, then swung her legs out of bed and reached for her coffee. She downed it quickly, and then stumbled down the hall into the shower.

A short while later she was ensconced at the kitchen table, tucking into a hearty breakfast. She'd filled Dorothy in on the events of the previous night, and Dorothy had tried to act casual but had clearly been distraught to learn that her daughter had found herself involved in yet another murder investigation.

She was sitting before her now, sipping a coffee, and looking distractedly out of the patio doors towards the bottom of the garden and the looming boughs of the Wychwood.

"Are you alright, Mum?"

Dorothy smiled. "I'm just a bit worried about you, love. That's all. You've already got so much going on, with Andrew, and your job, and now you're running around chasing murderers. I know you're following up on a story, but are you sure it's safe?"

"I know, Mum," said Elspeth. She put her fork down and reached out, touching her mum's hand. "It's safe. Peter's making sure of that."

Dorothy nodded, but she didn't look convinced. "Is

this what your life was like, down there? I always had this vision of you and Andrew curled up watching telly, and you going into the office to write up stories about burglaries, missing cats and local politics. I suppose that's a bit naive really, isn't it?"

Elspeth laughed. "A bit. But I suppose it was a bit like that, really. I'd found a groove. Maybe even a rut. And I was happy. But I have to face facts, Mum. That's over, now. If I go back to London, I'll be starting over again. A new life, a new job – if I can find one."

"No luck on that front?"

"A few freelance pieces to follow up on. No one's hiring permanent positions anymore, though. All this coverage of the murders is going to stand me in good stead, though. It's something I can point people to. Show them I can report from the scene, and tell the story as it unfolds."

"I suppose you're right," said Dorothy. "Just so long as you're being careful. You're my only daughter, Elspeth Reeves. I haven't got a spare."

"Then you'd better get me some more of that bacon," said Elspeth, sliding her plate across the table. "To make sure I don't waste away."

"You can get it yourself," said Dorothy, laughing. "This isn't a hotel."

Elspeth grinned and got to her feet. There was a knock at the door. "You expecting anyone?"

"Not today," said Dorothy. "I'm off out with the girls for dinner tonight, mind, so you'll have to fend for yourself."

Elspeth nodded as she crossed to the door. She opened it to find a rather ragged-looking Peter standing on the step. "Peter? You'd better come in."

He gave her a tired smile as he shrugged his jacket off. "Hello, Mrs Reeves," he said.

"Afternoon, Peter," said Dorothy. "I'll put the kettle on. There's some bacon left if you fancy a butty?"

The look on Peter's face was so grateful that Dorothy might well have told him he'd won the lottery. "If it's no trouble, Mrs Reeves, I'd appreciate that. I've been up all night again."

"All night?" said Elspeth. "I thought you were heading home after you dropped me off?"

"I was," said Peter. He pulled out a chair and sat down at the table, while Dorothy set about making him a sandwich. It didn't look as if Elspeth was going to get any more bacon, after all. "But I was called back out around three."

"Michael Williams?" ventured Elspeth. "DCI Griffiths said she was launching a manhunt. Did they find him?"

Peter nodded. "But it's more bad news, I'm afraid." He glanced at Dorothy, who was busily spooning instant coffee into a mug with her back to them.

"Don't tell me he was found dead, too?"

"In the Wychwood, not far from his house," said Peter. "Another apostle, another ritual 'sacrifice'."

Elspeth returned to her seat. She lowered her voice. The kettle was boiling noisily, and her mum was studiously ignoring them, although Elspeth suspected she could hear everything. "So the blood in the summerhouse was his?"

"We won't know for certain until we get the forensics, but it's probable, judging by the way he'd been wounded.

He'd been hit around the head with something solid, although we've not been able to ascertain what, yet."

"Which apostle?"

"The Master of the Pentacle," said Peter. He swallowed, looking decidedly peaky at the thought. It seemed even he was having difficulties remaining entirely objective. "He'd been posed just like the woodcut, mirroring the story. His hands had been nailed to the ground, and he'd had ritual markings carved into his back with something sharp. There was a knife in his heart."

Elspeth put her hand to her mouth. "That's awful."

It made a horrible kind of sense that the killer would select Michael Williams as The Master of the Pentacle. His knowledge of the mythology and symbolism of the Carrion King was detailed and thorough.

Dorothy stirred Peter's coffee, then placed it before him on the table, along with the promised bacon roll. "I can't tell you how much I appreciate this," he said, before tucking straight in. "I'm famished."

"You're welcome," said Dorothy. "Right, well I've got things to be getting on with. I'll leave you to it." She picked up her half-empty mug and wandered off into the living room.

"Everything alright?" said Peter, when she'd gone.

"She's just worried," said Elspeth. "And I can't say I blame her. We've pretty much had a murder take place in our back yard, and then Patricia Graves, and Rose, and now this. The TV news is getting everyone worked up into a frenzy, too. It would be bad enough even if I wasn't involved."

Peter nodded, chewing on his sandwich. "Are you

saying you want out? I wouldn't blame you. You didn't come back here for this."

"No, no, not at all. Just that I can see it from Mum's point of view, that's all. I'm seeing this through."

"Alright. But I promise you, it's not always like this." He grinned, and took another bite of his butty.

They sat in companionable silence while he finished eating.

"What did you tell Griffiths yesterday, by the way?" she said, when he'd finished. "Up at the Williams's place. She said you'd explained the situation. I was certain you were going to get into trouble."

"I told her the truth," said Peter. "That you were in the car with me when I got the call, and that I decided to respond as a matter of urgency. I didn't want to leave you alone with David Keel, as I wasn't sure I could trust him – he might yet prove to be involved in the murders – and so I kept you with me while I went into the house."

"And she bought that?"

"She bawled me out for not waiting for the squad car, but like I said – she's more interested in results. I expect I'll get a more formal warning at some point, but there's not much I can do about that now." He shrugged and downed his coffee.

"You want another?" she said.

"No. I'm going home to get my head down. Tell your mum thanks again for the bacon butty."

"I will."

"See you tomorrow?"

"I promised I'd go to the cinema with Mum," said Elspeth. "But then on Monday I'm going along to Patricia Graves's funeral in the afternoon, then over to Chipping Norton to interview Millicent Brown, the social worker on the Thomas Stone case."

"Okay. Well, give me a call if you need anything, and I'll keep you up to date, too." He stood, grabbing his coat from the stand by the door.

"See you," she said.

After he'd gone, she tidied up the plates and mugs, and then wandered through to find Dorothy watching an old Agatha Christie drama on the TV. She dropped into the sofa beside her.

"I thought you had work to do?" said Dorothy.

"I do," said Elspeth. "But it can wait a few minutes while I watch some TV with my mum, can't it?"

Dorothy smiled. "I suppose I'd better fill you in on what's happened, then."

CHAPTER THIRTY-TWO

It was cold in the crematorium, and Elspeth found herself wishing she'd brought a coat, rather than the thin, sober jacket she'd worn over her black ensemble.

She'd expected the place to be bustling with people, just as it had been the day she'd come here to see off her dad. Then, she'd barely been able to move for the well-wishers and mourners, who'd jammed themselves into the tiny chapel, standing around the edges and looming over those sitting in the pews.

The vicar had droned on about Jesus, Heaven, and the resurrection, and all the things her dad had done with his life – some of them she'd never even heard before – and her mum had cried, and dabbed ineffectually at her eyes with a handkerchief. Then the curtains had closed and the casket had been slowly drawn away, and she'd felt that dawning sense of loss all over again.

Afterwards, she had walked the chapel grounds in a dazed fug, staring at all the wreaths of pretty flowers and listening to further platitudes, and to people chatting, and even laughing with one another. She couldn't understand how they could all be so *normal* at a time like this, as if they didn't understand the magnitude of what had happened.

It was an experience that had stayed with her, and today, sitting there on the pew in that same chapel, all of those old emotions stirred again, and she felt hollow and forlorn.

Today, the chapel was almost empty. Aside from Elspeth herself, there were three elderly ladies, sitting together on the front pew, clutching their handbags on their laps; a liver-spotted old man; the vicar, and one other man standing at the back. He was in his late sixties, she guessed, greying at the temples but still with a fine head of hair, and a craggy, weatherworn face.

She watched the vicar take a final look at his paltry audience, and then step up to the lectern, unfold his notes, and welcome them. She didn't really listen as he began his sermon, too intent on her own thoughts.

Was this really it? Were these the only people left whom Patricia Graves had made an impression upon in her life? It seemed impossible that someone could live to the age of seventy-seven and have only six people – Elspeth excluded – turn up to her funeral.

The police had confirmed there were no living relatives, of course, and that her husband had died years earlier, but still – she must have friends, old colleagues, and neighbours. Had she really lived a life so devoid of companionship?

The vicar was in full flow, summarising the woman's life in a matter of a few sentences – and reading it from his lectern. He was insisting she'd been a good, Christian woman, particularly in how she'd helped those less fortunate than herself, taking in so many waifs and strays and helping to set them on the path of righteousness. Elspeth wondered why she'd never had any children of her own. Had she and her husband been unable to conceive? It was nothing but conjecture, of course, but Elspeth found herself wondering if that was why she'd taken in the foster children.

She glanced over at the three women, who were watching the vicar intently as he talked, their faces stoic as they listened to his brief soliloquy on Patricia's life. Now, he was talking about loneliness, about the disconnect between the aged and the youth, and how society had failed this woman by refusing to reflect back to her the kindness she had shown to others in her own life.

He urged them to stand for a hymn, and Elspeth joined in out of a sense of obligation, despite feeling like a hypocrite throughout.

Then, with no one having anything else to add, the vicar said his final prayer, the curtains were drawn and the casket was coaxed slowly back. It was over in a matter of moments.

Elspeth waited until the others had filed out of the chapel, and then followed them out into the gusty morning. Only three wreaths had been laid out in tribute, on a small patio area directly outside the chapel entrance. While the others drifted away to their cars, Elspeth stooped to read the labels.

One, a wreath of white lilies, was marked 'FROM BENJAMIN, WITH LOVE'; another, a fantastic spray of colourful violets and peonies, read 'WE'LL MISS YOU AT THE SOLITAIRE CLUB. MARGERY, CLAIRE AND

JACQUELINE'. This latter was clearly from the three ladies who'd been seated at the front, and were now clambering into a taxi by the crematorium gates.

The final wreath was bold and red, standing apart from the others. The card read, cryptically: 'THOSE THAT KNOW THE MOST MUST MOURN THE DEEPEST. GEORGE'. Elspeth guessed it had to be a quote from somewhere, although the name immediately leapt out at her. George Baker, the foster child who'd been in the Graves's care at the time of Thomas Stone's disappearance. If he was the George who had sent the flowers, it might mean he'd be easier to track down than she'd imagined.

She checked no one was watching her, and then slipped her phone from her handbag and took a quick snap of the card. It was probably nothing, but if Millicent Brown wasn't able to give her any leads, then perhaps she could call around the local florists.

She stood, watching the last of the cars pull away, stirring the gravel. It was quiet, save for the distant crowing of the birds in the trees.

She paused for a moment, allowing the memories to wash over her. Then, hoisting her handbag over her shoulder, she set off along the avenue of trees for the short walk to the car park, before setting out for Chipping Norton and her interview with the Graves's erstwhile social worker.

CHAPTER THIRTY-THREE

It was a pleasant enough drive along the Burford Road, through the sweeping green belt, which was peppered with the scattered remnants of the forest that had once carpeted the entire region.

It didn't take her long, and she hit Chipping Norton just before the school rush. It was busy, and similar in size, population and architectural appearance to Heighton. She'd visited before, of course, but not for some years, and the road system was largely unfamiliar.

She followed her satnav as it guided her through the town centre, past the old town hall, and out along a road lined with pubs, restaurants and takeaways. She turned off into a small side street, followed the road for a short while, and turned again to find herself navigating a warren of quiet suburban streets. Most of the houses here appeared to date from the late eighteenth century, and many of them had been turned into flats. Similarly to Heighton, the roads – built in a time before cars had proliferated, and thus with no provision for parking – were lined with stationary vehicles, filling every available space.

She found the right address, and then continued

down the road until she located a suitable parking space, into which she executed a parallel park that, twenty years earlier, would have wowed her driving instructor. She cut the engine, grabbed her notebook, and then paused for a moment, collecting her thoughts.

She'd been straightforward with the woman on the phone, explaining that she was a journalist who had recently had the misfortune to happen upon Patricia Graves's body, and was now engaged in trying to understand what had happened to her, and why.

The house was a ground-floor flat in a beautiful Georgian terraced house, with tall sash windows and a small set of steps leading up to the front door. Peonies, laid low with the rain, drooped across the flagstones in the front yard, and a little black railing separated the property from the street. She couldn't see anyone through the ground-floor window, which was obscured with old-fashioned lace drapes.

Elspeth mounted the steps, found the correct buzzer, and gave it a short burst.

A moment later she heard footsteps, and then a chain being slid into place on the other side of the door. The door opened and a wizened face peered out through the crack. "Yes? Who is it?" The woman sounded fragile and old, like ancient porcelain.

"Mrs Brown?" said Elspeth. "Elspeth Reeves. I'm the journalist from Heighton who contacted you on the phone."

The door closed again, and Elspeth's heart sank. Had she changed her mind? She considered ringing the buzzer again, but decided against it. She couldn't go pestering an old lady, especially on a hunch.

She was just about to turn away when she heard the chain being removed from the latch, and the door swung open again.

"I suppose you'd better come in," said Millicent Brown.

One more. One final reflection from the past; one last act of vengeance. He would relish this one. He had saved her until now, the woman who had shaped his early life, who had stood by, unmoved, while he faced such horrors. He would ensure this one was slow.

Just like Patricia Graves and Rebecca Williams, he'd studied the decrepit old woman, watching to establish her routine, to choose his best moment. And now the time was approaching.

Now, deep in the heart of the Wychwood, surrounded by the trees that gave him such strength, he felt his heart racing. Tonight, it would all be done.

He peered into the empty mirror, waiting...

The décor in the flat had once represented the height of sophistication, and while well maintained, seemed dated, now. A brown carpet ran throughout the hall, and the walls were covered in a bright yellow wallpaper, spotted with peacock feathers.

Millicent led her through to the sitting room, where she left her for a moment while she organised some tea. It was a crowded room, claustrophobic despite its size, with dark wooden panelling on the walls, a looming empty fireplace, and an ancient CRT television set in the corner. The leather armchairs were cracked and worn, but cosy, and there were numerous little tables dotted about the place, each of them cluttered with porcelain figurines, mismatched lamps, photographs in silver frames, sewing baskets and coasters. Boxes were stacked by the television, and a heap of old magazines had recently slumped into a glossy landslide by the window. It smelled of camphor and lavender. A large gilt-framed mirror hung above the mantel.

After a few minutes, Mrs Brown ambled through to join her, shakily carrying a tray. Elspeth jumped up to help her, taking the tray while Mrs Brown fetched out one of the tables for her to rest it upon. Then, with a satisfied sigh, she dropped into the armchair opposite Elspeth's and propped her feet up on a little round footstool.

She was in her eighties, and obviously lived alone. She walked with a slight stoop, and her skin was pale and paper thin, stained and creased with the passing of time. Her hair was wiry and a little wild, and Elspeth didn't suppose she'd bothered to brush it that morning. She was wearing a flower-print dress and a green woollen cardigan, and she smiled at Elspeth expectantly. "So, Patricia's dead, then. I heard talk on the television that it was murder."

Elspeth was a little taken aback by the directness of the question. "Well, that's what the police think, although they haven't yet been able to rule out suicide."

Mrs Brown leaned forward in her chair, turning her head and presenting her ear, as if she hadn't heard correctly. "Suicide?"

"That's right," said Elspeth. "That's why I'm here. I'm trying to get to the bottom of why she did it. There was no note, you see."

Mrs Brown shook her head in apparent disbelief. "She always was a selfish cow, that one. Never thought about anyone but herself."

"That seems an odd thing to say about a foster carer, someone who took other people's children into her home."

"Ah, well, that's presupposing she had any desire to help them, see? I was under no illusion, though. For her, it was never about the kids. It was because she couldn't have children of her own. It was her way of getting what she wanted. There was nothing altruistic about it."

"Was she a good foster parent?"

Mrs Brown laughed. "Well, she lost one of them, so what do you think?"

"But you still let her take in more kids?"

"Times were different then, love. People didn't want to know about foster children. They'd have rather pretended they didn't exist. Most of the kids were in orphanages or care homes. It wasn't a good life. Patricia Graves, for all her faults, offered them something better than that."

Elspeth set about pouring the tea. "What do you think happened to Thomas Stone?"

Mrs Brown shrugged. "God knows, poor boy. I suspect he's dead, if I'm honest. I've thought that for a long time. Life on the street for kids that age is no life at all. Kids need a guiding hand, a place to call home. And if someone picked him up, well... I hate to think what happened to him after he ran away."

"And what about George Baker, the other boy who lived with the Graves at the time?"

"He was a quiet one," said Mrs Brown. "At least after Thomas went."

"What do you mean?" said Elspeth. She sipped at her tea. It was lukewarm, but she drank it out of politeness.

"He idolised Thomas. They'd been in a children's home together before they moved in with the Graves, and they were as thick as thieves. Little blighters, they were, always causing mischief together. They gave us all the runaround, to be honest. It's not surprising that James Graves used to bark at them all the time, or give them a good clip round the ear now and then." She took a long draught from her teacup. "After Thomas ran away, though, George was never the same. He retreated into himself, wouldn't come out of his shell or socialise with other kids."

"That's not unusual, though, is it? For a boy from a disturbed home who'd lost his friend? Surely it was just his way of coping?"

"Well, the Graves didn't know what to do with him, really. That was the problem. Things got a bit tense, and came to a head one day when Patricia came home and found him dissecting a dead bird on the kitchen table."

"A dead bird?" said Elspeth.

"Turns out he'd been bunking off school, shooting them down with his catapult and then opening them up with the kitchen knives. When James came home there was hell on earth, as you can imagine, and that's when I got the call. They'd had enough. Couldn't deal with it anymore. They shipped poor George back to the care home, and dusted their hands of him."

"Poor child," said Elspeth. The image of the boy with the dead birds seemed to stick in her mind. "Had they always been like that with him?"

"Not always, no. I think at first Patricia wanted him to be her son. That's the mistake she made, you see. She thought it would be easy – bring them in, mother them. But these boys weren't ready for a new mother. They'd been bounced around through social services for years, and they'd grown calloused and hard. What they needed was stability, discipline. What they got was Patricia Graves insisting they call her 'Mother', and James, who'd never really wanted them in the first place. No wonder they were confused."

"I read the police file, and all the transcripts of the interviews that took place after Thomas disappeared. George changed his story. At first he said that Thomas had had a run-in with James. But later he went on record to say that he'd lied."

"Like I said, he was a bit of a strange child, but I'd be surprised if there wasn't half a truth in there, somewhere. James was a hard man, and he was always berating those boys. Not that they didn't deserve it, mind."

Elspeth could hardly believe the matter-of-fact way in which the old lady was reporting all of this; the nonchalance in the face of what could have amounted to child abuse. She supposed the world really had been a very different place in the late seventies, with a very different view of child protection. "What happened to George?" she said.

"Well, that's the one bit of good to come out of all this," said Mrs Brown. "George was sent off to an institution, and whatever they did to him there, they worked miracles. He came out of that place a new child. He changed his name, flourished at his new school, and earned himself a scholarship. I seem to remember hearing he'd gone on to become some sort of posh professor at the university."

Elspeth felt her pulse quicken. The reference to dead birds had been enough to set her mind racing, but now *this*. "You don't happen to know what that new name was, do you?"

Mrs Brown shook her head. "No, sorry, love. There were so many other kids. But you might ask Rebecca. She might know. I think she still lives around these parts."

"Rebecca?"

"Rebecca Wood. One of the neighbourhood kids at the time. They were good friends for a while. They used to play out in the woods together, running about, making up stories. After Thomas went, though, she wouldn't have much to do with George. I think it got to her a bit, too, like it got to all of us. She was too young to understand, of course, but George seemed to take it pretty hard. In the end he lost the only two friends he had in the world. No wonder the poor boy cracked."

Rebecca... It seemed like too much of a coincidence. "Did she marry?"

"I have no idea. I expect so. She was always a pretty little thing."

That had to be it. The girl, Rebecca Wood, was Rebecca Williams. The woman she'd seen in her gym the previous night with her skull caved in.

And George Baker, the foster child who had lost everything... he was Byron Miller. That explained the flowers, the wreath with the strange quotation.

"Excuse me for a moment," she said, placing her teacup and saucer gently back on the tray. "But I don't suppose I could use your loo?"

"Of course, love. Down the hall, through the kitchen, first door on the left. You'll forgive me for not showing you the way. My old hips, you see?"

Elspeth nodded, and grabbed her handbag. She hurried down to the bathroom and sat on the edge of the bath. She grabbed her phone from her bag, and thumbed through until she found the photograph of the card.

She peered at it for a moment, committing the words to memory: 'THOSE THAT KNOW THE MOST MUST MOURN THE DEEPEST. GEORGE'

Then, her fingers trembling, she typed the quotation into the search engine on her web browser. The hit came back almost immediately. It was a partial line from *Manfred*, a poem by Lord George Gordon Byron.

Byron.

When this was done, he would call for The Fool, and lead him on towards the final sacrifice in the Wychwood. Then the Carrion King's legacy would be complete. The five sacrifices would all have been made, and the last three tethers to his miserable past would be gone – all in the manner in which the story dictated.

Soon, he would traverse the underworld, imbued

with the power he had sought since those very first days with the pigeons and the ravens and the crows. And he would find Thomas's soul, and breathe fresh life into him, and undo what had once been done.

He saw the woman, standing over her tea tray, and he willed her to glance in the mirror, to fix her hair like she so often did, to let her vanity be her undoing.

She turned, and her eyes flitted across the surface of the silvered glass. He seized his chance, and locked them there. For a moment she stood, unmoving, agitation growing upon her face. Then, like a puppet master trying out a new toy, he shifted his arm, and the woman in the mirror traced his movements, dropping her teacup to the floor.

With a smile, he forced her to reach over to the little lace-covered table by her armchair. Her fingers closed around the letter opener.

Elspeth felt as if she wanted to throw up. She splashed some cool water on her face, trying to decide what to do.

Byron Miller was the Carrion King murderer. He *had* to be.

Even now, she could imagine his grinning face, sitting in The Reading Stop, calmly reciting his stories.

But how the hell did she even begin to explain it? There was nothing but circumstantial evidence to link him to the deaths of Patricia Graves and Rebecca Williams. The forensic reports had shown nothing. Nor was there any evidence he had been at the scenes of the apostle murders, apart from Rose's, but hundreds of other people had been there too. Yet it all seemed to add up. Just like the Carrion King in the story, the people who were supposed to care for George Baker had turned their backs on him as a boy, made him a pariah. He'd gone on to reinvent himself, to gather knowledge of the mythical and arcane, taking the Carrion King as his role model. And then, just like the character in his stories, he set about murdering people he identified with the apostles, and also meting out revenge upon those who, in his eyes, had wronged him – Patricia Graves and Rebecca Williams.

She had a sudden dawning sense of horror. The Carrion King had sought vengeance upon the ealdorman through the use of a mirror – by taking control of his reflection. Just like she'd seen in the play. Was that how Miller had killed Patricia Graves? Is that how he'd caused her to stab herself to death in front of her bedroom mirror? She could hardly believe she was even entertaining the notion, but it seemed to make a horrible kind of sense: the lack of forensic evidence, the fact the pathologist had said the wounds looked self-inflicted, the bloody handprint on the mirror. And Rebecca Williams, too – she'd been lying in front of the mirrored wall in her gym.

But how could it be real? It was ritual magic. Ancient, pagan *magic*. It couldn't really work, could it?

She had to take it all to Peter. She had to make him see what was going on. He'd probably think she was mad, but there was no other choice.

Elspeth dried her face and hands and collected her things, then hurried back to the sitting room. "I'm afraid

I have to go now, Mrs Brown," she called, popping her head around the door. "Thank you for your time. You've been incr—" She stopped abruptly.

Mrs Brown was standing in the middle of the room, staring into the mirror over the mantelpiece, a silver letter opener held to her own throat.

"Mrs Brown?"

She had her back to Elspeth, but Elspeth could see her expression in the mirror, grinning and malevolent. Her teacup was on the floor by her feet, broken where she'd dropped it.

"Mrs Brown?" she said again, cautiously edging into the room. "What's going on?"

She didn't reply, but turned her head so that her reflection could meet her gaze. She looked sinister, unhinged, not at all like the woman she'd met just a short while before. Elspeth felt the hairs on the nape of her neck prickle in fear. What was she doing?

"Mrs Brown, I think you should put the letter opener down, now."

Elspeth continued to edge into the room, slowly circling around to the side of the woman, ready to rush in and tackle her if she made a sudden lunge with the letter opener. It was shaped like a tiny sword, and the blade was making a depression in the soft flesh of her throat, just on the point of breaking the skin.

"You're scaring me now, Mrs Brown. What's all this about?" She could hear the tremor in her voice. "Is this about George Baker and Thomas Stone? What's going on?"

Elspeth had come around the side of Mrs Brown now, and she could see the sweat beading on her brow.

She looked panic-stricken, and she was clenching her jaw, the muscles working back and forth, as if it were taking a supreme effort just to stop her arm from plunging the letter opener into her throat. It looked almost as if the arm had a terrible will of its own, and she was fighting it with every ounce of her being.

Her hand was trembling, but otherwise she was perfectly still, locked in a strange, ungainly position.

Elspeth glanced at the mirror again, and the reflection grinned back at her, malign and self-satisfied. She knew then what had happened. She couldn't explain it, couldn't even begin to understand it, but somehow, Byron Miller was exerting a kind of malign influence over Mrs Brown. This was how he'd brought about the deaths of Patricia Graves and Rebecca Williams. Like the Carrion King before him, he had seized control of their reflections, and had used them to commit murder. It was just like the myths, like the ealdorman in the play. And now he was doing it again.

Elspeth wasn't about to let Mrs Brown succumb to the same fate.

Slowly, out of sight of the reflection, she reached down and slipped off her shoe, grateful, for once, that she'd decided to wear heels that morning for the funeral. She clutched the shoe in her hand so that the metal-tipped heel was pointing down, and then kicked her other shoe off so that she wouldn't stumble. Then, careful not to make any sudden movements, she inched closer to the fireplace.

She tried not to think about what might happen if her plan didn't work. She glanced at Mrs Brown. The strain was evident on her face. She couldn't hold out for much longer. It was now or never.

Elspeth took a deep breath, and then brought up her arm, leaping at the mirror and bringing the heel down as hard as she could against the glass.

The mirror erupted around the site of the impact, a spider's web of fracture lines moving out like a wave as the glass splintered into tumbling shards, raining down upon the mantelpiece, jabbing at her bare feet.

She fell back, dropping the shoe, turning to see Mrs Brown had collapsed to her knees, the letter opener lying on the polished floorboards before her amongst the shimmering fragments of glass.

Elspeth rushed to her side, dropping to her knees beside her and grabbing her by the shoulders. Slowly, the woman turned to regard her with confused, watery eyes. "What? What's happening to me?"

"Don't worry, Mrs Brown," said Elspeth, tears pricking her eyes. "I'll send for an ambulance right away."

He glowered in rage at the mirror upon the stump, which now reflected back nothing but the surrounding trees and his own fearsome visage. He resisted the urge to destroy it.

The girl had ruined *everything*.

He got to his feet, kicking angrily at the dirt, destroying the circle he had so painstakingly drawn in the soil.

If the old woman lived, his passage to the underworld could not be completed. He paced back and forth, opening and closing his fists, working his jaw.

No. He could still have his way. If he killed The Fool now, then he would just have to lie in wait for his next opportunity. Millicent would pass another mirror soon enough, and he would be waiting. He'd find another chance. He was so close.

For now, though, he had other work to do. He finished clearing away the evidence of his ritual, and quit the woods.

The Fool was waiting.

CHAPTER THIRTY-FOUR

"Come on, come *on*!"

The trilling ceased for the umpteenth time, and clicked over to voicemail. Elspeth stabbed at her phone and cut off the recorded message of a woman, brightly telling her, "The person you are calling is unavailable. Please leave a message after the tone."

She ground her teeth. She'd been calling Peter relentlessly, but his mobile was ringing out.

The ambulance and police were already here, and Elspeth had calmly explained to them what had happened – that she'd come back from the loo to find Millicent holding a letter opener to her own throat in the mirror. She explained that the woman had seemed transfixed by her own reflection, and that the only way to shake her out of it had been to smash the mirror.

The female police constable had eyed her strangely and written everything down, but it was clear from Mrs Brown's behaviour that something wasn't right. The experience had befuddled her, and she was having difficulty coming to terms with what had happened. To be fair, so was Elspeth.

The ambulance crew had checked Mrs Brown over, and concluded that she needed to be taken in for assessment. Elspeth was free to go – but all she wanted to do was speak to Peter, to tell him what had happened and explain everything she'd learned from Mrs Brown.

She'd been replaying their meetings with Miller in her mind's eye. The smug fool had laid it all out for them, and they hadn't even seen it. He'd told them everything – his entire plan – dressed in a mantle of ancient mythology. Worse, she knew it wasn't over. Miller had been clear – the Carrion King couldn't meet his full potential until all of his apostles had been sacrificed and all those who had wronged him had seen his vengeance wrought upon them.

She'd saved Mrs Brown – for now – meaning he'd already failed at the latter task, but it was possible he'd try again. It didn't seem in his nature to give up.

Additionally, that left The Fool, the final apostle. Whomever he had chosen to represent the Carrion King's final sacrifice still had to die for Miller's story to be over.

Her phone buzzed, and her eyes flicked to the screen. It was Peter. She jabbed at the button.

"Ellie? Sorry, I've been in with DCI Griffiths, going over everything from last night." He paused, and she could imagine him frowning. "Are you okay?"

She took a deep breath. "Peter, I'm at Millicent Brown's house in Chipping Norton. She's just tried to kill herself—"

"God – I'll get someone there straight away. Is she okay?"

"No, no. The police are already here, along with the ambulance. It's all over, and she's okay. But, Peter…"

"What is it?"

"She did it in front of a mirror. It was... it was like she was transfixed, and couldn't stop herself. Just like in the stories, like that scene in the play. I had to smash the mirror to stop her..." she broke off, fighting back a sob.

"Oh, Ellie. Look, I'll come and meet you. I can be there in fifteen, twenty minutes."

"There's more, Peter. Patricia Graves, Rose, Michael Williams, it's all linked. It's Byron Miller. He's the one behind the Carrion King murders, and the other deaths."

"*Byron Miller?* Ellie, where's all this coming from?"

"Look, get here quickly. I can explain. Byron Miller isn't who we think he is. He's George Baker, the Graves' sother foster son. He's orchestrated all of it."

"Alright, give me the address and I'll be there as soon as I can."

Peter's expression was unreadable as he sat in silence in the driver's seat of his car, listening to her outline her story. She told him about everything she'd learned from Millicent Brown, showing him the picture she'd taken of the card at the funeral and the results of her brief Internet searches.

She walked him through the relationship between George Baker and Rebecca Wood, the story about the dead birds, how Mrs Brown had explained that George had gained a scholarship to Oxford and gone on to change his name.

Finally, she explained how she thought Miller had affected the murders of Patricia Graves and Rebecca

Williams, and attempted to murder Millicent Brown. It seemed ridiculous to say it aloud – that he'd used some bizarre occult practice to temporarily bind those people to his will – but how could she deny it after what had happened inside?

She could tell Peter was uncomfortable with the idea, battling with the logic of it. He'd never been a man of faith, but now, faced with her story, he seemed lost, unable to fathom how to respond.

"Look, Ellie, what you've uncovered about Byron Miller – it's good detective work. You've found a link between the victims that we weren't aware of. But pagan rituals...?"

"I know what I saw, Peter. And you've got to admit, it makes sense. It fits the story of the Carrion King. And it explains why there was no DNA evidence at Patricia Graves's murder scene."

"Yes, but we haven't got forensics back from the Williams's house yet. We don't know exactly what happened there. And Millicent Brown... you've only just met her. We haven't looked into her medical history. She might have tried to do this before."

"I'm not imagining it. I know how it sounds."

"Look, don't take this the wrong way, Ellie, but you've been through so much recently. The breakup, the job, finding Patricia Graves, Rose... it's been a lot to process. And now all this with Millicent Brown."

"Peter – I'm not imagining this. Look, forget about the mirror stuff for a minute. Just assume I'm right about Miller. It's clear he's connected to Patricia Graves and Rebecca Williams, and might have a motive for their deaths. If nothing else, that should be enough to bring him in for questioning, shouldn't it? And if he did kill Rebecca Williams, what are the chances he's not connected to the death of Michael Williams, which happened on the same day, at the same location?" She paused, trying to judge his reaction. "We have to stop him before he kills someone else. There's still The Fool."

"Okay, let's work it through. So far the deaths of the apostles haven't been related to what happened to Miller – or Baker – when he was a boy. If your theory is right, Patricia Graves and Rebecca Williams were killed by some other means, out of a desire for revenge. That would match the Carrion King story. The apostles are different. They're people he's encountered more recently, and he's chosen them because of the role they play in his twisted story."

"Keep going," said Elspeth.

"Right. So we can assume he picked Rose as The Confessor because she was an agony aunt who knew other people's secrets. Geoffrey Altman was a local gamekeeper who'd helped Michael Williams with his research, so he fit the bill for The Master of the Hunt. Miller knew Lucy Adams through the theatre, and if he'd been keeping tabs on her and Michael Williams, he might well have known about the affair. Oscar Waring certainly had his suspicions, so they couldn't have been hiding it that well. So, she could have been seen as a 'fallen' woman, going behind her husband's back with another man. And then there's Michael Williams himself, who was killed in the manner of The Master of the Pentacle because of his knowledge of the Carrion King myths. That all fits, it's what we've already assumed, but there's no evidence to connect it to Miller."

"Not directly, I know. But if you connect it to the deaths of Patricia Graves and Rebecca Williams, it starts to build a picture that mirrors the story of the Carrion King."

"Okay, let's work it through to the end," said Peter. "Who else is there? Who might Byron Miller know that fits the bill for the final apostle?"

"Someone who'd walk ignorantly into a trap, blinded by their own ego and their attitude towards Miller and his knowledge of the Carrion King myths."

"As far as I can see it, there are three candidates. Oscar Waring, David Keel and Philip Cowper."

"Right. And even if I'm wrong about the identity of the killer, those are the most likely three candidates, aren't they? They're all connected to the Carrion King, they all have a passion for the story, and they all know and respect Byron Miller... When we met Miller in Oxford he called Cowper a 'fool'."

Peter nodded. "Alright. I'll call Griffiths. I'm going to get a call put out on Miller, see if they can bring him in."

"What are you going to tell her?"

"I'll tell her what you've found out about Miller's past and his connection to Patricia Graves and Rebecca Williams. I'm going to get cars sent out to the homes of Oscar Waring, David Keel and Philip Cowper. You're right. They're the most obvious candidates to be The Fool, and it's time we took some preventative measures. Whatever's going on here, the killer is not sitting idle, and if it is Miller and he learns we're onto him, he might attempt to escalate things, too."

He thumbed the screen and held the phone to his ear.

A short while later they abandoned the car in the small car park just off the marketplace in Heighton, not even bothering to stop for a ticket.

Late afternoon was sliding anxiously into evening, and the shops had all shut half an hour earlier, leaving the high street deserted, save for a handful of shop workers still closing up, or waiting for a bus home at the crowded stop outside The Old Dun Cow. Even Lenny's had closed for the day, although the lights were still on out back, where Elspeth supposed the kitchen staff were making preparations for tomorrow's early-morning breakfast rush. It smelled like it was going to rain again; she could feel it closing in, the weight of the coming downpour heavy in the air.

Peter had managed to get hold of Griffiths on her mobile, and had explained that new evidence had come to light suggesting Byron Miller might have played a part in the murders of Patricia Graves and Rebecca Williams, that they needed to bring him straight in, and that he was to be considered dangerous.

She'd questioned him at first, but Peter had patiently explained that it looked like Miller had been a childhood friend of Rebecca Williams and a foster child under the care of a potentially abusive Patricia and James Graves, and that there was a possibility that he could also be connected to the ritual killings in the Wychwood, in that if he was involved in the aforementioned deaths, he might be attempting to recreate the entire Carrion King story.

That seemed to be enough for Griffiths to agree to pull Miller in for questioning, and she'd put a call out to Oxford CID. Peter had also told her about Cowper, Waring and Keel, and she'd despatched cars to their home addresses, with a view to offering some protection until the killer was properly identified and restrained.

Now, Peter and Elspeth were on their way to Cowper's bookshop – their nearest port of call – in the hope of heading him off there if he wasn't already at home. Elspeth only hoped it would be enough; that one way or another they'd get to Miller before anyone else got hurt.

They raced through Clark's Yard and out onto Westgate. Like the high street, it was more or less deserted here, the only signs of activity coming from a lively tapas bar across the street. The light was beginning to fade beneath the brooding clouds, and as they hurried down to Westgate Books.

The shop was closed, the lights off and the sign turned around in the window.

"We're too late. He's gone for the night," huffed Elspeth, catching her breath.

"Hang on," said Peter. He tried the door, but it was locked. The bell jingled lightly as it rattled in its frame. It was dark inside, and all she could make out were the reflections of the other shop fronts in the glass. She felt spots of rain on her forearm. He knocked on the door. "Mr Cowper?"

Silence. He cupped his hands to the window and peered in.

"Alright," he said. "It doesn't look like he's here."

"Should we try the pub, or that restaurant he mentioned, Nightingale's?"

Peter shook his head. "Let's head back to the car. Uniform might have found him at home."

They hurried back to the car park. She'd left her Mini in Chipping Norton, on the promise that Peter would run her back there later to collect it. He blipped the lock and she ducked inside his car to avoid more spots of rain. He clambered in beside her and thumbed the radio.

"DC Cooper?"

"Yes, sir?"

"It's DS Shaw. Any word from the cars we sent out?"

"Yes, sir. Oscar Waring and Philip Cowper are both secure in their homes. DC Patel is with Cowper now, explaining the situation."

"And Keel?"

"No news yet, sir."

"Alright, I'm heading over there." He dropped the receiver and started the engine, and they roared out of the car park, turning off towards Wilsby-under-Wychwood, and home.

CHAPTER THIRTY-FIVE

David Keel flicked listlessly through endless scores of television channels, and then, feeling restless and unable to settle, tossed the remote on the sofa, prised himself out of his armchair and set about fixing himself a drink.

He'd left the TV tuned to some documentary about the fall of Constantinople, in which he supposed he might have been vaguely interested, if he hadn't been so preoccupied.

The play was ruined. All of his work these last six months had been for nothing. Of course, he felt terrible for the girl and her family – what had happened had been appalling – but he couldn't help but smart at his own misfortune. Why had it had to happen on opening night? The play hadn't even been over, the second half barely begun. He supposed he was unlikely now to ever see it performed in full; there was no way the Winthorpe lot would be persuaded to carry on, and he couldn't see any other local theatres touching it with a bargepole.

He glugged a large measure of brandy into a tumbler then took a swig, shuddering as the alcohol hit his palate. The play would become infamous, forever associated with the murders. It would colour everything, even his subsequent work. That stupid girl who'd been sniffing around all week had already posted a piece on the *Heighton Observer* website that was generating thousands of hits, and half the country's news channels seemed to be running the story on a loop.

The police statement had been brief, giving away only that the murder appeared to be linked to those of Geoff Altman and Lucy Adams, but that was bad enough. There'd been so many people there that the story had leaked almost immediately, giving details about the body, how she'd been posed like one of the characters in the play. As if it were somehow *his* fault.

He drained the rest of his glass, and then poured himself another.

There was a rap at the door. He ignored it, knocking back another slug of brandy. Knowing his luck, it would probably be one of those bloody reporters, wanting to get his side of the story. Well, he wasn't going to give them the satisfaction.

A moment later they rapped again. This time, though, when he didn't answer, they pushed open the letterbox, shouting through. "David? Are you there?"

Keel frowned. He recognised the voice immediately. What was *he* doing here?

He placed his glass on the cabinet and hurried into the hall to the front door. "Yes, coming," he called. He heard the letterbox snap shut as he slid the chain off the lock and opened the door. "Byron. This is unexpected." He stood to one side, beckoning the other man in. "Come in, come in."

Miller stepped over the threshold, a thin smile on his lips. "I hope it's not a bad time," he said.

"No, no, not at all," said Keel. "In fact, I was just fixing myself a brandy. Can I tempt you?"

"Why not?" said Miller. "One won't hurt." He was wearing a long grey overcoat, which he slipped off, hanging it across the banister where Keel's own was draped. Beneath, he was dressed in a smart black suit, although there was mud up the front of his trouser legs and knees.

"Everything alright?" said Keel, indicating the stains.

"Oh, yes." Miller laughed. "Puncture on the way over. Had to put the spare on by the side of the road."

"Sorry to hear that," said Keel. "Well, come on through. And forgive the mess. I wasn't expecting any visitors."

"I just thought I'd look in to see how you are," said Miller, following him through to the living room. He seemed to be taking a keen interest in the serried ranks of books that lined the walls, scanning the spines as he walked. "You know, after everything that happened at the theatre."

"Oh, don't," said Keel, fetching a second glass from the cabinet. "What an appalling mess."

Miller nodded, loitering in the doorway. "Not the sort of attention you were after, I imagine. It's a shame. It's a story that deserves to be told. The journey of the Carrion King towards transcendence, the betrayals and the settling of scores, the rituals and magic, the vengeance... I've always thought it deserved wider recognition, and your script was really quite admirable."

"Thanks," said Keel. Coming from Miller, that was

high praise indeed – as much good as it would do him now.

"So what'll you do?"

"Write something else, I suppose. Let the noise die down a bit – if you'll excuse the expression." He laughed, suddenly self-conscious. "To be honest with you, I wish I'd never got started with the whole ruddy Carrion King business." He crossed the room and handed Miller his drink. "No offence. I mean, it's fascinating and all, but look where it's landed me."

"You couldn't have known you'd get caught up in all this. I suppose you were just in the wrong place at the wrong time. You should remember that. These things are rarely personal."

"Story of my life," said Keel. "What does it take to be in the right place at the right time?" He downed the rest of his drink, and then eyed the bottle. There was no point in stopping now. And besides, he had company, which gave him an excuse. He poured another.

Miller sipped at his drink. "Do you mind if I smoke?"

"We'll have to step outside, I'm afraid. It'll set off my asthma otherwise. Hope you don't mind."

"Not at all. Through there?" Miller indicated the door back to the hall.

"Yeah, there's some patio doors off the kitchen. Hang on, I'll open them up for you." Miller followed him back out into the hall, through the study, and into the expansive kitchen. Keel crossed the room and turned the key in the lock. He opened the door, shocked by the sudden chill coming in off the garden. It was beginning to spot with rain. He stepped out onto the patio, and

Miller came out behind him, pulling the door to. He searched out his packet of cigarettes and lit one.

"I didn't realise you lived so close to the woods," said Miller, strolling to the bottom of the garden. "It must be nice, having them so close."

Keel shrugged, following. "To be honest, these days I tend to wonder what's lurking out there in the shadows. I mean, it's pretty, and nice to take a walk in the springtime, but with everything that's been going on…" He walked across the lawn to the low wall at the bottom of the garden, skirting the rockery. "They found Lucy Adams somewhere over there."

"Yes, I know," said Miller.

Keel took another swig of brandy. He was starting to appreciate its calming influence already, the warm feeling spreading through his chest, suggestive of the cosy numbness that would follow. He'd sleep well tonight, at least, even if he risked a headache in the morning. "Well, I've got to say, I appreciate you coming ov—" He stopped suddenly, mid turn, as a large rock, wielded in the fist of Byron Miller, collided with the side of his head.

Dazed, confused, his head pounding, he dropped to the ground. Blood was trickling down the side of his head. "Wh… wh…" He tried to look up, to ask Miller what had happened.

But then there was a second blow, and everything went black.

CHAPTER THIRTY-SIX

Keel's house, it transpired, really was only a few doors down from her mum's.

A police car was waiting for them when they pulled up on the roadside, and two uniformed officers – a tall man with a shaved head and portly belly, and a woman with blonde hair scraped back into a tight ponytail – approached Peter almost as soon as he set foot out of the car.

"Catton. Grant. Is he inside?" said Peter.

The man shook his head. "No, sir. We can't get a response. The TV is on in the living room, and his car is on the drive, but he's not responding. We've been around the back via the neighbour's garden and can see the patio doors are open."

Peter ran a hand through his hair. "And that red car on the drive, who does that belong to?"

Catton shrugged. "I'm not sure, sir."

"Well get on the bloody radio and run the number plate, then!" said Peter.

"Yes, sir." He huffed away back to his car.

"Stay here," said Peter. "Or better still, go home. I

can see to this. I have backup."

Elspeth glowered at him. "You think I'm backing out of this now?" She looked round to see PC Grant eyeing her with interest. No doubt all of this would end up in a report. Well, good. At least it would show Peter had tried to do the right thing.

"I'm going to try the front door again," he said, heading off up the path. Elspeth followed behind.

Peter peered in through the front window. The curtains hadn't been drawn, and Elspeth could see the reflection of the TV playing in the glass.

"Anything?"

"No. Nothing. No sign of him." He tried the front door, but it was a Yale lock and wouldn't open. He knocked loudly, three times. "Mr Keel? It's the police, Mr Keel. If you can hear me, open up."

He paused, but there was no response. After a minute, Peter peered through the window again. He turned to Elspeth, and shrugged.

Elspeth heard a car door slam, and looked round to see Catton had joined Grant at the other end of the garden path. Peter hurried over.

"Well?"

"It's registered to a Professor Byron Miller," said Catton. "There's a general call out for him."

"I *know*," said Peter. "I gave the ruddy order. Get on and call for backup, *now*!"

Catton nodded meekly and reached for his radio.

Peter strode back up the driveway. "Is there any other way to get round?"

"Not unless you go through one of the other gardens

and go round through the woods," said Elspeth.

"We haven't got time for that," said Peter. He took a deep breath, flexed his neck, and then charged at the door, throwing all of his weight behind his shoulder. The lock burst with a tremendous splinter, and the door swung open violently, crashing against the wall inside with an echoing bang. Peter was inside before Elspeth or the others had even had chance to take stock. They all hurried after him.

Elspeth found him standing in the living room, just off the main hall. It was unnerving how much the house resembled Dorothy's, but dressed in an entirely different way. The living-room walls were lined with reams of overstuffed bookshelves, a small desk, and a sideboard, along with only two comfy-looking armchairs. There was a half-drunk bottle of brandy on the sideboard, along with the scattered pages of Keel's play script.

Peter wandered back out into the hall. "Mr Keel?"

He turned to Grant. "Check upstairs."

"Yes, sir," said Grant, and hurried up to search the bedrooms. Peter walked through to the study, and then on to the kitchen, where the patio doors were hanging open, their hinges creaking noisily in the breeze. The lights were off. There was something ominous about the scene, about the way in which it looked as if Keel had just upped and left through those patio doors, heading out into the garden, drawn towards the darkness of the beckoning Wychwood beyond.

"Nothing upstairs, sir," came a voice from the hallway, startling Elspeth. Grant came hurrying in to join them.

"Alright, thanks, Grant," said Peter. He crossed to the doors. A security light blinked on when it sensed his movement. "Hang on, what's that?" He stepped out onto the patio, and crossed to the bottom of the garden, stooping low and using the end of his pen to poke at an object he'd seen lying on the grass.

Elspeth stepped out behind him, bracing herself against the cold. "What is it?"

Peter looked round, as if remembering she was there. "A broken brandy glass," he said, "and a rock that looks like it's stained with blood."

"Oh, God, we're too late."

"Not necessarily." He turned towards the trees. "They might still be out there, amongst the trees."

She heard a noise and turned to see Catton standing on the patio behind her. "Backup's on the way, sir."

"Good. But we don't have time to wait for that. If we're going to stop him, we have to act now. We're going to take our torches and spread out in a line."

"In *there*?" said Catton, bristling. He was pointing at the Wychwood.

"Yes, in there," said Peter. "We're trying to stop a murder here, Catton."

"Yes, sir."

Peter turned to Elspeth. "You're going home. Right now. No argument. I'll not put a civilian in jeopardy. Especially you."

"But surely more hands…"

"No." He was absolutely emphatic. "Go now. Please, Elspeth."

She took a deep breath. She wanted to tell him to

stop being ridiculous, to stop underestimating her – but she knew he was just looking out for her. And he was doing what he had to do as a policeman, too. "Okay," she said. "Alright." She backed away. "I'm going. But you *promise* me you'll be careful."

"Scout's honour," said Peter.

"You were never in the Scouts," she countered.

"Policeman's honour, then." He grinned. "Grant, see her home. She only lives a few doors down the road. Then straight back here."

Elspeth hurried back through the house, out through the broken front door, and along the road to Dorothy's house. Grant jogged along beside her, and then stood at the bottom of her garden path until she'd watched her go inside.

Elspeth closed the door and fell back against it, taking deep, stuttering breaths. Could she really let this go on without her? After everything that had happened?

"Oh, hello, Ellie love." Dorothy came out from the kitchen holding a wooden spoon. "Everything alright?"

"Yeah, fine, Mum," she said.

"Only, I saw there was a police car a few doors down, outside of David Keel's house."

"Yeah. Routine enquiries, I think," said Elspeth.

Dorothy nodded, and turned to head back to the kitchen.

"Mum, have you got a torch?"

"Of course. In the kitchen cupboard with the screwdrivers. Why?"

"Is it okay if I borrow it?"

"Elspeth – what's going on?"

"I'll tell you later, Mum. I won't be long." She kicked off her heels and ran through to the kitchen, digging in the cupboard until she found the torch. It was large and weighty, but it blinked on when she pushed the button. She found her boots on the mat by the back door, hurriedly shoved her feet into them, and then opened the patio doors.

"I don't like the look of this, Elspeth," said Dorothy from behind her.

She turned and smiled. "Don't worry, Mum. I know what I'm doing."

She only hoped that was true.

CHAPTER THIRTY-SEVEN

Elspeth swung her legs over the wall, dropping down into the mulch below. It was still trying to rain. Her breath was fogging before her face, and the Wychwood smelled damp and fresh around her.

A few doors down, she could see three torch beams, flickering eerily amongst the trees, stabbing out into the darkness. She switched her own torch on, and set out towards them, using the beam to scan the undergrowth so she could see where she was treading.

Out here, everything seemed heightened – the crunch of her boots, the rustle of the breeze through the leaves, the distant cawing of a crow. The darkness, too, seemed absolute, impenetrable, as if the feeble beam of her torch would never be enough to penetrate it. It was as if the Wychwood itself was closing in around her, warning her to stay away.

She knew what she was doing was stupid, but she felt as if she couldn't stop, now – as if she were being inexplicably drawn towards some final moment, to bear witness to whatever the end of this terrible affair might be.

She pressed on, hugging herself as she walked. She

was gaining on the others, now. They'd spread out in a line as Peter had suggested, and were slowly advancing ever deeper into the gloomy Wychwood. She could see Peter up ahead, faintly illuminated by the beam of his own torch. He looked ghostly and unreal, like a spectre drifting through the gnarly boughs of the trees, searching for prey.

She waved her torch in his direction, catching his eye. He twisted suddenly, shining the beam of his torch in her face. She blinked and recoiled, raising her hand as if trying to ward off the piercing light.

He lowered his torch and came crunching over to her, the displeasure evident on his face. "I told you to stay at home!" he hissed.

"No, you said to 'go home'. There's a difference. I did go home. And I got a torch."

"This isn't a game, Elspeth."

"Don't you think I know that?"

He frowned. "Look, we haven't got time to argue now. You're here now. Stay next to me."

He turned and marched off, and she hurried to keep up.

She had no sense of passing time out here. It was almost as if they'd progressed into another realm altogether, where everything had stopped. She imagined the backup would be arriving soon, and then the woods would be flooded with light and the sound of trampling policemen and dogs – but right now, with just the four of them traipsing along in a line, she might have been able to believe that time had somehow stopped.

Up ahead, she caught sight of a glimmer of light

amongst the trees. She tugged on Peter's arm and pointed. He lifted his torch and focused the beam, and the light was suddenly extinguished.

"Over here," he hissed to the others, setting out in the direction of the mysterious light source. "Stick together, and watch your backs."

They crept forward, closing ranks, Elspeth beside Peter at the front, Grant to the left, Catton to the right.

The trees here were thinning, giving way to a natural glade. Peter stopped beside the bough of an immense oak tree, and swung his torch from side to side, searching for any sign of Miller or Keel.

As his beam crossed one of the trees, Elspeth caught a glimpse of a man's pale, staring face, and almost yelped in shock. She raised her own torch, and the spear of light fell first upon the trunk of another tree, and then, as she swung it slowly to the right, upon the dangling body of David Keel.

"Over there," she said, her voice cracking at the sight.

Keel had been suspended from one of the overhead branches by a rope that had been looped around his neck. His eyes were closed, and blood had run freely from his head wound down the side of his face – evidently where he'd been struck by the rock Peter had found in the garden.

His body was still twisting slowly back and forth on the rope, as if he'd only just been suspended. A church candle had been set on the ground nearby – evidently the source of illumination they'd seen earlier.

Elspeth felt sick.

Peter rushed to Keel's side. "He's still breathing.

Catton, quickly, get me something we can use to cut him down. He's unconscious, but there's still time." His fingers scrabbled for the knot.

"Hang on, Peter," said Elspeth. "Something's wrong. If Keel's still alive, then Miller might still *be* here."

"Oh, you're too clever for your own good, Miss Reeves."

The shadows behind Peter stirred as if they were alive, and Elspeth watched in horror as they appeared to detach themselves from the boughs of the nearest tree, slowly resolving into the form and shape of a man. He'd been lurking there all along, this nightmarish apparition, this man draped in a thick black mantle of crow feathers.

He turned toward her and she almost recoiled at the sight of him. He'd daubed his face in stark white stage paint, smearing it on so that, in the low light, his face took on the aspect of a fleshless skull. His cloak of crow feathers was draped across his shoulders, tied around his throat by a thick golden cord. She could see that there were scores of dangling crows' heads nestled amongst the downy feathers, as if he'd stitched the carcasses of whole birds into his gruesome, totemic cloak.

He wore a necklace of bone fetishes – presumably more animal bones, strung on black string – and from his belt hung other bizarre shamanistic tokens: a rabbit's foot, a sprig of holly. He was clutching a sword, and pointed the wavering tip at Peter's midriff. "Get away from him, DS Shaw. It's too late to stop me now."

Peter held his ground, but didn't say anything.

Catton stepped forward into the glade, fixing Miller in the beam of his torch.

Elspeth took a step forward, and Miller reacted by jabbing the sword in Peter's direction, warning her to keep her distance.

"It's over, Byron," said Elspeth. "You must realise that. The police are looking for you. No matter what you do here, you won't get very far."

Miller smiled. "Soon it won't matter. Keel's a fool, but he has to die. For that, I'm truly sorry. He doesn't deserve it, but there's no other option. Believe me, I've spent years trying to find one. This is the only way."

"George," said Elspeth. "Listen to me."

Miller paused. "Don't you dare use that name!"

"I know what happened. I know what they did to you after Thomas went missing. I know why you're so angry."

"Went *missing*?" He practically spat the words. "You know nothing about it. You have no idea what they did. But I'm going to save him. I'm going to bring him back."

"Back from where?"

"From the dead."

Elspeth gaped. She glanced at Peter, but he wasn't taking his eyes off Miller. The tip of the sword was only inches from his gut.

"Thomas is dead?" she said, trying to keep Miller's attention on her.

Miller shook his head. "Not for much longer. There's only Keel, and Millicent Brown, and then no one will be able to stop me from bringing him back."

He was clearly delusional. Had that really been what all of this was about? All those murders? A missing boy from nearly forty years ago?

Peter looked as if he was preparing to make a move.

Elspeth knew she had to keep Miller talking.

"Tell me what happened?"

"They *killed* him," said Miller. "They killed him and hid his body in the Wychwood, Patricia and James. They were the ones who were supposed to protect us, but they took him away from me. They hid him from the world and told everyone he'd run away. They made me lie to the police. They were going to kill me, too."

"Why, George? Why did they kill him?"

Miller looked pained, as if the very act of remembering was like reliving it all over again. "We'd been playing in the woods out the back of the house, just like we always did; me, Thomas, and Becky. We'd come home late, covered in mud. But Patricia and James were having a party that night, and James went apoplectic when he saw that Thomas had traipsed mud up the hall carpet."

She had Miller's attention now, and out of the corner of her eye she saw that Peter had begun to slowly inch away from the sword tip.

"What did he do?" she prompted, hurriedly.

"He forced Thomas to get down on his knees and scrub it. He wouldn't let me help. He said it was Thomas's mess, and he had to clear it up. Thomas was there for over an hour, scrubbing at the carpet with a wire brush until his fingertips bled. But James wouldn't let him stop. He just stood over him and bellowed at him to keep on scrubbing, or else he'd send him back to the care home he'd been dragged up in.

"That was what did it, you see? Thomas turned around and said that he wished James *would* send him back to the care home, that anything would be better than living with *him*, and James just lashed out. He hit Thomas across the side of the head, and Thomas fell. He bashed his temple against the edge of the radiator. There was blood everywhere. I saw everything from the top of the stairs."

"Why didn't they call for an ambulance?"

"Thomas was already dead, and James was terrified he was going to get the blame. So Patricia wrapped him up in a bundle of towels and snuck him out to the Wychwood. They buried him right where we used to play." Miller's voice had risen in pitch as he'd talked, as the fury boiled up inside of him. "Can you imagine that? Can you? They took our special place, and they *desecrated* it."

"And now you're going to bring Thomas back to life?"

"Only the Carrion King can do it, you see? Only the Carrion King can obtain mastery over life and death."

"Is Thomas still out there, in the woods?"

"Beneath the sacred tree," said Miller. "Sleeping until the Carrion King comes to rouse him."

"What about Rebecca?" said Elspeth. "Why did she have to die?"

"She abandoned me!" said Miller.

"She was just a *child*."

"I hated her for leaving me. I had no—" He was cut short as Peter leapt at him, grabbing him around the shoulders and sending them both sprawling heavily to the ground.

"Cuffs, quickly!"

Miller grunted as Peter struck him in the jaw, and the sword tumbled from his hands. Catton rushed forward to grab it, while Grant emerged from the trees behind them, where she'd obviously been creeping round, ready to grab Miller from behind. She stooped low and snapped the cuffs around his wrists while Peter pinned a squirming Miller to the ground.

"Get Keel down!" called Peter. "He might still be alive."

Catton hurried over with the sword, and Elspeth went to help him, taking Keel's weight while Catton used the blade to saw through the rope. Keel slumped forward suddenly, and she staggered under the burden, but then Catton was helping her, and together they lowered him to the ground.

Hurriedly they loosened the noose around his neck and checked his airways. He still had a dull pulse.

"He's still alive," she said. "Barely." In the distance, Elspeth could hear the wail of sirens.

"Finally," said Peter. "Catton, make sure the paramedics find him and get straight to work." He got to his feet, and dragged Miller up behind him. Grant was standing over him, her baton clutched in her fist, ready to step in if he tried anything. It was clear the fight had gone out of him, though. He looked distraught, his eyes flicking about him, tears streaming down his cheeks, white paint running in long streaks down his face. He bowed his head. "What about Thomas?" he mumbled. "I only wanted to see him again."

"Thomas wouldn't have wanted you to become this," said Peter.

He stooped to retrieve his torch, clicked it on, and led Miller away towards the oncoming sirens.

Dazed, emotional, and elated, Elspeth leaned back against a tree and sank to the ground. Finally, it was over.

She hugged her knees to her chest, took a deep breath, and then looked to the sky as the heavens finally opened, and the rain came, pattering down upon her upturned cheeks.

CHAPTER THIRTY-EIGHT

The remnant of the Wychwood close to Patricia Graves's house – known locally as Heighton Woods – was just as Elspeth had imagined it.

Softly decomposing leaves formed a thick carpet that came up around her ankles, and the smell of the damp earth filled her nostrils. She'd always equated that scent with a feeling of wellbeing, and finally, now it was all over, she thought she might be able to reclaim that, to learn to enjoy the woods again.

She walked slowly, avoiding the low hanging branches, the mossy creepers, the fallen logs. Beside her, Peter trudged through the undergrowth like a truffle hound, eager and intent on his target.

They'd followed the instructions that Miller had given in his interviews, parking the car on Windham Road and tracing the meandering public footpath around the back of the terraced houses and up into the Wychwood. She could see why it had appealed to Thomas, Rebecca and George as children; like the woods at the back of her parents' house in Wilsby-under-Wychwood, it reeked of adventure.

She thought back to the days of her own youth, playfully dashing about with Peter and the others, splashing in the stream, scrambling up trees. She wondered what might have happened if they'd faced the same situation as George Baker, how *they* might have behaved. She and Peter were lucky – they'd been happy, and they were happy now. All that stuff with Andrew, with the job in London, everything, really – it paled in comparison to what George Baker had been through, and what he'd done to the people whose lives he'd cut short.

Peter found it hard to understand how she felt pity for the man, but it wasn't about condoning, or even trying to understand what he'd done. It was about recognising the horrors he'd lived through as a young boy, and seeing how those events had shaped him.

It hadn't taken much prompting to get him to open up during questioning, by all accounts, and he'd outlined the whole story in exquisite detail – how Patricia and James Graves had cornered him in his room and threatened him with the same fate as Thomas if he didn't change his story, and the years of psychological torment that followed.

It was no wonder, then, that he had retreated into a fantasy world, basing his stories on some obscure local myths, searching for ways to forget, to be closer to the only real friend he'd ever had.

He'd made regular pilgrimages up here, to their 'sacred tree', visiting Thomas, promising that one day they'd be together again.

The SOCOs had been and gone, and Thomas's bones had been recovered and taken away for reburial. She'd asked Peter to bring her up here all the same, to get a sense of what had happened, what it had all been about. She felt she needed that, after everything she'd seen. She needed an end to her story. One that she could write up, certainly, but more than that – a personal one, too. A moment of closure.

She was still struggling to come to terms with everything – the shift the entire episode had caused in her worldview. She'd seen what Miller had done to Millicent Brown, the way he'd somehow managed to control her, to puppet her, to will her to do herself harm. She'd hoped for the police to find a rational explanation for how he'd done it, but the SOCOs had found no evidence of drugs, or hypnotism, or any other means by which he might have influenced those three victims, except, perhaps, for a book of scrawled rituals, which he claimed to have pieced together from ancient texts. She'd begun to face the realisation that she was going to have to accept it at face value – that Miller *had* used an ancient ritual to carry out those horrific attacks.

Peter had visited his house after the arrest. They'd found all the evidence they'd needed to prosecute him for the ritual murders of Geoffrey Altman, Lucy Adams, Rose Macauley and Michael Williams – the means by which he'd made the costumes, the tools he'd used, receipts for the nails he'd driven through Michael Williams's hands, and the ligature he'd wrapped around Rose's throat to throttle her.

But they'd also found a gilt-framed mirror, and a diary detailing the precise routines of Patricia Graves, Rebecca Williams and Millicent Brown. He'd clearly been stalking them all for some time, watching, waiting for the perfect moment to strike.

He'd freely admitted to all of the murders, but despite pressure from his solicitor and the police, he was still maintaining he'd used the mirror ritual to effect the deaths of Patricia Graves and Rebecca Williams, and was claiming responsibility for the attempted murder of Millicent Brown, despite the fact the police hadn't charged him with it.

The police – Peter had explained – were convinced he had killed Patricia and Rebecca, but maintained that he had done it in person, and had somehow managed to stage it in such a way that he could claim his wild tales of ritual magic were true – an act of exquisite showmanship, executed by a master. He always had seemed theatrical.

Up ahead, the trees had begun to thin around the edges of a natural copse. She pushed her way through spindly branches, emerging into the small glade. Pale sunlight slanted through the overhead branches, dappling the compacted dirt beneath their boots.

The 'sacred tree' was just how Peter had described it. It formed the shape of an upturned palm, the fingers questing for the sky. She imagined the children galumphing about, scrabbling up the branches, digging in the mud. Rebecca, Thomas and George, gleefully misspending their youth, bruising their knees and scraping their elbows as they forged new adventures together.

Together, they silently approached the tree.

The hollow was small, and formed from a gnarly misshapen root. Miller had long ago exhumed the corpse of his childhood friend, and had moved him here, beneath the tree itself, in a hiding place they'd used as children for passing notes, or secreting catapults and other precious childhood treasures.

"This is where they found him?" said Elspeth.

Peter nodded. "Not a bad resting place, really, if you think about it."

"You're right. It's peaceful up here," said Elspeth. She turned on the spot, taking it all in. "What do you *really* think?" she said.

"About what?"

"You know what. About the magic."

"Ellie, I'm a police officer. I'm a rationalist."

She pulled a face. "That's not an answer."

"I know. But look at it this way. The first whisper of 'magic' in the official case and it falls apart. It could never stand up in court."

"I didn't ask about court. Or about your professional opinion. I asked about you." She prodded him in the chest with the tip of her index finger.

He frowned. "I… I don't know. It's not that I don't believe you. I do. I know that's what you think you saw…"

"It's what I *did* see. Believe me, I'm not wild about the idea either. It's terrifying to think that there are people out there that can do things like that. But it was *real*. I know it was. And I'm not going to stop digging until I know more about it."

Peter sighed dramatically. "Ever the journalist."

She laughed. "Thank you."

"What for?"

"For being here. For being a friend. For being one of the good guys."

Peter smiled. "Now you're just talking rubbish," he

said. He put out his hand, and she took it. "Come on. You've got work to do. Those applications aren't going to write themselves."

Elspeth rolled her eyes in mock defeat. "Okay, okay. You're as bad as Mum. Home, then, so I can be chained to my desk."

Peter laughed. "Don't forget – you're the one who started all this."

Elspeth sighed. "I suppose I am, aren't I?"

CHAPTER THIRTY-NINE

Meredith was waiting for her at the bar. When she saw Elspeth coming, she beckoned her over, grinning, and waved at the barman. "Hang on, there's a latecomer. What'll it be?"

"Oh, a gin and tonic, please," said Elspeth, squeezing in beside her.

"Make it a large one," added Meredith. She beamed at Elspeth while the barman clinked ice cubes into a glass. It was busy tonight, and the after-work crowd was still in the process of giving way to the students and more serious night-time drinkers. Elspeth still hadn't decided which camp Meredith belonged to. Probably the latter.

Evidently, The Old Dun Cow was a typical haunt of the gang from the *Heighton Observer*, who had taken up residence in the far corner by the jukebox, dragging three tables together and surrounding them with a mismatched collection of chairs.

Tim was standing at the jukebox now, feeding in twenty-pence coins. It was an old-fashioned affair, filled with vinyl singles from the eighties. The Jam's 'The Eton Rifles' had been playing as she walked in, but now it had rolled over to The Cure's 'The Lovecats'. Elspeth felt right at home.

She realised Meredith was talking. "Sorry?"

"I said: have you decided if you're sticking around yet, or what?"

"Why?"

"Well, I've got a problem now, you see." Meredith pulled a 'you're not going to like this' expression – the one Elspeth had seen so many times before, on the faces of so many different editors. Her heart sank. "After publishing your story, people are going to be expecting something a bit different from the *Heighton Observer*. We've spent so long running local interest pieces that we've forgotten what serious journalism looks like. And now there's this expectation, and you're the only person I know around here who's cut out for it."

Elspeth frowned. "So…?"

"So you see my problem," said Meredith, passing over her drink. "I couldn't possibly let you go, even if I wanted to. I'm going to have to chain you to a desk and keep you writing. I might even look at increasing your rate. You got a problem with that?"

Elspeth laughed. "No problem at all."

"Good. That's settled, then." She grabbed her vodka. "Come on, the others are waiting. You can carry Caroline's cider."

They joined the others by the jukebox. Copies of that week's edition were laid out on the tables, now soaked through with slopped beer. Meredith had dedicated the first twelve pages to Elspeth's large retrospective feature on the Carrion King case.

Dorothy had already framed the front page.

"I think it's time for a toast," said Meredith. "To the newest member of the team, and to a damn fine job, too." They raised their glasses and bellowed their cheers, much to the annoyance of the couple at the nearest table.

"And to Rose," said Elspeth. A murmur of appreciation went around the small group.

"So, what's the next big exposé going to be?" asked Richard, a tall, thin man with a beard, whom everyone in the office called Dick.

She shrugged. "I guess it depends on the leads. At the moment, I've got nothing."

"I doubt it'll be too long, around these parts," said Caroline, one of the layout team. "And besides, I get the feeling it might be a romance story, about a strapping ginger copper and his childhood sweetheart."

Elspeth felt a hand on her shoulder, and turned to see Peter standing behind her, grinning. She glanced at Caroline and pulled a face, causing the other woman to hoot with laughter.

She turned back to Peter. "Glad you could make it."

"Drink?"

"I'm okay, actually." She sipped her gin. "Look, give me a couple of minutes and we can get out of here if you like? Go somewhere a bit quieter?"

"Sounds perfect. I'll wait for you outside." He slipped away into the crowd.

"I do hope you two are going to get on with it," said Caroline, when he'd gone. "I could cut the sexual tension with a knife."

"It's not like that," said Elspeth. "We're old friends.

We've been through a lot together, that's all."

"Mmmm hmmm."

Elspeth shook her head. It was useless trying to argue.

She downed her drink, and placed the empty glass on the table. Meredith put a hand on her arm. "Go on, you get off. Don't worry about this lot. Go and have a nice time with your... *friend*."

Elspeth groaned. "Thanks, Meredith."

"We'll see you soon, okay?"

"Absolutely."

Outside, the evening was cool and clear.

"You seem to have your feet well and truly under the table there, now," said Peter, as they crossed the road and followed the path down to the marketplace.

"I suppose I do. They're a good bunch. Meredith's asked me to write some more pieces for them. It'll tide me over while I look for something more permanent."

"You really proved yourself with your coverage of the Carrion King case, didn't you?"

"Well, a lot of that's down to you. I really do owe you one."

"Don't mention it," he said.

"So, since you've made such an impression on the readers of the *Heighton Observer*, do you think that means you'll stick around for a bit?" She couldn't help but notice the hopeful tone in his voice, and it made her think of Caroline, and what she'd said in the pub. Sooner or later she was going to have to face up to everything she'd left behind in London, to Andrew, but knowing that Peter was here... it made it all seem so much more achievable.

"I reckon so. I've already started looking for a place of my own."

"That's good news," said Peter. "Really good news. Won't your mum be upset, though? She seems to like having you around."

"She'll be fine," said Elspeth. "And I'll still be here. But I need a bit more space of my own, and I'm sure she wants her house back."

Peter laughed. "So, do you want to get some food? We *are* celebrating, after all." Elspeth stopped to sit down and he sat beside her and nudged her playfully with his elbow. "We could try out that new Mexican place, if you fancy it? Or somewhere a bit more upmarket?"

"You know what I really fancy?"

"What?"

"A dirty kebab," she said. "With lots of garlic sauce."

"God, you really are the perfect woman. Next thing I know you'll be challenging me to a game on the Xbox."

"Bring it. Game on. I'm pretty mean with one of those remote paddle stick things."

He burst out laughing. "Yeah, alright."

"So, where can we get a really greasy kebab? One that we're going to regret in the morning?"

He leapt up and took her hand, pulling her to her feet. "Come on. I know a place."

They ambled along, side by side, neither one of them feeling the need to fill the silence. Cars purred past, headlamps glinting, and a cool breeze ruffled her hair. For the first time in a long while, she felt truly alive. Despite everything, despite the horrors of the last couple of weeks, she was starting to believe that she might, at last, be starting to feel happy again.

She looped her arm through Peter's, and together, they walked off into the night.

ACKNOWLEDGEMENTS

This one's been germinating for a long time, and I have a whole bunch of people to thank for their help and support. First and foremost my family, who cheerfully put up with long days being driven around rainy Oxfordshire scouting locations for the book, and then gave me the space and time to write it while I ignored pretty much everything else that was going on around me.

Cavan Scott was his usual, steadfast self, pushing me on and encouraging me whenever I hit a wall. Thanks must go to my editors Cath Trechman, Miranda Jewess and Cat Camacho, who have supported the book since the very first time I mooted the idea, and likewise my agent Jane Willis, and publishers Nick Landau and Vivian Cheung. There are too many others to name, but you know who you are, and I hope you also know that I appreciate it.

Elspeth listens to a lot of music in this book, and all the artists are personal favourites of mine. The soundtrack of the book is the soundtrack of the writing of the book, the playlist I had on in the background while I plotted all the crucial scenes. If there are any bands or artists mentioned that you've never listened to, I urge you to give them a try.

ABOUT THE AUTHOR

George **Mann** was born in Darlington and has written numerous books, short stories, novellas and original audio scripts. *The Affinity Bridge*, the first novel in his Newbury & Hobbes Victorian fantasy series, was published in 2008. Other titles in the series include *The Osiris Ritual*, *The Executioner's Heart*, *The Immorality Engine*, and *The Casebook of Newbury & Hobbes*.

His other novels include *Ghosts of Manhattan*, *Ghosts of War*, *Ghosts of Karnak* and *Ghosts of Empire*, mystery novels about a vigilante set against the backdrop of a post-steampunk 1920s New York, as well as an original *Doctor Who* novel, *Paradox Lost*, featuring the Eleventh Doctor alongside his companions, Amy and Rory.

He has edited a number of anthologies, including *Encounters of Sherlock Holmes*, *Further Encounters of Sherlock Holmes*, *Associates of Sherlock Holmes* and the forthcoming *Further Associates of Sherlock Holmes*, *The Solaris Book of New Science Fiction* and *The Solaris Book of New Fantasy*, and has written two Sherlock Holmes novels for Titan Books: *Sherlock Holmes: The Will of the Dead* and *Sherlock Holmes: The Spirit Box*.